The BUTTERFLY and the SQUID

C.G. Matteini was the recipient of a Literary Titan

gold award for *The Peace Quaternity*, a collection

of two poems and two historical fiction short stories.

He published a book of poems, entitled *Us*, and an

illustrated children's book, entitled *Cloud Jumping*.

His writing on sustainability can be found in the

CPA Journal, and his short story "Tooths"

was published in the *Mug of Woe*,

edited by Jenn Dlugos and Kyle Cranston.

C.G.'s blog (on writing and what inspires his writing),

poems (about light and dark), and other writing

can be found on his website

www.cgmatteini.com.

The
BUTTERFLY
and the
SQUID

C. G. MATTEINI

ISBN: 979-8-9886642-5-3 (paperback)
ISBN: 979-8-9886642-6-0 (ebook)

Any references to historical events, real people,
or real places are used fictitiously. Names, characters,
and places are products of the author's imagination.

Cover design by Laura Duffy
Book design by Karen Minster

PRINTED IN THE UNITED STATES OF AMERICA
FIRST PRINTING, 2025

www.cgmatteini.com

This book is dedicated to

my mother and father,

who taught me that the truth

is in the love.

It is the wind through the trees

It is the light flickering on the leaves

It is the way she looks at me

It is speaking through my dreams

INGEO
(Long Ago)

Ingeo dreamed of a man who was lost:

Overlooking a wooded valley; in the forest below, dying; on a crescent sandy shore searching for someone; in white space, in black starry space, in fantastic glass buildings that reach the sky, on an island, in his mind. In all these places the man is lost, and Ingeo shares his confusion and budding terror but cannot not help, only follow . . .

. . . into a dark alley where Ingeo senses, as the man does, a change. Something coming. The man grabs a hand, his lover's, and yells in a language not Korial. They run through a maze of alleys growing tighter and darker. They drive through an invisible thickness, hanging on to each other for life and love. The ground rumbles, the building cracks. Ingeo screams from above for them to reach and take his hand, he will pull them out of their world, but the building collapses, and they choke on the dust as they fall.

Ingeo sees now through the man's eyes: stars. The woman's hand slips through his fingers. Sanity spills from his ears like warm water. Three fireballs tear through the black sky and blot out the stars, roaring the tri-roar of some otherworldly nightmare. The hot smell of fire and death singe his nostrils as the meteors strike and concuss the world.

Ingeo awoke in a cold sweat. Nurin shone in thick, soft beams through the panes of his window. He was inside the light, warm, hovering like a dust mote, wavering between realms. He was cold and sad.

They were real, he thought.

He could still hear their harried footsteps.

No, just a dream.

The footsteps were coming from outside. He knew their gimpy rhythm. He jumped out of bed and threw open the window as Gideon limped around the corner, talking to himself and laughing. Ingeo wiped the tears from his cheeks, dressed, tied his shoes tight, and ran downstairs, nearly running into his mother.

"What's it about?" she asked in Korial. She blocked the hall with one thick arm. Her hair was a tangled nest, her gray eyes exhausted and alert. She was still in her bar apron.

"Don't know," he replied in earnest. He ducked under her arm and took his coat.

"What have I said?"

"What's the worry? He's likely here for supplies."

"'What's the worry?' the young man asks," she said, glancing over her left shoulder and appealing to Ingeo's dead father. "Winds are shifting."

He'd heard it from her many times. He opened the door and backed out. "I know." And he did. But Gideon was no dissident. He was a scientist; and Zinsa, however steeped in the faith she'd become, however pickled by its juices, surely still recognized the difference. Still, Ingeo was neither oblivious nor reckless. He'd been content with no one knowing about his visits to the planetarium. He'd be content now just to observe the old man from a distance.

He didn't need her consent, but he waited for it. She gave it by slamming the door shut.

He sprinted down the street, cut left into the first alley, then right onto the south road. It rose and curved. The Seven Spires pierced the sky above the steepled, rowhouse rooves and slid around each other in parallax as he ascended. The market murmured from over the hill, wafted its bouquet of meat, sweets, incense, and feces. The sounds and smells of home. His thighs burned. He topped the hill in time to see Gideon stumble into the throng. He followed him into the shadow of the castle.

He weaved through a packed aisle, vegetable and jewelry carts down one side, clicking clocks, greasy engine parts, and lowing reemas down the other. Two women in Gideon's wake pointed to the sky and laughed. A boy and a girl jumped up and down and reached for the blue. Ingeo squeezed the boy's shoulder. "What's it about?"

The boy's eyes were big and dreaming. "Another world!"

Ingeo tingled through his core, over his scalp, out to his fingers, and down to his toes.

He's done it, he thought.

Gideon climbed onto the base of the statue of Zinsa, leaned on his good leg, and flapped his hands to quiet the crowd. Few noticed him. "Remember my telescope!" he hollered, jabbing a finger over their heads, over the rooves and the city wall, across the fields to the wavy green hills and the small white bump on the highest crest. "My telescope! Remember!" A few more turned, curious about all the shouting. He looked from one to another, nodding his head and grinning, as though they were all in this together. His gray hair was wild, his spectacles slanted, his pants and long coat yellowed and threadbare. Ingeo burrowed closer.

"I've mastered it just in time!" Gideon proclaimed and paused for a reaction. Someone hit him in the chest with a fruit core.

A man, a roofer from east quarter (Ingeo could hardly remember a name, but he never forgot a face) shouted, "Nice treat! Tell us all about it!" This drew the first laughs.

Gideon's eyes widened. "I mean to! For twenty turns I've refined my instrument and waited. I told you my theory, here, two turns past. Some of you must remember. This one does!"

The accused, a quiet woman, pious, faithful, gaunt, a weaver of some sort, turned a few heads, turned red in the cheeks, and made for safer space. A smelter from north quarter standing on Ingeo's right hip, a squat boulder of a man, heavy drinker, crossed his arms over his chest and flared his nostrils.

Gideon wrung his hands. "Hear it again. You should *listen!* The dull star, the one that floats alone, is no star at all. It is another world. I trained my telescope and saw the surface."

More people laughed now, and from deeper down in their bellies. Merchants shouted for the attention being drawn from their goods and slung a few choice words at the one drawing it. Ingeo liked the look and feel of none of it. Gideon went on, undeterred or unaware of the growing sentiment and the guards seeping into the crowd. "Our planets have converged. Close as they come in their orbits. Now close your eyes," he commanded and was the only one who did, as far as Ingeo could tell. "Step onto the ladder. Place an eye to the eyepiece. See inside, the dull star. Turn the dial. No, let me turn it for you! I draw the star closer. The light fades to gray. A gray surface. A continent, and an ocean."

Guffaws and backslaps. But not all were amused. Some frowned. Some shuffled their feet and eyed the sky. Ingeo looked up and crafted his own rendering on the blank blue canvas, not for the first time or the hundredth. Only now he had textures, elements, and pale colors to paint with. It was nothing to fear. It was not impossible. It was science and discovery, history being made. But Gideon's story took a strange turn then.

The astronomer's eyes popped open. "There's more," he warned. "There is nothing to do but say it. There are three volcanoes along the coast. Six dark squares, evenly spaced, in an arc around the center volcano. Massive structures. Impossible without intelligence."

Ingeo's throat dried. The good people of Teles fell silent. They looked at each other with tilted heads, furrowed brows, and scrunched noses as if asking one another if Gideon had indeed just said what they thought he said. Then they exploded with laughter, applauded him, and pelted him with a hailstorm of paid-for and unpaid-for produce.

A calm, sharp voice penetrated the ruckus. A single word. An invocation: "Heresy."

Ingeo shrank. The full weight of this came crashing down like the building from his dream, the one that buried those lovers. The coarse, black robe of a hooded Mind Dreamer brushed his side. "Heresy," she said again and was answered with prayers, boos, and one screaming cackle.

A middle-aged woman, a farmer and baker, came to Gideon's defense. "Too much time alone is all," she said. A hunched man, new to Teles, spit at her. Twin sisters Ingeo's age—Joli and Ry, he remembered *their* names—shoved the man.

Rough currents formed, some people pushing closer to the statue, others getting out of there. Ingeo ducked and rode a frothing stream to the base. He tugged on Gideon's pants. They locked eyes. Gideon's were untamed. *Yes, Ingeo, Yes!* they seemed to say. *Believe it!*

"Rescind!" Ingeo pleaded.

Mind Dreamers formed a black circle around the statue. They closed sunken eyes, mouthed prayers with pale lips, lifted bony arms, and wiggled bony fingers. Gideon turned this way and that, shooing them away. A small boy, perched on his father's shoulders, tapped Ingeo on the head, and pointed at Gideon. "Blood," he said.

Gideon's back had been to the statue. No one had noticed. But they saw it now, the dark patch of matted hair. Gideon touched the back of his head and grimaced. "Nothing serious," he said. "I was startled, and I fell. Imagine how *you* would have fared! Or *you!* Any of you!"

See, Ingeo thought to the shaken mass. *He hit his head. He doesn't mean it.*

A desperate voice took up the call of heresy, and more joined in. A brave, fierce minority booed. Gideon jumped from the statue, looked quickly and severely into Ingeo's eyes, and passed him a crumpled piece of parchment.

Ingeo tunneled out of the crowd and turned. Guards led Gideon up the fanned castle steps. Zinsa stood in her high window in the Spire Stilter, watching, still, a blank white face atop a green sea of cloth.

Gideon tore his arms away from the guards, limped forward, and shouted: "We are not alone in this space around Nurin. Is it so hard to believe? Could the Mind not dream of life outside of Qol? The Mind has. Prepare yourselves!"

A cold wind whipped over the hill city as Zinsa stepped back into the dark of her chamber. The heavy castle doors opened, then shut behind the astronomer.

Ingeo sat on a windowsill watching the sky darken and thinking that Nurin must have slowed its descent just to stretch his nerves. The bar was overcrowded and too quiet. No songs, no scuffles, no drinking games. Only muffled conversations, looks passed between tables, sides being formed: sympathy for the astronomer versus none. The air was thick, the smell of sweat and sour ale as potent as ever.

Ingeo risked another glance at the parchment. It was covered in scribbled formulas except for a small island of coherence in the bottom right corner, a solution, an alignment, a number for each of the telescope's dials. Ingeo had seen many such combinations before, but he didn't know enough about the instrument to know if this one was special. Maybe it was. Maybe Gideon had seen another world. These "structures" were easily explained. A trick of the old man's eyes in the heat of the historical moment. A concussed fantasy.

But the way he'd looked at Ingeo as he passed him the parchment. The mad thrill in his eyes. The warning.

Ingeo felt his mother staring at him over the heads of her patrons. He hadn't tried to hide his intentions from her. He knew he couldn't, just as she knew she couldn't stop him. It was, after all, her inherited curiosity that had nudged him across the fields and up the green hills that first time and every time since. It was her obstinance now propping up his decision to go again. He met her eyes, slid off the windowsill, and left.

The sky was blue-black. The first stars were out. Lanterns burned in the windows of the row houses. A family eating. A man reading. A couple quarreling. Two little girls with their faces pressed to the glass, looking up.

The guards at the south gate were drunk and engrossed in a game of tiles. They accepted Ingeo's bribe without looking at him. He passed through the gate, turned west, traced the wall until he was out of sight, then took off into the field. He looked up as he ran and found it easily, the hole in space, the black lake with sparkling shores and a lone dull light in its center, the oversized star that maybe wasn't. Ingeo thought of the lovers and didn't know why.

He reached the hills, caught his breath, and looked back across the field at the shadowed, ringed, torch-speckled hill city with its seven-spiked crown. Home. It looked very far away. He started up the path.

Two guards sat and one stood on the crumbling, semi-circle rock wall outside the planetarium. A fourth, holding a torch, paced the overgrown grass. Ingeo crept out of the trees, close enough to pick up their tone but not their words. They were arguing, three men and one woman.

The one with the torch paused in his pacing as though having come to some conclusion, then barked something with the air of being in charge. All four looked up at the telescope protruding from the dome. *Pointing.* All four looked away. The lead spoke again. The others sighed, grumbled, and squeaked, respectively, then followed him around the planetarium to the door on the far side.

Ingeo snuck up to the near window, the very same he'd tapped on his first time here roughly one turn past. Gideon had been polishing his telescope and talking to it. It had seemed so big to Ingeo then, so *portentous.* It did still. It gleamed with starlight. It loomed.

The door opened, and the guards entered in a tight bunch behind the torch. "Find another light," said the lead. Ingeo recognized him now, the scar above his left eye. He was an infrequent visitor to the bar but a hard and silent drinker when he came. "Watch the mess," he said, pointing to a dark, dried puddle a body's length from the foot of the ladder.

"Blood here!" screeched the smallest of them, a big-nosed, nine-fingered man who'd lost the tenth cheating at tiles.

"Keep it down. That's Gideon's blood."

The woman, from west quarter, mother to three young boys, approached the telescope like it was a wild animal, held out a hand as though to let it sniff her. She stroked it and looked up its smooth back through the opening in the ceiling. "I just wonder why Zinsa is bothering to come at all," she said.

The fourth guard, unfamiliar to Ingeo, tall as the woman and three times as wide, leveled a fat finger at her. "If you have questions, why don't you be the one?"

The small man grinned. The lead nodded. The woman took a sharp breath in, let it out, and approached the ladder.

She climbed. She glanced at the dials. She tapped the eyepiece and cringed, as though afraid it might shock her, then lowered her eye.

"What what?!" squealed the nine-fingered man.

"Nothing," she said. "Black."

"Ha! Maaad Gideon!"

The three men exhaled in unison and shared a laugh. There was nothing to worry about. They were living in the world as it had always been, the one world. All four walked out of the planetarium and turned left toward the wall. Ingeo went right and was quickly inside. Too quick without a light. His foot caught the sticky edge of the dried blood puddle. Pulse pounding in his temples, he cursed himself and climbed the ladder.

Qol was a full spin further along in its orbit since Gideon had last cast his searching eye into space. Nor had the other world, if that was what it was, stopped its endless circuit around Nurin. The guards had failed to consider this and wouldn't have known what to do anyway. Ingeo took the parchment, a candle, and a match from his coat pocket. He read the solution by the light of the flickering flame, adjusted the dials, swallowed, and looked into the eyepiece.

Inside was a glowing gray dot. He turned another dial, and the dot grew and darkened. Shadows formed, contours, the impression of movement. A dark gray continent and a gray-blue ocean. Three volcanoes along the coast. Six black squares, evenly spaced, in an arc around the center volcano. Ingeo trembled. Ingeo muttered the things he saw. He jumped off the ladder, ran out of the planetarium and down the hill.

His mother was sitting on the stairs when he arrived home. She stood. He buried his head in her chest, squeezed her, and cried.

"Unbelievable," she said.

He thought he would never sleep again. He slept for what felt like an instant. In that instant, the dream returned, a version of it. The lovers ran through catacombs, chased by a machine that smashed through the subterranean rock walls and shook the ground and shook their brains.

He awoke to guards shouting and banging on doors up and down the street. There were guards downstairs. He slipped out of bed and searched for his shoes. They were in his closet, lined up and cleaned of Gideon's blood. A guard threw open his door, ransacked his room, examined his shoes, tossed them, and left.

"What did they say?" Ingeo asked his mother when they were gone.

"Someone at the planetarium in the ninarc," she said.

"The planet?"

"Zinsa went. She looked. There was nothing."

The castle horns beckoned from atop the hill in a minor tune that sent shivers up Ingeo's spine and paled his mother's face.

"She can't," he said. "It's the truth."

"It doesn't matter. It's heresy."

"I have to—"

"Please, Ingeo."

"I have to tell people."

She looked at the floor and sighed like it was her last breath.

The hills to the west were smaller than he remembered, the wooded canyon beyond it narrower, the river slower and shallower. He'd taken these trails only once before, with his father, when he was young. Everything seemed bigger then. But he remembered the way. It was slow going, but he would not risk the road. It took him all of the arc hiking at a strong pace to reach Golla.

The lake sparkled through gaps in the tall trunks. Nurin blazed red above the tepid watery horizon and cast a trail of fiery light straight to Ingeo. The stilted wooden city was a bed of glowing embers, the boats a swarm of flushed waterbugs slipping in and out of docks, sliding under boardwalks, cozying up to warehouses. Motorbarrows rolled over boardwalks, thin trails of smoke rising from growling engines.

Ingeo had intended to avoid the city, to go around it through the hovels and then follow the road from a safe distance on the other side. There was less chance of running into guards or Mind Dreamers that way. But now he considered taking the risk. He'd hiked well and might be ahead of them, ahead of the message he'd left in Teles on his way out. He could leave it here too. He could catch a ride. He waited for Nurin to sink into the lake.

A flame appeared in the forest as he skirted the muddy shore. Then another, then more. The air was spiced. The hovels were alive with families cooking, eating, drinking. Children played chase. A baby wailed. Ingeo kept his head low and nodded to any who noticed him, but few did. They were busy living. They were still on the safe side of *knowing*. He left strips in dark corners for them to find in the early arc. He left one on the boardwalk beneath a torch that had gone out, in an empty barrel outside of a warehouse, in a flower box outside a lodge, in a doorway, in a bag slung over a shoulder. He stayed in the shadows. He listened for talk of Teles. The few guards he passed seemed tired and bored. The few Mind Dreamers did not hiss of heresy.

The bars were raucous. Ingeo shoved through the crowd and came to the depot. There were plenty of drivers but few sober and none interested in traveling through the ninarc. Except for a white-haired, one-eyed woman. "Don't look at me like that," she said in Korial, pointing to her patch. "I see farther and better than all these fools." She pocketed his coin and shoveled coke into her engine.

They rumbled over a boardwalk. A long, low barge slipped underneath them. The sky was clouded over and starless. Ingeo sat behind the driver, atop the engine. He took a risk. "Is it true, an execution in Teles?" He didn't know for sure. The horns had played that black song, yes, but perhaps Zinsa had stayed her hand. Perhaps she'd let Gideon and any who supported him off with a grim warning.

The driver "looked" back over her shoulder with her patched eye. "Is it?"

He regretted opening his mouth. "Just a rumor," he said and sat back. He told himself not to sleep, not yet, stay alert. But he'd had a long hike, and the seat was warm.

The guard spilling the contents of his rucksack was a dream. He was safe.

No, it was real. His heart stopped. It was over. They'd kill him and the old woman too. Or she'd turned him in. Another guard was rummaging through the trunk beneath her seat. She stood behind him staring into the back of his head. Ingeo stepped down and inched away, ready to bolt. But there were no strips of parchment in the small pile of his belongings. The guards went back to their hut and their game of tiles. The ferry into Marra chugged across the river toward them. Ingeo breathed. "Well," said the woman, picking up a canteen and a loaf of bread. "Don't just stand there."

They crossed the prairie and snaked through the forest. They were on the road now, after all, and Ingeo missed his mother terribly. They'd been this way not more than three phases past. They'd come twice a turn for as long as he could remember to buy the wheat for her ale. He wished the driver was her. He wished this was one of those routine journeys.

They turned south at the fork and climbed. Miwa's tapered wooden tower rose from the grassy hilltop, and the city, a lumpy, rusted, green metal blanket, spread out around it. There were guards at each of the narrow, slanted openings. There were Mind Dreamers roaming the ceilinged alleys, reminding anyone they passed and any listening behind the windows and doors of their shops and homes that the Mind dreamt only of Qol. So, word had reached. The driver drove with a stern calm, the controlled urgency of everyday business.

"There was something in my sack," Ingeo said when they were through the city and back on the road.

The woman turned and eyed him with her patch.

"Did you read them?" he asked.

She said, "'I am Ingeo, Gideon's assistant. I saw what he saw. Zinsa lies. Impossible without intelligence.' What did you see?"

He told her. And they were quiet for the remainder of the arc and through the ninarc, all the rest of the way to the Academy.

"The buildings themselves are experiments," his mother had explained to him the first time they'd passed through here, the last stop before the farms to the north and east. "Always changing. The scientists and students always tinkering." Ingeo recognized it now in the early, slanted light by not recognizing it. The buildings were shapes he could never have thought of. Many were shapeless. They were all sizes. Some were layered and turned in on themselves so that it was difficult to perceive their size. They were made of wood and metal and many types of stone. It was a hodgepodge, a brainstorm of structure, nestled into the hills behind a curvy river moat. It was very much itself. That was how Ingeo thought of it that first time, and that was how he thought of it now. It was open-minded. It was hopeful, and so *he* was hopeful. But he never made it inside.

The bridge was clogged with guards shouting, Mind Dreamers hissing, and students and scientists protesting this intrusion on their neutral reserve, their intellectual island, faithful as they were to nothing but the results of their tinkering.

The driver lifted a plank beneath her feet, reached down, pulled out a stack of parchment strips tied with a string, and shoved them into Ingeo's chest. "Off. Go."

She would not be the last stranger to help him on his soul-bending journey, but she was the first. "Thank you," he said and buried the strips in his rucksack.

She pointed to her eyepatch. "I see you. Good luck."

He slipped out of the cart and scurried upriver through the bush. The river bent and narrowed. He thought he could cross up ahead without being seen from the bridge. His foot caught a root, and he stumbled into a small clearing. Three girls—young women, he if was a young man, as his mother had very recently declared him—were sitting beside a tree and staring at him. "I'm sorry," he said. "I'm just—"

"What is it, man?" one said. She had freckles on her nose.

"Speak up," said another with no hair on her head.

"I need to get across," he said.

They looked over at the bridge at the same time, then back at him. "Some trouble?" asked the purple-eyed third. The other two nodded.

"News from Teles," Ingeo said.

All three brows wrinkled.

"Is it true?" asked the one with the freckles. "Executed the astronomer?"

Ingeo buried his face in his hands and wept. He'd held onto hope. He'd allowed for other possibilities. But of course Zinsa had gone through with it. She was too far gone in the faith not to. The women shushed him. Purple-eyes patted him on the back. "Easy," she said.

"What is it?" asked the bald one.

"Tell us," said freckles.

He wiped tears and snot on his sleeve. "They'll kill you," he said.

Freckles looked at the bridge again and snarled. She leaned into Ingeo. "Say it, man. This is still the Academy."

He told them. They listened without blinking. When he was done, they looked at each other and seemed to agree on something without speaking. "Hand over some of those strips," said purple-eyes.

He passed them half of what he had left. "Careful," he said. "It's all true." He ran.

The guards hunted him through the forested hills. He stayed ahead of them but never by much. He moved northeast because it was a direction to go and because of something he remembered from the dream. The valley where the man had been dying. Ingeo recognized it only now, as though the dream became clearer as he drew closer.

He climbed a steep slope, hiked through a rocky pass, and found himself looking down on the valley from halfway up the south range.

The north range veered off into the distance and faded into the Shole.

A hoverbird zipped into his field of vision and floated at the end his nose, its wings a thrumming blur. It flew east, then stopped, turned back, and looked at him as though asking what he was waiting for. He followed it.

A circle carved into a half-buried boulder and another carved into a tree trunk farther along hinted at a long-overgrown trail. A shimmer in the valley hinted at water. They rounded a bend. A guard came from the opposite direction. The hoverbird fired itself like a dart at the guard's face, and he fell to the ground, holding his face and screaming. Others shouted from ahead and below. The bird took off up the hill, and Ingeo climbed for his life, for Gideon, and for the truth.

The bird stopped and hovered in front of a cave. Ingeo ran past it and backed into the dark, trying to disappear. He slipped on a pile of seeds and nearly fell into a crevice. Deep down was an orange glow, a tiny pool of light or a flame, a revelation or a hell. Ingeo felt a terrible need to find out which. Guards filled the mouth of the cave. The bird dove at their faces in slow motion, their screams silent, their blood suspended in drops and rivulets. Ingeo looked down into the glow. It was part of the truth. He thought of his mother and father as he jumped.

PART ONE

MANIFEST DESTINY

1

(109 cycles by; 166 spins past; 158 days ago)

Grugreera paced his hollow, rubbing his arm stump and willing his heart to slow and his skin to soften. They wouldn't listen. Three short steps from the rear stone wall to the curtain, back and forth. He put an ear to the curtain and held his breath for the first announcement. Nothing. He added a trroorra coal to his flare, breathed, and watched the wavering green heat rise into the flue.

This anxiety was shameful. It was selfish. He'd do well whatever placement he received. He could build. He was strong in alchemy. There was something he liked about farming. But diggers! Diggers unearthed new dens, lakes, and rivers. Diggers expanded the hive, and so, MaGog. Diggers tapped the raw materials that would become the ships and fuel that would propel them. Diggers channeled the fire, the nectar, the life-giving heat of the Core.

A trilled holler echoed through the den, and a wave of hope collided with a wave of fear inside Grugreera's chest. He threw open his curtain and gripped the net. From seventh level, highest in the den, beneath the stalactite forest ceiling and overhanging the crystal black lake, Grugreera watched as other second-ring Primes in burnt orange cloth and first-rings in light yellow filled the mouths of every flare-lit hollow from flat shore to spiked ceiling and around the striated walls. Two-hundred and forty-eight lives, half on the blade edge of change. They whipped their heads around or craned their necks or dropped to their bellies and looked down, all hunting for fellows in dark blue.

Grugreera spotted one on the far side of the lake crawling across the net on fifth level. He spotted another, down and to his left, stepping off a ladder onto a path on third. Two walked out of a shore-side common and went in opposite directions. Each of these fellows bore a satchel heavy with wafers—with *futures*—and necklaces for the females. Each stopped in front of a second-ring Prime's hollow.

Orria, directly beneath Grugreera on sixth level, shouted "Farmer!" in their native Vrrgrrul and in her brightest trill. Another cried "Relations!" from the far side of the cleft. "Builder!" "Alchemist!" "Miner!" echoed.

Grugreera stepped back into his hollow, sat on his mat, and listened to the rising vibratory wave, a tremolo cocktail of elation, rapture, confusion, shock, and humble, chest-filled acceptance, reverberating through the den and through his head.

It doesn't matter, he told himself. *Just not—*

The thought parched his skin.

A census male climbed up the net into the mouth of his hollow. The male clung with his toes and left hand, reached into his satchel with his right, and pulled out a thin metal square. Such a simple little thing, Grugreera thought. Such a potentially devastating thing. And there was nothing special about this male's face—slender and pale with big, black, circle eyes; he could have been any fellow—but Grugreera would never forget him. Or the strange way he looked at Grugreera's stump like it meant something to him. Or his nervous trill.

Just not the surface, Grugreera begged silently.

"Grugreera," the male said, reading the dots and dashes on the wafer.

"Yes," Grugreera confirmed in a whisper.

"Digger," the male said, then tossed the wafer onto the floor—*clang! rattle!*—and quickly climbed away.

Grugreera's heart stopped. He screamed relief and joy. He shimmied through the net, hung from it, raised his stump, and shouted his new life. Fellows nearby congratulated him. Fellows everywhere shook the nets, whistled, ran along the paths, swung from ropes, jumped from rope bridges and splashed into the lake. Orria climbed up from her hollow and hugged him. "You'll do well," she said.

"Digger," he said and could hardly believe it or fathom the strength and depth of his pride. "And you, fellow. Your necklace suits." A small chunk of yellow-orange rruvik hung from her neck on a string of black cloth. A beautiful piece in its simplicity and humility. A beautiful tradition to celebrate the females. She smiled and put a vile to his nose. Cooks in dark brown cloth were popping in and out of hollows, handing out dust and liquids. Grugreera took a deep pull and was quickly as high as he'd been in as long as he could remember. Koren provided good dust for Placement!

They climbed down the net to the path on fourth level and joined the flow of fellows rushing toward the common. Someone shoved Grugreera from behind. It was Obudud, flanked by Murrimir and Iorra. All second rings, all moving on. Obudud flashed a grin. "Grugreera, those eyes!" Theirs too had the bright, cold sheen. "You may even have fun."

A pit formed in Grugreera's stomach. He would miss that raspy trill. He would happily forget all differences. "Get what you wanted?" he asked his fellow.

Obudud shrugged his too-broad shoulders. They were shoulders stuck in the past, unevolved. He was deformed in his way, as Grugreera was deformed. It's what had bonded them in their first ring of Prime. "Sure, sure, fellow," Obudud said. Murrimir and Iorra kissed him on either cheek. Iorra wore a nugget of blue vivanum around her neck.

"We're grateful," Grugreera said and was embarrassed by how somber he felt. Some fellows had to forage. Some had to live the short surface life. Grugreera shouldn't be so troubled by it. "You'll do well," he said.

Obudud scoffed and took a hard pull of dust. "I'm proud, sure." And that was it, that sarcasm and apathy. That was the gap that had grown between them during second ring: Grugreera working harder at each successive apprenticeship, increasingly anxious to move on and make his mark, and Obudud increasingly disaffected. Grugreera looked around for watchers, traced the wire lining the wall, and marked the nearest black glass eye. But there was nothing to fear. There was no harm done. He knew Obudud. He knew that his fellow was just more afraid than he let on. It was a natural thing for a new forager. "Let's go," Grugreera said. "One more rip together."

They staggered down the path and through the rainbow archway of the common. The tunnel at the far end was black. All fellows hushed as they entered. The crowd grew tight and tense: one coiled MaGog.

Came the booming of the drums. Came the hollow, ringing, syncopated strikes of the pipes and bells. Grugreera laughed from his dust-numb throat, as he shuffled around the corner and into the green trroorra light spilling from the mouth of the dome.

The fellows of den 53 of Zone 14 made a single, primal shadow writhing around the blazing pit. Grugreera stepped into the rip, waved like a worm, and grinded with a fellow. The cold chemicals. The drums and pipes and bells. The manic-happy MaGog. Grugreera closed his eyes, flowed and reflected. Could Prime really be over? Could Gog have made two rings around Gorr in the time he'd been living in this den with these fellows? A fifth of his life gone in a blink. He could barely remember who he was when he crossed over that threshold from Youth to Prime. And now he was a digger? It was hard to believe, his great fortune.

He opened his eyes and saw Obudud sitting on a ledge above the crowd, alone, this fellow who'd worked hard for one thing during Prime, his reputation as an insatiable ripper. Grugreera grabbed two tubes of liquid from the nearest cook and worked his way through the crowd. "You should be swarmed," he yelled to Obudud over the music, as he climbed the ladder.

Obudud shook his head, overly wide like his shoulders. "One arm and always climbed faster, built better," he said.

"And dug," Grugreera said, smiling. "Here." He handed Obudud a tube and sat. Obudud took the tube but didn't drink. His gaze lifted slowly, tracking the wavering heat rising from the pit in the center of the churning MaGog, up into the flue, up to the surface. He was scared. It was understandable. "Takes great courage to forage. Not many can," Grugreera said.

"Maybe I don't have the courage," Obudud replied, tensing those shoulders.

"You do. You will."

"I don't want to die."

"You asked for forager."

"Only so I could see it again."

Grugreera sighed. This sentiment and obsession. It was all too common among fellows, increasingly so. The closer they came to the destiny, the harder it was for most to bear the wait. But they were a generation or more from starting the migration, and all but the current Young would be too old by that time to survive the crossing. Besides, life in the hive had improved so much under Koren. "Just to see a blue spark in the sky?" he asked his fellow. "What about MaGog?"

Obudud's lip curled. "You just accept it all."

Grugreera scanned the dome for watchers and wall-eyes. "I accept MaGog. You must. Every sacrifice strengthens the whole."

"Do well, Grugreera?"

"Of course."

"For Koren and her machinations?"

"For MaGog. Don't force me," Grugreera said. He was hot now. His patience for this discontent had run thin.

Obudud awoke to the danger. He grabbed Grugreera's left, whole arm. "You'd call me out."

"What don't you understand?"

Obudud let go and stood.

"Do well, Obudud," Grugreera said. "Do your part, and MaGog will remember you."

Obudud climbed down and disappeared into the crowd. Grugreera drank one of the tubes and shook his head. Why wasn't it enough for fellows to play their roles? Why did so many not feel fulfilled by this mended life here in the underworld? But he let it go. He let his frustration dissolve into the warm liquid kicking in. The drums and pipes and bells were a beautiful blur of sound. His fellows were a rumbling, ripping mass, and he loved them above all.

A female by the pit caught his eye. Her red cloth. A hazy, pleasant memory. Another rip in another den? Yes, he remembered her. He remembered it being somewhat… different. He remembered convincing himself that it hadn't been.

He climbed down and tunneled into the crowd. Swaying bodies parted, and there she was, beside the pit. Her lithe shoulders rolled to the beat. Her back muscles rippled. Those waves, they resonated. He tapped her shoulder, and she turned. Her blue-green arradir necklace, a jagged splinter like a stroke of lightning, swung on its string. "You and me," he said. "Once."

She looked at him kindly, as at any fellow come to dance. She noticed his stump. "Hm, yes. You were first ring Prime, I was second."

Her trill was a higher form of music. Why did it affect him so? Why this tightness in his chest? "I forget your name. I'm sorry." And he was, more deeply than was rational.

She smiled at his embarrassment. "I forget yours. Hrulora."

"Grugreera," he said and realized in speaking his own name what had changed and why he was so moved by the memory of their one time together. *He* had changed, of course. He was not the careless, virile, first ring Prime he'd been back then. He saw life and the world differently now. He took it all more seriously, and he wanted her to know that.

"Have you birthed?" he asked her.

"Once."

"Was it mine?" he blurted without thinking.

She shrugged without a break in the slow cycles of her shoulders, half-time to the pounding beat.

He looked away. "It doesn't matter."

"No," she said, acknowledging his mistake but not judging it.

"How are you here?" he asked, troubled by the error in the system. Females could choose their roles and dens after birthing, but they had to choose another Zone to live in. Bringing Prime fellows who may have conceived back together—that type of tension was the seed of others that had caused so much pain for so long. Grugreera felt the sting of it now.

She plucked at her red cloth, providing the obvious answer. "Past Prime. In relations. I'm with the group orienting the new first rings for this den."

"Oh," he said, relieved. The system was intact. "You birthed. MaGog is grateful."

"One MaGog," she said with perfect humility. "What did Koren give you?"

"Digger," he replied, grateful that she asked. "What I always wanted."

"You're strong with the Core. I remember."

She remembers, he thought, and was scared of her for reasons he was sure he would never understand.

A fellow turned her around and put a vile to her nose. She took a pull and danced with her. Grugreera watched, mesmerized, swaying himself, caught in their motion. Hrulora looked back over one slim, perfectly evolved shoulder. Her eyes were black round coals, her head smooth and slender. "Do well," she said and was swallowed by the crowd.

2

The bells were not coming from the rip. They were offbeat and relentless. Grugreera shot up from his mat. It was next cycle. It was time. He'd almost forgotten in the joy of receiving his Placement and the foggy bliss of the rip about this greater joy: they were going to see her.

He stood and nearly fell over. His head swam and throbbed. He steadied himself against the wall and looked hopefully toward his curtain. There, just inside, was a stoppered tube, a regenerative delivered by cooks as he and the other Primes slept off the rip. He thanked Koren as he gulped down the spiced, blue liquid. His headache eased, his skin softened. A hairless jijurra the size of his hand had its tail wrapped around one of his jars and was scratching at it with its single tooth. He shooed it away, opened his jars and filled the inside pockets of his cloth with dried worms and chunks of dried vine flesh. He held his wafer in his teeth and opened his curtain. Fellows everywhere were scrambling over the nets, along the paths and bridges, and up and down the stairs and ladders. Grugreera climbed out, hung from the net, and looked back into his Prime hollow for the last time. It was no longer his. It was over, just like that. He was ready. He was all simmering nerves.

The station reeked of excreting chemicals. The line for the carts was long but moved quickly. Very few fellows talked. They shared looks of boiling excitement, fear, yearning. Females fingered their necklaces. Grugreera got into a cart with three others, closed his eyes, and chewed some vine.

To see her at all was a rare gift. To be addressed by her in one's Placement Meeting was something Grugreera had imagined many times and now found almost unbearable to imagine. The fellows in his cart attacked their jitters with talk of anything but Placement. Grugreera nodded and smiled and wished they would be quiet. They rolled through the dark behind the familiar glow of green trroorra headlight mixed with purple rreever flaring in the engine. The ride was interminable. Then it was over. A sharp prick of yellow light at the end of the tunnel pierced the green-purple aura and grew bigger and brighter (and threatened to surface Grugreera's headache; he'd never get used to these electric lights). The clang and grind of cart strings and the nervous trilling of dozens, hundreds, thousands of fellows, grew louder.

It was madness at the dwell station. Carts crawled over every track and bridge, in and out of every tunnel. Fellows in burnt orange from every den in the hive leapt from bridges, slid down ladders, jumped over tracks, and formed a growing mass pushing toward the entrance halls. Grugreera was swept into a foaming current. He feared a stampede as fellows flooded the nearest hall. But inside, they used their breath, calmed themselves, and helped each other along. Grugreera clung to a fellow and kept his eyes on his feet, safe from the blinding lights. Had the station been wired when they'd last come here, as Youth on the doorstep of Prime? Could Koren, *would* Koren have wired the entire dwell? But Grugreera was relieved to see trroorra-green, the soft, true light of one thousand sixty-one rings of life in the underworld, emanating from the far end of the hall and swallowing the false yellow.

Fellows poured from the halls and sprinted across the floor of the dwell as though for their lives, laughing and crying. Grugreera ran faster than he knew he could and skidded to a halt at the back of the growing congregation, halfway to the high, flattened wall where the giant black eye—the eye through which, by some secret miracle of progress, they would see her—waited dormant. Beneath it was the smaller eye for seeing them and the two grated holes for the exchange of their voices. This was happening. This was real. Grugreera turned. Several thousand had arrived. The floor was nearly full, and fellows were now dashing up the stairs and around the semi-circle stone benches, thirty-three rows up to the smooth ceiling. His emotions were volatile. His skin was hard and dry, soft and damp, hard and dry. A raspy laugh startled and then comforted him. Obudud. A chance to reconcile before never seeing each other again. Grugreera worked his way over to his fellow. "Feeling better?" he asked.

Obudud turned. "Grugreera! Yes, do well!" He lowered his head and took a fat pull of dust.

Grugreera recoiled, looked around for watchers. "Put it away."

Obudud came up eyes shining. He wiggled the vile down by his side. "For your last moments of Prime?" he goaded.

A few fellows around them laughed nervously. A few slipped away.

Grugreera seethed. "You want to see the blue world?"

"Raise your voice, and I'll take your other arm off," Obudud answered casually.

But Grugreera was done with this cowardice and insubordination. "How will you die, Obudud? On the surface or in a cage or worse? Look around you. Look up. You get to see her one more time. Think of what she's done for us. Think of what you'll do. The final push. We get to be a part of it." He stared into Obudud's eyes and saw the cold and false confidence there melting. He hated him and pitied him and felt strong in knowing that he could love him again as MaGog if he overcame his fear and did his part. "Do well," Grugreera said and walked away.

"Do well," Obudud called from behind him, his voice a small, scared vibration in the sibilating MaGog sea.

Grugreera found a place. The dwell was all but full. Ten thousand or so fellows in burnt orange cloth soon to be exchanged for the colors of their Placements. Ten thousand trying to hold it together. A male squeezed Grugreera's hand and looked at him with eyes that seemed like they would never blink again. His teeth were chattering. Grugreera nodded reassuringly. "Use your breath, fellow. We made it." But he struggled to take his own advice.

Ear-splitting cracks discharged from the grated holes beneath the great eye. The silence that followed was deafening. Grugreera's heart hammered, and for a terrifying moment he thought it would burst and he would die there and never see Koren or the liquid fire again. The male holding his hand fainted. Grugreera waived for watchers, and two came and pulled the male out. He would not be the last.

The pupil dilated, revealing a string of trroorra coals on a curved wall. Koren stepped up into the light, and the Primes roared and shook the underworld. Grugreera put his hand to his face and looked on through his fingers at her freakish, towering, black-robed frame, her blade nose, her huge, consuming eyes, her cleaved mouth of rotting teeth and sharpened stones—smiling at them! pleased with them!—her scythe, as tall as she, the symbol of her domain, the peace she brought. "Happy Placement," she said. And oh, her whirring stone-metal voice! The Primes were twice as loud. She paced behind the eye and let them have it out. They tried to stop and couldn't. Grugreera grew lightheaded from screaming and had to drape his arm over a fellow's shoulder. Many were linked in this way. Koren stepped up again. "Breathe," she said.

They tried. They failed. Eventually, they quieted. Grugreera went up on his toes and looked out over the sea. Heaving chests made choppy waves.

"Look at you," she said, coming forward, leaning in, filling the artificial eye with hers, which were now the size of tunnels sucking them in. Grugreera went willingly, gladly, into her pits. "Largest class in our history, true. Think how far we've come." She pulled back, releasing them from her eye depths and displaying again her long, withered face, ridged head, thin neck, thin scar running down the cylindrical protrusion of her throat, and the thicker, marbled one crossing it. Grugreera pictured the stone-metal fans spinning in the tube behind the vertical scar, giving her a voice for the one taken from her when she was a Youth. She and Grugreera were the same in that way. Both maimed. Both had over-come. "Thank you," she whirred. "I am grateful for you. Be grateful for each other. We are MaGog."

Yes, Grugreera thought.

"One with the Core," she scintillated.

Yes.

"United in our love for her for keeping us warm."

Yes!

"United in our goal of leaving her."

Oh!

MaGog howled. Koren sharpened her voice and cut through it. "You know how close we are." She smiled and turned away.

Ten thousand, less one, looked up at the ceiling, looked through *it,* to the blue world and the life of plenty for future generations. Grugreera dropped his eyes to the floor and looked through it to the Core and the flowing nectar. He felt it moving through his veins.

"Now," she said. "One thing first."

Silence again. An instantaneous, shared tension. A hunger in the collective belly.

Koren shook her head. "Simple values." She reached long, white, meatless fingers into one side of the eye and pulled a male into view, a first ring Prime. He was shaking. The skin on his face and neck was parched and peeling.

"Hit a female, very sad," Koren said with a slicing whiz that Grugreera felt in his chest. It will be good, he thought. A reminder before moving on. Prime was a strange and difficult time in many ways. The intensity of the apprenticeships, the rips, the *urge.* But this could not be tolerated.

Koren stood behind the male, taller by the length of her head and scarred neck. She spun her scythe once, twice, then stopped it dead with the curved black blade in profile. "We make mistakes but not this kind. It's not fair. We've worked too hard. Every life is precious. I take no pleasure."

Blood seeped from the cracks in the male's fear-dried face. Grugreera felt the rightness of this, the morality, the natural law. He looked around and nodded. Some fellows nodded back. Some looked away.

Koren gave her verdict: "But a first offense. You know how I feel about second chances. One more."

A collective exhale. A mix of empathy and disappointment. Grugreera marveled at her mercy and methods. He felt a heavy, crushing love.

Two armored, collared Dondarra appeared and led the male away. Koren hummed. "Let's begin," she said. "Females, let me see you."

Mothers, to-be Mothers, and to-be workers of all types, lifted their arms and the stones tied around their necks, whistled and blew kisses to the one who'd freed their half of the race from centuries of subjugation hardly three generations ago. Free, at least, here in this growing hive, south of the crater, north of the twelve-fingered mountain.

"Ahh," she buzzed, "you're beautiful. You keep our world together. You always did, even in the long dark time. Especially then. Males, show them how you feel."

Grugreera and every other male took a knee, took the hand of the nearest female, and held it to his lowered forehead.

"Up now. Females, recognize our males. They've come a long way."

The females looked into the males' eyes and touched their faces. Some kissed. Grugreera accepted a passionate peck on his lips. His heart was full. He wondered how many children he'd conceived in two Prime rings and where they were now and what they were doing. He remembered very little about being Young other than losing his arm.

"Now," Koren crooned. "Where are our diggers?"

Grugreera lost his breath.

Called first!

It was confirmation of his very life, the choices he'd made, his reason for being. He raised his arm and turned in a circle. One in twenty fellows had their arms up, more males than females. Everyone would start keeping a rough count.

"You," she said, and Grugreera could swear she was looking at him, that she *knew* him, his passion and ability.

"Discover," she implored. "Untap our mineral rainbow. Untap the fire. Untap new dens and lakes and rivers. Expand our hive of love. Do well. We thank you."

Grugreera reached for her with his five fingers, his mind, his heart, and his soul. All the new diggers reached together, then lowered their arms and accepted hugs and kisses.

"Glome," she said.

A full quarter of the fellows raised their arms, a big number even for glome, half males and half females.

"A large group, yes," Koren said. "It will all make sense. Glome, your formers fought for the peace we enjoy. You will fight to keep it. And to, hmmm," she purred, "expand our territory." Her mouth twitched as though she'd nearly laughed. Grugreera wondered if anyone else saw it. "We are grateful," she said, and fellows embraced their new glome.

"Foragers," Koren called. A small few raised their arms, lonely pairs of worms in the big sea. Grugreera looked back for Obudud and didn't see him. "MaGog is in awe of you. You will live your short lives in honor and privilege. Bring us the rare gifts of the surface. Take time to look into the expanse. See the blue world." And now she did laugh, and it seemed to Grugreera a strange, sharp laugh and a strange time to laugh. "Picture the future you are helping to create. Die with it in your minds, knowing how high we hold you." MaGog were loud for the foragers. Koren gave extra time for tribute to them.

"Hunters," she hailed, and Grugreera's skin dried. His phantom limb burned. The worms were eating it in tiny bites. They were eating the screaming caretaker who was trying to save him. A watcher put merciful darts in her chest. Another set her and the worms on fire. Another seared the worms off of Grugreera's mutilated arm and fingerless hand.

He was back in the dwell. His limb tingled as MaGog celebrated the new hunters.

"Watchers," Koren called, her voice a darkened, low motor. A smattering of fellows raised their arms, more males than females. "Keep them up," she said. "Now, census." A larger number, more female. "Lower them. MaGog, all of you, let us confront a hard truth. It will happen to some of you. You will be ambushed in subtle or violent ways by the resistance. You will be fed false histories and false futures. And some of you will eat." She shrugged her peaked shoulders. "You know the truth. You know the nature of the blue world peoples. They will share nothing, even with each other. They've proven it again and again. Still, I try. The rumors are true. I'll be speaking to their Council again. I wish I could tell you I expect progress."

She sighed, and Grugreera sighed as well; but not for the same reason, he feared. His faith in MaGog was immovable. Their history and the blue world peoples' apathy toward their suffering saddened and angered him as much as any fellow. He'd always and forever put his whole heart into MaGog's unalterable destiny. He only wished that his fellows could nurture within themselves and each other more gratitude for the present. Even Koren seemed at times to underestimate what she'd done and continued to do for life in the underworld and the very soul of MaGog. Imagine the possibilities if more societal energy was poured into the future here at home!

"Watchers, census," she said. "You have difficult roles. Smoke them out but never assume. Never be rash. Never abuse your position. Our system relies on our ability to trust you. Give us respect." The watchers and census fellows bowed in all directions. "We give you respect." Grugreera joined in bowing to them.

She called the builders and bid them go out and craft efficient infrastructure and comfortable homes for the expanding MaGog population, now over six hundred thousand strong. Alchemists she beseeched to unleash and transfigure the latent beauty and power of their world, the power to propel them to a new one. Forgemasters she urged to pour not just the stone-metal but their spirits and love for MaGog into the molds of the rockets that would eventually carry them. Farmers she named the heart of the hive, handlers the touch, relations the voice, strategy the brain. The sea churned according to the modulating frequencies of her voice. Grugreera sensed something in it as she drew near the end, something that troubled and excited him, something unsaid. He would remember that feeling the next time they saw her and everything changed.

"Engineers," she cried with finality and a cragged smile. All expected a small number, but the arms that went up were difficult to spot in the crowd of ten thousand. "It will all make sense," she assured them. "Engineers, you revered few, look around. You will never see us again."

They would disappear into Zone 3.

"I regret it, the effort spent just to protect our technology."

It was a very difficult thing for Grugreera to fathom, the maze, the cocoon of tunnels and process and secrecy, the giant, cold, mindless shells multiplying and filling their trestles beneath the silos, waiting for the engineers to build their brains and engines and teach them how to fly.

"But our system, it works," she said, and no fellow could deny it. No fellow who went into Zone 3 ever came out. Leaked rumors were rare and unreliable. "Our enemies know only what we want them to know. My only hope for myself is that I live to see it."

Grugreera's love for her swelled. Such selflessness. Such self-sacrifice for a goal she could never obtain for herself.

"We are MaGog," she said.

Yes.

"United in our love for the Core for keeping us warm. United in our goal of leaving her."

The Core!

"I started with our females, and I end with them."

Grugreera's chest tightened at the sudden, intrusive memory of Hrulora.

"All the pain before MaGog, the chaos, all grew from the mistreatment of females and Young. Males, show us your love again."

Grugreera pictured an infant with his own high brow and flat nose and Hrulora's perfectly lithe form and round eyes. He choked down a cry. This feeling, it was some close relative of pain! It was what the system protected against, and rightfully so!

He started burrowing out to beat the crowd.

"Prime is past," Koren said from behind him. "Do well. You are declared."

3

Grugreera awoke to a tortured, hissing whine, a single voice made of many tiny sub-voices like air leaking through holes. Rows of vines flickered past on his left beneath a low, toothed ceiling. Farmers hacked and stuffed chunks of dripping, gray-purple flesh into gray cloth bags. Seeds oozed out, sterile ones. Vines could grow from foraged seeds under trroorra light but could not reproduce. Grugreera would, unfortunately, become intimate with certain parts of this centuries-old process before long. The vines squirmed and cried.

Three farmers waited on the platform with crimson cloth draped over their arms. Two fellows in burnt orange stepped out of separate carts up ahead (fellows rode alone to their first placements, another tradition that Grugreera appreciated; he was grateful for the space to rest and reflect after the excitement of the last two cycles). Someone touched his shoulder. Sugorra. He hadn't even noticed her behind him. But he was happy to see a fellow from his former den. "Beautiful necklace," he said. "You'll do well."

Her skin, she was nervous. She smiled. "Grugreera, it was good," she said and walked off into her new life.

Farmers handed out seasoned vine, crispy pulge, and fleshy crawler legs to Grugreera and the others passing through. Grugreera accepted all with love and thanks. Two builders in light purple cloth took the empty carts up ahead. An alchemist in dark purple, an old male with sagging shoulders and eyes faded to gray at the edges, shuffled past Grugreera and took the cart behind him.

"I'm done," the male said.

"Oh," Grugreera responded, turning. He was moved. He'd met very few fellows headed to retirement. "You did well then. Thank you."

The male nodded. "I'm grateful. Spacious den, spacious hollow. All amenities. Says right here on my wafer."

It was a very nice thing to hear. It was yet another rational and humane feature of Koren's system that elders were set up to live out their lives in comfort and dignity after fifteen to twenty rings of service, depending on their roles. Under Marradar rule, for more generations than Grugreera cared to think about, elders were neglected at best, discarded at worse. It had been a simple, physical reality of that long dark time that any fellow deemed useless in protecting the territories and riches of that small, warring elite were expendable. But Koren changed all that. Koren opened eyes to that Self-destruction.

"You're just entering," the male said.

"Digger," Grugreera replied with a full heart.

"Hm, can be hard work," the male said, looking at Grugreera's right half-arm.

Grugreera was very used to such looks. "I'll do well. They'll send me deep."

"Hm, you do it."

They nodded to each other. The carts started up and rolled out of the farm.

They rode through a thin, dark tunnel for a long time. Grugreera was nodding off when the violent grinding of a bore roused him. The carts slowed into trroorra light. A cloud of dust twirled up into a flue. Purple rreever flared. They passed through the legs of an unfinished bridge.

Two diggers in the dark green cloth that Grugreera would soon wear guided the bore into the left wall. The right tunnel had already been dug, the track laid and connected to the bridge. Two other diggers shoveled rock chunks into metal buckets and lowered the buckets on wires to ground level where two more fellows emptied the rubble into carts. Runners would come at some point and drive the carts to the nearest quarry to be chopped and ground and sifted for minerals. Then they would drive the waste to a pit or to the surface to be dumped. It was a fairly efficient process from start to finish, certain steps of which Grugreera had participated in during his digger apprenticeship, joyfully or reluctantly, depending on which step. But there were things he would do differently.

As for roles, he would gladly mine scrap for minerals. Give him a pickaxe, yes. Give him any role where he could *feel* his work, feel the contact and vibrations, the unique tactile signatures of each species of rock and ore.

Just not these bores, please.

These machines. This dusty digging of tunnels.

The string stopped not far past the bridge. The driver whistled. The green-purple glow of headlight and engine flare illumed a wheel in the ceiling just inside the black mouth of a tunnel. Grugreera and his fellows pulled the metal arms up from the sleeves in the center of their carts and clamped the claws onto the wire running above them. The driver pulled a chain hanging beside the wheel, and the wire pulled them out of the tunnel, up off the tracks, up to the ceiling, and through a path in the stalactites. They dipped, then rose toward another wheel, dipped and rose. They traced a wide river gurgling through a deep crevice. The shores were lined with trroorra flares and water tanks, the walls with patches of white lichen. Fellows waved up at the carts. Grugreera and others waved back.

The river poured into a wide fissure in the high, stone wall, and they followed it. Before long, it poured from the fissure into a vast black lake, and they rode the wire up and up across a yawning, jagged ceiling. Constellations of trroorra flares marked buildings on far shores. Six bright white jorronda flares made an arc of stars floating in space. The carts were ships, and Grugreera was crossing the void, after all. He was moved and conflicted. He hadn't expected to come this way. He'd seen the pyramid replicas once when he was a Youth but from the shore. Now the carts skirted the star-topped peaks.

It pained him—had his entire life—to think of the sacrifice made to build the real things, so many times larger. Tens of thousands of fellows? Hundreds of thousands? He couldn't recall and didn't want to. Whatever the number, it had been far too many for far too long dying of heat and cold and radiation to build monuments to the dream. But why did the dream need monuments? Imagine all the good those people could have done for the hive. But that was so long ago.

A rainbow-rimmed tunnel in the far wall marked the entry into Zone 12. It dilated as they approached and whispered the bustle of the border station. They rolled onto the tracks, stopped to unclip their claws and lower their arms, then started up again and pulled in. Grugreera double-checked his wafer, stretched, turned to congratulate the old male on his retirement once more, and found him dead asleep. "Do well," Grugreera said, and stepped out of the cart.

He showed his wafer to three drivers before finding one headed in his direction. He took the lone empty cart in the string. The female in front of him turned and smiled in a way Grugreera wasn't sure he liked. She wore crimson, a farmer. She was middle-aged. "I can guess," she said.

He smiled politely. "What, fellow?"

"Digger," she said.

It startled him. It was a wild guess, especially given his half-arm.

"You have a look," she said. "Contrary. Determined. You want to do what fellows think you can't. And there's something else."

He straightened his back and changed the subject. "Where are you traveling to?"

"I foraged. Returning to my farm now."

He didn't believe her. She had no blotches in her eyes, no sores on her skin.

"A short reassignment," she explained. "But listen, I saw a lightning storm!"

"Oh, fellow." Now he knew for sure she was lying. He would have heard if there'd been another. Everyone would have heard. His fellows were nearly as obsessed with these phenomena as with the blue spark.

"Not the one, though," she said.

She meant the one felt on the southern edge of the hive several cycles by. These storms were not brand new. They'd been occurring since Grugreera was a Youth, once or twice a ring, symptoms of the atmosphere's apathetically slow rebuild, an electro-magnetism fired out of it and conducted down the southern mountain's icy, twelve-finger peaks. A strong charge might transmit through the source rivers and lava veins underground. But eventually they expended their energy, and a charge had never reached as far as the MaGog hive. Until this one, which had killed, along the way, some unfortunate number of river tamers in the hive beneath the mountain. A sad moment for MaGog's precarious ally. A regrettable event that Grugreera had spared little thought on before and would be happy to forget about again.

The carts left the station and passed into darkness behind the green-purple aura. Grugreera relaxed into his seat and closed his eyes. The female spoke again, a voice in the dark, a choked trill over the squealing wheels. "I wish I wasn't," she said.

"Wasn't what, fellow?"

"Reassigned back."

Grugreera swallowed his disappointment. He chose sympathy for this fellow, yet another willing to die for the opportunity to stare up at the blue spark for brief windows. "Did you birth?" he asked her, steering the conversation in a different direction again.

She was silent. She seemed struck by the question. "Three times!"
she cried.

"Thank you," Grugreera said.

"It's hard giving up a Young," she said.

His stomach flipped.

She sniffled. "You birth and then give it up."

"No. It becomes MaGog. We are one."

"What if I want to decide?"

He shook his head. Tried to shake away these feelings. They were
no use!

"Have you conceived?" she asked. "Do you know?"

He sharpened his trill: *"Please."*

"Listen!" she cried.

To the little voices!

They rolled out of the tunnel into a nursery. Young swam and
splashed in a twisting stream. Others climbed nets and walls and ran
from laughing, scolding caregivers. Some sat in a circle taking their lessons. A trio danced on a kaleidoscopic mosaic set into the stone floor.
Grugreera's heart trembled. It was beautiful. A beautiful peace. But the
farmer was right, it could be even better. He scanned the little faces for
his likeness. He smelled her, a scent memory: Hrulora. He felt a surge
of loyalty, a bursting warmth like the Core inside him, only different.

4

Life after Prime was not consistent or inconsistent with Grugreera's prior imaginings, because he did not allow himself to compare it to his expectations. He did not allow any disappointment. He only lived and served and kept his mind and heart tuned to his intention, every shift working himself to exhaustion and then shuffling to his lead, straightening his back (a harder and harder thing to do), expressing his lifelong passion for MaGog and the Core, and respectfully requesting a reassignment. He had faith it would come, if not from his lead then from census or even from Koren, who would catch wind of his hard work and passion and send him deeper. Fifty-one cycles digging tunnels with a bore. Fifty-one cycles waiting and knowing it would happen. When it did, he couldn't believe it.

He lived the next cycle in a stupor of joy and nerves. Time was strange. He was on a cart again. He was thinking back and looking forward. An older male named Burdrr, short, broad-shouldered like Obudud, was leading him around to different places, including a hollow and a common. They walked down a long, steep ramp into a wave of heat emanating from behind a stone-metal door, and Grugreera was suddenly very aware of and very overwhelmed by his surroundings. He was wearing yellow cloth, and Burdrr was explaining what would happen next and what he was to do.

The wait meant nothing in the end. He would have waited a hundred rings.

Life was a dream. Time was not measured in cycles. Time was the flowing of a river of fire.

Grugreera stepped out of his hollow and onto the path on second level. He was smiling. He was walking but not really seeing where he was going. He was more tired than he had ever been and sore in places that he didn't know he could be. He climbed the net to the common, which overlooked the den, which was small and shapeless and waterless, and he loved it. The common was empty except for a fellow putting out bowls of dried purple-green pulge, vine flesh, lichen, worms, and rrooma legs. She shooed away a pair of scavenging jijurra, who hissed, flicked their fleshy tails, and scampered off. Grugreera realized only then, with an internal smirk, that he'd gotten up before the bells again, despite his exhaustion. He grabbed some food and thanked his fellow, who looked at him like most fellows in the den had since his arrival three cycles by—or was it four already?—like she wasn't sure what to make of him. He walked without a flare down the tunnel. He sat outside the stone-metal door and fell asleep waiting for Burdrr to arrive with the key.

Burdrr lifted Grugreera's apron off the hook and lowered it over his bowed head. The straps settled into the bruises on his shoulders and delivered a delicious pain, the pain of good hard work. Burdrr had told him, during his first shift, that he would get used to the weight over time. It already felt like his true skin: stone-metal body with a core of fire. He ran his hand over the scales. "Burdrr," he said, "I feel so... MaGog."

Burdrr shook his head. He was a funny, older fellow. He was hard-working and loyal and gave himself credit for neither.

"You must feel it too," Grugreera said with a knowing smile.

"Fair work here," Burdrr admitted, as he held up Grugreera's glove.

Grugreera slipped his hand into the cool stone-metal. He made waves with his fingers. The joints squeaked. "Where is the oil?"

"Ran out," Burdrr said.

"Where's Dirra?" Dirra was late again.

Burdrr shrugged. Grugreera helped him dress. They grabbed their helmets and shovels and stepped out of the dressing room into the depot.

"Wait, Burdrr. Quiet. Please, fellow."

The lava slid across the back of the black room. It sizzled. A bubble grew and popped. "We should see it this way and listen, the three of us," Grugreera said. "Once at the beginning of every shift, once at the end. Huh, Burdrr?"

Burdrr didn't answer, but he felt inspired too, Grugreera was sure of it. Grugreera walked to the channel. "Could be wider," he said, looking around and observing the depot's simple layout and infrastructure with a clear mind for the first time. He'd been delirious since starting here. Rapt. Lost in the work, swimming mentally and emotionally in the Core's heat. Now he was waking from the initial joy. He was noticing things and having ideas. "Or we could split a second channel. More fellows could work at once."

"You're lead after a few cycles?" Burdrr grumbled. "Don't need it. Been slow."

"Slow?"

It wouldn't stay that way. It couldn't. Every engine cart, bore, and rover needed three ingredients for fuel, and lava coal was one of them. And surely the engineers in Zone 3 used it at times to test their infantile rocket engines. MaGog was working harder than ever, and Koren did not fill the gap in this depot with an impassioned fellow like Grugreera for no reason!

His sense of urgency was at once exhilarating and calming. There was peace in taking action. He looked around. The track there needed patching. The storehouse was a mess and lacked any logic. Full stone-metal boxes could be stacked on top of empty ones, and it was impossible to tell which was which without unstacking them and lifting the lids. But these were small problems easily fixed with muscle and spirit. He put his hand on Burdrr's shoulder. "Fellow, I'm grateful for you. We'll be the greatest depot. Koren will hear about us."

Burdrr looked bewildered. "Haven't had someone like you."

Dirra walked in, dropped her helmet and shovel on the floor, and sat against a wall. "You missed it, Grugreera," she said. She was heavy and misanthropic, with eyes as small as a Qol's, and Grugreera adored her for no other reason than that she was alive and working here with him and Burdrr.

"Missed it, fellow?" he asked.

"Half a ring by," she said and flicked the piece of purple rreever hanging from the string around her neck. "Couldn't keep up. Runners coming all the time."

"Half a ring by? Why then?"

"How do we know?"

Burdrr pushed a cart stacked with empty boxes out of the storehouse and toward the channel, and Grugreera forgot what they were talking about. He put on his helmet and leaned over the channel. He stared into the gooey, burning, ambient flow and imagined he was staring into the Core itself. He dipped his shovel. "Come, Dirra."

"We have plenty," she moaned.

"We have to be ready."

He was proven right that instant. He was proven to be in the exact right place and time in MaGog history, exactly where he was meant to be. A runner rolled into the depot on a string of empty carts with an order for Zone 3. Grugreera jumped into action. "Burdrr, Dirra, come!" They filled the order too slowly. They had to look inside nineteen boxes to find nine full ones. Grugreera apologized profusely to the runner and assured her that things would be more efficient next time. She seemed befuddled by his energy.

The shift ended. Grugreera begged Burdrr to let him stay on and start reorganizing the storehouse. Burdrr looked at his stump, shook his head, and tossed him the key.

Each cycle Grugreera woke up more inspired. Each time Burdrr or Dirra pleaded with him to slow down, he declined with a smile and a "Thank you, fellow." He didn't fault them for not feeling his hunger to improve and ramp their efforts. He only did what he could to make his passion contagious. It poured from him. It overflowed. So that on his eighth cycle in the deep he was pained beyond description—and his faith in the system sustained a near fatal blow—when the census male, the *very same* who'd delivered his original placement sixty-four cycles by and Zones away (he would never forget that forgettable face or that nervous trill) came to the depot and handed him the second reassignment of his young career.

5

(earlier that cycle)

Droodroovid sat at his slab scanning wafer after wafer, searching for signs in the columns of dots and dashes to the clickity-clack white noise of more wafers being stamped: reports, profiles, and case histories on every fellow in Zones 11 and 12.

Mind open to inspiration, he picked up another wafer off his stack and read: Zone 12, dens 50-59: 58.231 left farm to birth, second time ··· 55.12 discovered large trroorra deposit, promoted ··· 56.76 spoke publicly against MaGog, second time, excommunicated ···58.199 approached by resistance, reported it, promoted ··· 54.23 unsanctioned consumption of dust, first/last warning --- 56.187 served sixteen rings as digger, retired ··· 50.51 reassigned from miner to glome.

He read facts, but he saw much more. Facts were links in chains, pieces of patterns. The numbers were fellows, and he rarely forgot one. His memory was his gift. His store of context only grew. Each new fact added to the shape of a fellow, and Droodroovid saw: exemplary MaGog; consistent psychological troubles; first time stealing with high risk of repeat; regular complaints about placements; passion for Koren (true or contrived—sensing *that* was a trick); isolation from fellows (Droodroovid could empathize); first time speaking publicly against MaGog with low risk of repeat; interest in the surface; suicidal tendencies.

Of course, any census analyst worth the role could string facts together. All of these others were prepared to identify candidates likely suited to particular assignments. They had views on who showed signs of passionate loyalty or potential defection. But most fellows showed signs of both at times. They were human, after all.

Sensing who was *truly* loyal, who would *actually* defect, who was *genuinely* intrepid and would welcome death for the short, thrilling surface life, who would enjoy the murder required of a glome expansion and assimilation force; executing, with minimal friction, a group reassignment involving multiple roles—all of that required something that Droodroovid simply had more of, an artful, mathematical understanding of how isolated behaviors recorded in dots and dashes added up to personalities and *potential*. It was a form of compensation in his nature. He saw things in the wafers that he'd never been able to read in faces or body language or hear in voices. In the patterns, in census, he'd found a way to understand his fellows, and to help them.

He read: 56.73 ··· stalked a female, second time, same female, reassigned to glome. He remembered this fellow. There was something there maybe. He walked into the stacks to retrieve the fellow's profile and case history. He was leafing through the wafers when the next assignment came and with it the twist in his belly. Hruma waved him over. Her loose, wrinkled skin jiggled.

Soon enough, Droodroovid thought, as he approached her. Any cycle now, some watcher would walk in here, announce Hruma's retirement, and tell her to name her successor. Droodroovid would have to be careful. He'd have to make a couple of mistakes, minor things to keep himself off the top of the list but without risking his current position.

Hruma rubbed her drooping face. "Pirrit vine, large tangle above 12, near 129."

Good, Droodroovid thought. The surface. His mind started racing. "12-129," he repeated.

"Ten fellows," Hruma said. "No engineers, no glome."

Very good. A group reassignment and fairly large. No mistakes on *this* one. "Understood," he said and took the wafer.

He paced between the analysts reading at the slabs that ran down the center of the room and the others punching wafers at the machines that lined the wall, together building the system's knowledge of its fellows one dot and dash at a time. He waited for a number to jump from his memory, something in the 12-120s, 130s, 140s. Nothing did. Seventy-five thousand fellows in Zones 11 and 12 were a lot to sift through in preparation for these moments. But he couldn't let them slip away. 12-110, 12-100, 12-150, 12-160—there. There was one there.

He tapped Llerroda and Noorra and gave them the instructions. He followed them into the stacks but hung back, buying time for a second *potential* to bubble up in his mind. It was simple for the other two. They'd find their candidates quickly. It was a short surface assignment with minimal risk of permanent sickness. Many fellows would jump at the chance, especially now, with Gog and Qol both just past perihelion and Qol nearly as big in the sky as it ever got. But Droodroovid was looking for more than the typical expressed interest in seeing the blue spark.

He walked the stacks, running his fingers over the wafers. He plucked one here and there, skimmed. Llerroda and Noorra waited for him at the edge of the stacks. Hruma watched. But Droodroovid needed one more. Always two for group assignments of any size. That was his goal. And if they could turn one out of every two ...

It came to him. He'd limited his search to Zone 12, but the 12-120's shared a border with the 11-230's, and he had one there. An odd profile, a bit of a gamble, but a fellow with true markers *and*, though the fellow didn't know it, connections to the resistance.

Droodroovid found the fellow's bin, plucked his profile wafer, and left the stacks. Llerroda and Noorra handed Droodroovid their suggestions. He placed his and theirs down on an empty slab, read through them quickly, and selected his ten: three builders, two diggers, one handler, two farmers, and two forgemasters. He shuffled them so that the two potentials were not on top of each other, then returned to Hruma.

Hruma made a cursory review of the first several wafers but stopped on the handler. "One arm," she said.

Droodroovid was ready with his rationale. "Means he's had to work harder. And manual digging skill translates to the assignment. Deeply loyal too."

"Passion for the Core," Hruma pushed back. "Works deep. Won't like leaving." She was right. And she had another point too, though she didn't realize it. Tucked into the male's history, which Droodroovid had read a good chunk of—he remembered it well; he remembered delivering the male's initial placement—was a report of the male fainting when seeing the surface during the pre-Prime ritual. A poor choice then, perhaps. An odd profile, a gamble. But the markers were there, and the ties to the resistance. And the best candidates, in Droodroovid's experience, were those different from the herd, physically or mentally, willingly or unwillingly. Droodroovid, a member of the latter categories, couldn't read a face, but he could read personalities in the dots and dashes, and he could see a half-arm. "I find the ones who talk fearless about the surface aren't up to it. Ones who seem unsure end up moved. This male works hard. And deeply loyal." He shut his mouth, held his breath, and waited.

Hruma grumbled, brought the wafer closer to her graying eyes, put it down, skimmed the others. "Approved, go."

Droodroovid left quickly. In the tunnel, he exhaled.

The eight went as expected. It was a short assignment with minimal risk of permanent sickness. The fellows expressed their loyalty and gratitude, whether they felt it or not. They believed that he would report them if they didn't. He gave them their wafers and left them to find their way to their new sites. He touched a few corners of Zone 12 over the course of most of a cycle before meeting the first *potential*.

He always saved them for last, and he always leaked confidence on the way. No matter his intentions, he was delivering them into ambush.

Half would turn. Half would scream for watchers or glome and wake up later in resistance cells with aching heads. Each attempted conversion meant lives and the resistance at risk. But they'd learned from many mistakes. They'd refined their criteria and tightened their methods and processes. Besides, this was a long game. There was time, a generation or more.

The cart string pulled into a narrow, curved den being built alongside a narrow, curved river. The air was thick with chalky dust rising slowly into the flue in the spiked ceiling. Bores and pickaxes ground, crushed, and clanged. Droodroovid stayed in his cart. He could leave now and tell Hruma that he'd made a mistake. But he always told himself that in these moments. It had devolved into a superstitious ritual.

He stepped out, cleared his throat. "Karramar?" he called, his voice drowned by the sounds of the tunnels and paths being cut. He waited for a lull. "Karramar?" he yelled again. A female three levels up a scaffold paused with her pickaxe raised, looked down at him, observed his blue cloth, and seemed to curse. She took her time climbing down.

"Well? Glome?" she said. "Reassignments all the time. Impossible to get things done."

Droodroovid had no insight into her tone, but the words she chose expressed frustration and were consistent with her profile. She'd spoken against Koren publicly once before, once that they had a record of. He handed her the wafer. "Short assignment. Vine tangle. Minimal risk of permanent sickness."

She looked at the wafer for a long time. She ground her teeth. Those were typically good signs. "For MaGog, right?" she asked. "Do well?"

He nodded and left. He felt confident that he had his one out of two. That meant the odds were against him for the second.

He found the one-armed handler alone in the depot, hammering away at a track by the low, orange light of the lava stream. The handler didn't see him, and he stayed in the shadows, wavering in his conviction. Perhaps he shouldn't push his luck. He likely had his one already.

He almost left. Almost.

"Grugreera," he said.

"Yes, fellow," the one-armed male confirmed without looking up. "Can I help?" He turned and froze.

Droodroovid's pulse quickened. His skin dried.

Grugreera swooned, leaned against the trough. "Why are you here?"

Droodroovid was thrown. The utter misery on this fellow's face crashed through the mental wall that had separated Droodroovid from his fellows for his entire life. He read a face for the first time and felt what was behind it. He was destroying a life. It called everything into question. How many other lives had he ruined? And for what? A slow trickle of defections? What did it amount to when compared to Koren's growing hundreds of thousands?

But the markers! Droodroovid thought. The unalloyed passion for the Core and the underworld. The long history of questioning why the blue world. The recent lack of interest in coupling, and the strong feelings for one female, Hrulora, a member of the resistance. Ties to another member. If only this fellow knew!

But no, how terribly wrong. The "markers" meant nothing. This male's live, contorted expression could never be written in dots and dashes. And if Droodroovid could be this wrong in reading the wafers, what good was he? How completely alone!

"I know you," Grugreera said. "My first placement. It was the best moment of my life."

The utter sadness in his trill. The disbelief in this as coincidence. This was a grave error, and they hadn't yet come to the worst part. Droodroovid couldn't go through with it. He couldn't move. Grugreera took the wafer from his hand, read it, laughed and coughed, a sound like he was hacking up a broken heart.

The surface. The antithesis of everything this male loved.

But the markers!

Grugreera waved Droodroovid away, turned, and stared into the lava. Droodroovid left defeated.

6

The lift jerked and rose. "Helmets," said the forager lead.

Grugreera and the other extras—ten of them in all—put their helmets on and snapped them into the collars of their mollirra metal suits. Grugreera saw his dulled reflection in another fellow's suit and had trouble believing it was him. But this was very real. The cold was leaching. His breath was sharp and loud over the steady hiss of stinking air coming from the pack on his back, the off-gas of some mineral and chemical concoction he'd learned the ingredients to in his alchemy apprenticeship but which he now lacked all interest in remembering. He saw, through the thin strip of glass in his helmet and the leader's, her burned, blotched eyes, wide, restless, and *smiling*. A dark, open sore on the bridge of her nose glistened. She coughed, and Grugreera flinched.

He would battle through this. He would. He wouldn't faint again. He was older now, stronger. And the system wasn't broken, no! Koren needed diggers for this work. The best diggers. Pirrit vine did not respond favorably to being axed, and its skin was harder than many minerals. There were few roles more fundamental to MaGog's survival than replenishing its stock of vine seed. Koren needed Grugreera *here*, and only for a short time.

"Once more," the leader said, her trill muted by their helmets. "Remember it: cold hurts, heat kills. Light will start faint. Won't be sure it's there. Feel better than you've ever felt. Start back *then*. Don't hesitate. *Help each other remember.*" She looked from one to another with her ravaged eyes. Grugreera looked up at the ceiling. "Lean in," she said, but Grugreera remained outside the circle of helmets. "Not much time. Take our radiation in small doses." She winked horribly. Puss leaked from her sore. "Do the job, but look around. Look up. The *horizon*. The *spark*."

The lift screeched to a halt. The door groaned opened, and they filed out into a long, low-ceilinged, mollirra metal building. Two rovers sat idling to the left. Five suited foragers—full-timers living on borrowed time—stood by a rack of axes to the right. They motioned to Grugreera and the other extras to hurry over. Fire pits along the back wall cast frenetic trroorra light and shadows and did nothing to temper the biting cold.

Grugreera and five others were given axes. Four were given sacks for collecting. The full-timers took axes, and the fifteen fellows hustled to the rovers where the lead was waiting. It was dark inside. No flues or holes, so no flares. No windows except a small circle for the driver. Maximum protection from the elements, though a few layers of mollirra metal cut the cosmic radiation in half at best. They'd commenced dying bit by bit. Grugreera sat on a bench and held his helmeted head in his gloved hands. He tried to breathe away the knot in his chest and only managed to tighten it. The building gates screeched open. The engine fired, and they were off rumbling across the surface.

"Not long," said the lead.

It felt very long to Grugreera. He was sure he felt a sore forming over his left eye already and another on his neck. Fellows shifted in their seats, laughed nervously. The rover skidded to a stop. The leader slid the door open. "Go!"

Nothing changed. It was black traded for black. Then the wind cried, the stars resolved in the glass strip of Grugreera's helmet, and it hit him like it did the first time: the immensity, the unbounded plain of rock and dust, the incomprehensible infinity of space. His mind was stretched to its physical limits. He whipped his head around in search of

Qol and found it hanging between two of Gog's five misshapen moons, little, pale green Brreev, and big, yellow-with-red-veins Rrin.

The leader grabbed his arm, and they ran up a gentle rise. Trroorra light shone from beyond a ridge. Fellows were shouting over a chilling, hissing whine. Grugreera reached the edge and looked down on a long, shallow trench lined with writhing pirrit vine. Fellows hacked for seeds. It was carnage. It was life. It was oddly stirring.

He skidded down the slope into a space between fellows. He raised his axe and brought it straight down. A shock fired up his arm. The vine, barely scratched, cried and reached for him. He looked to the leader and mimicked her angled strikes. Soon the vines were recoiling from him. The exposed, moist, gray-purple flesh iced over. The seeds oozed out and froze in their flow. He chopped the seeds out, called for a collector, and moved a few steps down the edge of the tangle.

The vines enjoyed some revenge. A leg snapped; a fellow screamed. Grugreera and a few other fellows hacked him out, and the leader and another carried him back up the slope. Grugreera resumed a feverish slashing. A fellow put a hand on his shoulder. "Pace, fellow," she said. They would not be out long. They would take their radiation in small doses. But this was not quite a sprint. Grugreera slowed his pace to hard and steady.

The cold stopped bothering him. He forgot what that meant. Someone banged on his helmet and pointed to the sky above the ridge. It was gray-black. They ran up the ridge and down to the rover. Before getting in, Grugreera and all sixteen of his fellows turned and looked back. An insidious rainbow stretched across the horizon, climbed the sky, and drowned out the stars. Gorr breached and scorched. This was meant to be part of the experience, part of the draw of these assignments, seeing the brilliant, red, killer dome. To Grugreera, it was simply a waste of life.

A silver silhouette against the red was a lost fellow. No. "Scavenger!" Grugreera yelled and pointed. The leader yanked him into the rover.

He was afraid again next cycle, but he was in control of his fear. He knew that the sooner they met their quota, the sooner he'd be back in the deep. He expressed his love for his fellows as they rode the lift. He learned their names. He offered his observations about how the vines moved. The leader confirmed what he said and added a few tips. The others smiled and nodded.

The cold was pain. It was not something one got used to. But Grugreera relished it. He relished suffering alongside his fellows. He hacked like MaGog depended on it, which it did. Other extras stuck close to him and followed his lead, and they made good progress down the crevice.

When Grugreera no longer felt the pain, he knew it was time to go. He tapped shoulders, and the group executed an organized departure. They saw two resistance scavengers in shimmering silver suits fitted to their bodies. Qol suits. He pointed them out to the leader, who countered by pointing to the burning horizon. Grugreera slammed his mollirra metal fist against the side of the rover and stepped in.

He sat with the other extras but was quiet during the meal, which was excellent once again. Fresh cuts of vine flesh. Spiced pulge. A wide variety of worms and crawlers. It was true that foragers lived well in exchange for their shortened lives. The food. The large common. The mosaic on the far wall depicting images of the surface *before*: green and yellow hills, brown and black herds, blue-gray lakes, towering, pale, metal towers, all beautiful in its way. The viewing eye, which Grugreera knew would not open during his short time here but within which he pictured Koren telling them that MaGog was fine, the system was fine, everything was progressing, they had plenty of seeds now, go back to your homes. The dust in ready supply and startlingly good, judging by the shimmering eyes and face-stretching smiles of his fellows. He did not partake, but he went to the dome to dance. He thought it might do him good. It did him something.

The music was a rich tonal tapestry of drums and pipes and bells, and Grugreera quickly fell into a trance. He danced and reflected. He pondered his life and its turns. He lamented the resistance, the lost souls. He looked to the future, to changes in the system, adaptations for a time when the migration would be humming and the underworld evolving into its new epoch. His ideas flourished.

He opened his eyes and saw her. Her rolling shoulders: a rhythm signature. She turned her face into the halo of a trroorra flare. Her lighting-strike necklace swung.

Hrulora.

He went to her, heart in his throat. She saw him coming. Her perfectly round eyes widened.

"How is this?" he asked. He needed to know. Was he in control of his life? These things kept happening. These feelings!

"In relations, remember," she said. "I'm sent all around." But she also seemed unsettled by the coincidence, in a hive of six hundred thousand.

"Relations cover one zone or two," he said, trying to understand.

"Most do," she said, swaying to the beat.

"Please stop." It came out sharper than he intended.

She didn't stop, but she forgave him with a look that saw through him, through his flaws. He wanted to confess them to her, every single one.

"You were reassigned," she said, her trill a melody weaved into the syncopated braid of percussion.

"Forager."

She stepped closer. Her breath! He remembered the taste of her mouth! She looked into his eyes, searching for burns.

"Only two cycles so far," he mumbled.

She stepped back. "So many reassignments. Many to glome, Zone 3. Fellows moved from where they have passion."

"Yes," he said. She understood. "Loyalty first, but sometimes—"

She put a finger to her lips, which turned up in the slightest, most dangerously beautiful smile he'd ever seen and ever would. "One MaGog," she said. "The next of our next might go."

"*Our* next?" he blurted. Had she birthed his after all? Could she know?

"I can't know," she said, answering his thought. She glanced around for watchers and wall-eyes. "Not ours. Magog's."

"Of course," he whispered. And that was true. That was right. This need was perilous. This utter distraction. "MaGog. The destiny."

"We crossed again, fellow," she said, as though that was all that really mattered. But she didn't believe that, and he knew it.

"We did," he said.

"I have to go."

She *had* to. And he *needed* her to.

"Yes, Hrulora."

She left. She was gone. Her body, her mouth, and the things unsaid. A question she hadn't asked, the one that any other fellow would have. Had he seen the blue world? She knew him better than that.

Grugreera imagined that the vines were stone-metal with lava inside, and he lost himself in the pleasure of splitting them open. He looked back and saw that he had carved a path through the middle of the tangle and down the crevice. The others were far behind. A wounded vine hissed and tried for his ankle with the last of its life.

He paused with his axe lifted. A tapping sound? There again. He turned. A silver-suited scavenger motioned with a finger, then disappeared around a bend. Grugreera took off without thinking. Another scavenger grabbed his arm, and a third threw an arm around his neck from behind and squeezed. The one he'd chased ripped the axe from his hand, shone an electric light in his face, and then turned the light on his own rounded glass helmet. It was Obudud.

"Grugreera, I came for you," he rasped. "You can have a better life."

Grugreera's head swam with rage. He couldn't speak. There was nothing to say.

"The oasis exists. We'll go there."

The one holding Grugreera's arm pointed to the gray-black sky.

"We have a rover. Suits like these, Grugreera. Come."

But Grugreera was deaf to this sad treachery.

Obudud gripped his shoulder. "Grugreera, males and females match there. Raise their young together."

Grugreera lost it. He ripped his arm away from the first traitor and shoved him into the vines, then bent his knees and launched himself backward, falling hard on the second. Obudud jumped on top of him. "Grugreera, it exists!" Grugreera palmed Obudud's helmet and smashed it against a rock. His head hit the splintered glass with a thud.

The one in the vines screamed. The other crawled away. The light was coming. Grugreera heaved Obudud over a shoulder and lumbered up the crevice, calling for MaGog. His skin tingled, then itched, then burned. He fell to one knee, lifted himself and his dead weight with the strength of not wanting to die, of not accepting that. Against the deep blue sky above the crevice: his fellows sliding down.

The rover was glowing by the time they reached the station. Every fellow was peeling from head to toe. Grugreera stared at Obudud's crumpled form on the floor of the lift and heard him say, over and over as they descended: *Grugreera, males and females match there. Raise their young together.*

7

Grugreera filled stone-metal boxes with lava and stacked them to cool in the storehouse, which was filled from wall-to-wall and floor-to-ceiling and thus a source of anxiety. No runners had come since he'd returned. He didn't know exactly how long ago that had been. Having seen and felt how cycles start, he had little interest in time. There was only the work, and he was working.

"Rest," old Burdrr said again.

Heavy, little-eyed Dirra sat in a corner chewing on a crawler leg.

"Come, fellows," Grugreera said. "Help me with this one."

Another glome came, and Grugreera sighed. Two had come already and asked him the same exact questions about what had happened on the surface. Now a third. A glaring inefficiency. But this fellow was not here for him. "Go to the nearest common with a viewing eye," the fellow said. Grugreera looked at Burdrr and Dirra to confirm that they'd heard what he'd just heard. They shrugged.

The nearest common with a viewing eye was theirs, and it was packed to the walls with a few hundred MaGog of every color cloth: a squirming, speculating microcosm of the hive. Dirra and Burdrr tunneled into the crowd to get closer to the eye, but Grugreera stayed at the back, finding comfort in the space behind him. Skittish chatter bounced off the stone walls and fed on itself until it was more than Grugreera could bear. Then the dark aperture opened and cut it off. Koren stepped forward. "We are MaGog," she said.

Her metallic trill sliced Grugreera's heart. His love for her frightened him. Everyone held their breath.

"One with the Core. United in our love for her for keeping us warm. United in our goal of leaving her."

The trilled roar shook Grugreera's brain. He did not contribute to it. Koren stomped her scythe and silenced them.

"I can see some of you, not all," she said. "I have a lot to tell you. I know you will help each other stay calm."

It was a wide broadcast if she couldn't see all of them. It was said she had fifty or more eyes built into the wall that she faced behind the device that sent her image and voice to them from somewhere in the maze of Zone 3.

"Nearly all together. All MaGog except those in critical positions."

It was hard to believe. It was unprecedented. Grugreera's skin moisture vacillated.

"Rare times," she said, pushing a low (amused?) whir through her fans. "I start with our history. You'll understand why. Where did we come from?"

Every fellow in that common and, Grugreera assumed, every fellow in every other packed common and dwell in sixteen Zones, said it together: "The surface."

But Grugreera didn't say it. It was too fresh.

"The surface," Koren echoed. "The vast. Mountains, forests, lakes, and rivers. Proud, strong cities. You know the stories. The caregivers taught you. They're all true."

MaGog made sounds of collective dreaming. Koren allowed them a brief indulgence, then sobered them. "That world ended. Close your eyes now. Do it. Imagine it. Just try."

Grugreera kept one eye open. He'd seen and felt enough of the surface recently to empathize with the ancestors. He had no desire to relive it.

"A sea dried," she said and brought her face closer to the eye. Did she see Grugreera? He might have been the only fellow in the hive looking into those bottomless holes at that moment. They dragged him down. She closed them, and he wavered, the spell broken. "A continent burned. Everything else choked to death by the poison smoke shell, which ate the atmosphere and then died of starvation when there was nothing left. Sentenced then. One thousand sixty-one rings. I want you to see them, the survivors. See them looking back into the suffocating haze. See them walking into the caves in search of a future for their Young and for the race. For us. Consider what they went through. Remember them."

Fellows sniffled and reached for each other through the darkness behind their eyelids. Grugreera took a groping, dry hand in his. Another touched his stump and recoiled. Koren lifted them up again. "Remember, too, what they found. Life enough if they lived together. And they did. They took the offerings and made a new world. And whose offerings? Who took them in?"

Grugreera whispered along with the MaGog shout: "The Core."

"The beautiful irony of our survival," she said, sharpening her pitch, cutting into Grugreera again. "The strange designs of life: that the very killer, that soulless, lifeless, random wanderer through space should activate our Core and drive up her heat. See it spewing from the long-dormant volcanoes on the western shore!"

Fellows wept. Grugreera dropped the hand he'd been holding. There was something going on. The irregular timing of this meeting. Her passionate telling.

"But we were destined," she purred. "It was only time in the way. Four hundred rings in the underworld, then the Pramma."

"The Pramma!" MaGog echoed.

"The Pramma," she said. "The vision. Arrarra saw the blue star, saw it as an afterlife. But I like to believe—yes, fellows, I *do* believe—that MaGog knew it from the start, deep down. That it grew as a seed in the collective mind, the knowledge that we would reach it in *this* life. And oh, fellows, open your eyes."

Fellows did. They struggled to breathe. They held each other.

"We are close, yes?" she goaded. There was laughter in those eyes and in her tone, Grugreera was sure of it. Did no one else notice? She paced left, right, stopped in the center of the eye, and spun her scythe. "What stood in our way?"

"Greed!" fellows yelled. "Oppression!" "The Marradar!" "Ignorance!"

"Yes," she said, the stone-metal sibilating in her throat. "Above all, the mistreatment of our Mothers and Young. Too long. Just too, too long. I think of all the lives and time wasted."

Grugreera felt that loss in the depths of his soul. He thought of Hrulora. He pictured a tiny version of her giggling in a nursery somewhere, and it crushed him.

"*But,*" Koren said. "If not for the time wasted, it would not be us."

Grugreera exhaled and nodded, grateful for this return to the present and the task at hand. The final push. But wait—

"Why do we live as we do? With eyes in the walls and watchers and our technology safe inside the maze?"

"Spies!" fellows cried. "The resistance!" "The Qols!"

Koren nodded, reached into the side of the eye, and pulled Obudud into view. He was gagged. His eyes bulged with terror. His cracked face seeped blood.

Grugreera's stomach churned. He knew he'd killed Obudud by bringing him in. He just hadn't expected to see it happen. It was right. It was just. He only wished, sometimes, that life could be simpler.

Koren drummed long, sinewy fingers on Obudud's shoulder. "I feel for the resistance, I do," she said. "Troubled, misguided, lied to by the Qols. But we will come to *them*. Every life is precious. I take no pleasure." The scythe went up and down. Obudud's back arched, and his eyes widened in disbelief at the pain. He screamed into the gag. Koren grabbed him with one hand by the back of the neck, turned him, and showed MaGog the flayed flesh and severed spine, the two curved marks in the shape of her weapon. She dropped him like a sack.

It's over, Grugreera said to himself and to his fellow. *Goodbye, Obudud.*

But it wasn't. She'd yet to come to the true purpose of this meeting. She hadn't called the entire hive together just for an execution.

"The resistance is a limb," she said. "A tool. A pet. I was there. I was a Youth—you all know the story—when the first Qols came. I saw what happened. Still, I didn't hate them. They were only afraid, I told myself. And I came to power knowing I would reach out in a different way than the Marradar had, that I would secure our destiny through cooperation. I've tried."

She paced again, stopped, jabbed her scythe at the ceiling.

"A spacious and fertile world!" she said. "And they came to ours, why? To help a humble race? No, to keep us below the surface. To deny us the right we were born into when the meteor hit. Cowards. Fearful by their nature. I've offered peaceful terms. I've bent to some of theirs. They've answered with greater demands, espionage, and murder. *That's* why the maze and the system. They couldn't know."

She took a deep, vibrato inhale, sucking the breath from Grugreera and his six hundred thousand fellows, then breathing it back into them. But it was rank.

"I lied to you," she said.

Grugreera's head throbbed. He wished this was a nightmare. He needed to wake up and feel the relief of knowing she hadn't really said that.

"Think of your life," she went on. "Everything you know is true. Everything but one thing. *One.* You can't know how much it has hurt me to keep it from you. You can't know how hard it's been. But MaGog, it will *please you.*"

Grugreera felt in himself what he saw in his fellows all around, temperatures and moisture fluctuating, a shared terrified-excited tactile pulse.

"MaGog, you know us to be a generation or more from going. So do they. *That is why.*"

Grugreera realized it then, but it was in his sub-mind. He couldn't name it.

"I want you to close your eyes once more."

This time, Grugreera did.

"See the twelve-finger mountain to the south touching the edge of space. *Feel* the ice."

Grugreera's skin froze.

"Now *feel* it melting as Gorr touches the horizon, the water trickling down and seeping into the underworld."

It seeped into his skin, now soft and cool.

"Now picture a lightning storm."

Streaks behind his lids. Fellows oohed and aahed.

"Picture the most recent, ferocious one. Eighty-five cycles by. Hear it like the sky tearing open!"

It tore his mind down the middle.

"*Feel* the electric shock, down through the drenched fingertips, the arms, into the underground, into our rivers and *magnetic magma,* our *veins.*"

His blood was charged, burning lava.

"Some of you felt it. Some of our friends beneath the mountain died, sad, but we were waiting. We'd come to know what the storms do to their satellites. *That* was the moment. Now open your eyes and look into mine."

Grugreera did and was tortured by not knowing if he could trust them.

What lie, Koren?!

"Eighty-five cycles by, on the back of the storm that touched us here and blinded the Qol satellites, your Dondante launched with a glome force. Four cycles by they landed and fought the oppressors and won."

Seizures. The throng a wracked, hysterical mess. Grugreera stumbled backward. Her voice faded as he ran. "Breathe now, help each other," she said. "Fellows, this is only the beginning. We need each other now more than ever..."

PART TWO

AFTERMATH

8

Towering black pillars of smoke dominated the ashen sky. Fires ravaged the forest. Nima lake, between the village and the prophet's island, was a churning red- and purple-black muck of Tiralee and vramen blood and body parts. The stench of burning and death. A Tiralee bellowed.

Kade lowered Dawlis onto the floor of the boat, lifted Orly by his scruff, and tossed him in, then Fred, then Jackson. Piper shoved the boat off the rocks and jumped in. Kade grabbed the wheel, turned the engine, and dropped the throttle.

They tore across yet unstained royal blue water, rumbled over the back of a vramen and stained it. They hit the mouth of the narrow in-flowing river to the south and carved along the curved bank. The engine screamed. Dawlis slid across the floor in a pool of his own blood. The groos stood over him licking his face and wound, white paws and snouts soaked red. The river widened and straightened. "Piper, take the wheel," Kade yelled in Korial.

Kade tore off the top of his suit, dropped to his knees, and wrapped Dawlis's cleaved collarbone. Dawlis expelled a breath. His eyes rolled. Kade slapped him in the face. "No, no, no." He put a hand on the boy's chest and felt nothing and realized that the Mind was insane. It was beyond any semblance of reason that it should end this way, that Dawlis should spend his life on another world and come back only to witness Gog's first attack, be central to it, and die; that Lorel should search for her son for four turns on Qol and seventeen on Earth and speak to him only once before sending him back to this fate; that Shaw should never see his son alive again; that the Mind should speak to Peis—surely dead too by now, and for what?—through prophecy of such a dramatic and pointless return.

Pointless and insane. That's how Kade felt as he tried to pump Dawlis's heart back to life. In vain. All in vain. He sat back against the side of the boat and stared into the streaming trees. The groos howled over the shredding engine. Piper's shoulders convulsed with sobs. Dawlis jolted awake.

Kade lost time in a laser focus. There was only the driving as fast as possible, the listening for Piper to tell him when to turn, the growing of the space between them and what had just happened, the knowing that it would be forever right behind them and closing.

The river narrowed and bent. Pale, aquadynamic heads bobbed on the surface up ahead. Canoes on a muddy bank. Kade cut the engine and ran the boat aground. Tiralee swam forward. Nimar came out of the trees and waded into the water. Kade crouched down, draped Dawlis's good arm over his shoulder and stood him up. "Take him. Help," Kade said in English.

A Nimar man and woman thrashed through the water, wailing. Piper's parents. He jumped down into their arms. Dawlis's blood washed off his feet and ankles and swirled in the royal blue. Tiralee waved it away, pearl-white brows furrowed.

"What came?" a Nimar woman screamed.

"Take him," Kade said.

"Where are the others?" rumbled a Tiralee man.

Kade lowered Dawlis back down onto the floor of the boat and jumped off.

They closed on him.

"Speak!" demanded an older Nimar man, voice cracking, eyes blood-shot, hand on the hilt of his sheathed machete.

Kade put a hand on his xim. "Ships," he said, and the truth sounded strange coming out of his mouth. Maybe it wasn't the truth. Maybe a warrior hadn't traveled here in a meteor, and ships hadn't crashed into the forest. Maybe a swarm of vramen, the great green fish, kept out of the southern waters for generations and denied their seasonal migrations and feasts, hadn't spilled into the lake and exacted their revenge.

"Ships from where?" asked a Tiralee.

"Gog," he answered.

"He's lost his mind," said a Nimar. Kade wished she was right. He wasn't sure she was wrong.

A rubbery, webbed hand squeezed his wrist, an older Tiralee woman. "Where are the others?"

The others. Those who'd been left behind to gather food and sup-plies after the meteor hit, enough to last them until the ash no longer rained on their village. Kade looked into the woman's wet eyes and said, "Mos' if not all of them are dead."

Miserable gasps. Groaning and weeping. They may not have believed it was Gog, but they knew their loved ones had met with something ter-rible. They had eyes to see the pillars of smoke rising from the direction of what had been, until very recently (it already felt like a past life to Kade), their sublime home. They had ears and hearts to hear and feel the crashes.

"Not all!" a Nimar man shrieked from the shore, desperate for that to be true. "We have to go back."

"We were attacked by Gog," Kade said with an edge he hoped would cut through their disbelief and spare them a drawn-out waking up to the horrific reality. "I'll tell you what I know. Dawlis needs help."

"Dawlis," a Tiralee said in a tone of remembering.

"The prophecy," said another.

"Did they come for him?" asked a third.

They tightened around Kade and the boat, muttering to themselves and to each other, jabbing fingers up at Dawlis. The groos leaned over the side of the boat and growled.

"They knew!" shouted a Nimar woman.

"Back up," said Kade. He was starting to worry about himself, about what he might do. He took his hand off his xim.

"You knew this would happen!"

"No, back up!"

Isulu, Nimar matriarch and one of three people in Nima who knew where Dawlis had spent the last eighteen turns of his life, a celestial truth that did worse than nothing to explain what had happened here, elbowed her way to the front. "Quiet!" she screeched. "Don't let that one die. Bring him down."

Kade helped Dawlis out of the boat, and two Nimar led him ashore. The groos leapt, splashed, and followed. Red stained the royal blue once more, and now there was too much of it for the Nimar and Tiralee to avoid. It licked them with its tendrils.

Isulu stuck a bony finger into Kade's chest. "Speak," she said. Her gray hair was wild. Her eyes were dark and hard. "Someone get him a cloth."

She was looking at his nose. He touched it and felt the split bridge, the caked blood. He'd come that close to losing his eyes or half of his head to Radin's black sword. "They're out there," he said. "Go deeper into the forest. Send scouts."

"Who?"

They still couldn't believe it. They looked like their minds were breaking along with their hearts.

"MaGog," he said.

"MaGog," Isulu whispered.

"They came in ships. Their leader came first in the meteor. The shadow from the prophecy."

"Came for him?" she asked.

"Yes," Kade said. Another wholly irrational truth. "They came for him as a boy too. We never knew why."

Kade saw then the red- and purple-black churning muck. He smelled the billowing fires.

Eaten and burned and blown apart, his merciless thought.

"Where is Peis?" Isulu asked.

"Dead," he said. "Likely."

Dawlis shuddered on the muddy beach. He lay with his head on a log, staring up at the sky, his eyes soft, curious, questioning. What was he seeing? What had he seen from the floor of the boat while his heart was stopped?

The Nimar and Tiralee backed away. They held each other. They looked at Kade and waited. They needed him to tell them more, though they were terrified of what they were going to hear. And Kade suddenly needed to exorcise it.

To expunge and analyze it, to probe it for meaning. "The meteor," he began. "A man inside." The melting, black, red-glowing meteor; the scaffold and sparking electronics inside; the footsteps in the ash leading out of the crater; his fight with this Harbinger, the Archfiend of Gog, Radin, the Dondante, tall and gangly, tree-strong in black, metal-scaled suit, narrow head and big, round, opaque yucs sucking to a bone white face, fighting with xim and wave—*yes, waves on the dark planet!*—from speeding boats; the vramen trailing the Harbinger's boat; the two Nimar boys tied to the back of it (Kade spared the survivors nothing; he gave them violent closure); the vramen pouring into the lake; the ships thundering down; the Tiralee and Nimar giving all; the Archfiend walking up the face of the island like doom; Dawlis shattering his black collar as he split Dawlis's collarbone; Peis standing with his xim raised in one bloody hand, as Radin rose from where he fell, and as Piper, the groos, and Kade, with Dawlis draped over his shoulder, made their escape.

They wheezed and sobbed, vomited and cried. They asked no questions. They didn't know what to ask.

A weak bellow upriver turned every head. Three Tiralee floated down on their backs, their heads barely above the water. One was Vinson. Kade swam to him and held him up by one arm, thick as Kade's thigh and cut with a wide, seeping grin of vramen teeth marks. A Tiralee woman took his other arm, and a man tended his wound. Kade stared into the stormy, gray depths of his eyes and tried to see what he had seen, as though if he was still picturing it, Kade might find it playing there and might learn something important. That's all they could do. Relive it from all angles.

Vinson, another of the three who knew where Dawlis had lived his life, looked at Kade, looked around at his people, and spoke in a scratched, bass tone of finality: "The rest of us are gone. I don't know about the Nimar."

They learned that moment. A Nimar woman covered in dirt and blood stumbled out of the trees. It was Jovi, the woman who'd ridden in the canoe with Dawlis on the ninarc of their arrival in Nima. She was alone.

"Bring her down!" Kade yelled. Her perspective would be critical. She could tell them about MaGog.

Dawlis rolled over in the mud. He planted a hand, then a foot, and stood. Slumped to the side of his severed left collarbone, he looked directly into the eyes of a whimpering, shattered Nimar woman standing next to him. *His* were full and empty. They were guilty and accepting of his guilt for dragging his shadow into this land. They were knowing and somewhere else. He looked at a man, who looked away; at another woman, who also couldn't bear it; at a child, who stared right back. And Dawlis looked ancient and childlike. He went down on one knee and bowed his head to the peoples of Nima.

Piper, the third burdened with the celestial knowledge, burdened too with having witnessed the carnage from the island's plateau, the hero who'd shoved Radin with a wave allowing Dawlis to land his blow, pushed through the crowd, fell to his knees in the mud, and threw his arms around Dawlis. Dawlis embraced him with his good arm. Nimar and Tiralee wept terribly.

"South," Kade said in English. He looked back to make sure they weren't being followed. Jackson did the same. There'd been threats. There'd been some whose grief cried for justice and blood and who were willing to go machete against xim for the principle of not letting Kade and Dawlis simply walk out there. But cooler heads had prevailed, and Isulu and Vinson had sent them off with provisions. They were more use to the Nimar and Tiralee alive and as far away as possible. Maybe MaGog were still hunting Dawlis. Better to draw them away.

"A small port, only one in Nima. The guard will be there but maybe not in numbers. Maybe we can slip out on a flyer or boat or risk a message to Ayn." For now, Kade kept his glasses off and thus undetectable.

There was a clearing up ahead. Dawlis, leading, headed straight for it. "Dawlis, don't." But the boy was already standing in the grass with his groos and looking back. Guard ships hovered over the island a few kels away, ten or eleven of them, green and blue metal triangles. One dropped out of the ash ceiling and joined the herd. Another split off from it and flew east. "Keep moving," Kade said. "Keep to the trees."

Dawlis looked at him as though surprised he was there, nodded, and led on.

"The meteors," Kade said, his mind racing, grasping. "The firs' one. Came down in the Fenti hills one turn after you were born. This foreigner going in and out of the hills, bald woman with a limp. We never drew the connection. There was nothing to draw. No one suspected. No one had any idea it was possible." Kade shivered. His head pounded. "We followed her across continents. Firs' the three of us, me, Lorel, and Shaw, then just me. Every time I almos' gave up, there'd be something. A clue, or I'd feel the person. Once a turn, maybe. Eyes on me in a station, in a shop, on a street, a ferry. I didn' know who was following who."

Kade's regret was of suicide-inducing proportions. How much of this could he have avoided if he'd gotten his hands on this foreigner, this first arrival from Gog? And what had she been doing here for nineteen turns other than toying with him? Preparing for the attack? Infiltrating the guard?

Oblivious. Blindsided. Failure.

Kade lashed himself. He saw Lorel and Shaw clawing through the dirt looking for their young son in a sunken hill. He saw the churning red- and purple-black muck. He was on a beach at night, and the sand was cold and coarse beneath his feet. There were sticks poking out of the sand and leaning against each other in a crooked structure, a web. There were billions of cold crystal stars in the black sky surrounding towers of green and copper space dust growing out of a dust mountain. Four towers. A four-fingered hand.

He slammed his shoulder into a tree, here in Nima. "The second meteor," he said, rubbing the shoulder. "Who was in the second?" He was asking himself, and he was asking the Mind. "Earth," he said to Dawlis. "Think back. Something you saw, maybe. Someone you knew." Anything that could shed the faintest light. Anything at all. But Dawlis had nothing to offer. He wasn't ready to talk about Earth or share his singular version of the last half spin. He wasn't ready to leech that poison, and Kade wasn't ready to cut it out of him.

"The assassin," Kade continued, desperate for understanding, analysis, planning. "The man who tried for Ayn. Tha's where we start looking. Tha's—" He stopped. His voice sounded strange to him. A feminine tinge. An odd taste in his mouth. "The port," he said cautiously, as though inching over to a mirror afraid of what he might see. "We scout it," he said in the voice he knew. "We wait. Long as it takes for things to quiet down."

Dawlis led with Fred and Jackson on his flanks, Orly on his heels. He looked back over his split shoulder to acknowledge that he was listening, or at least that he was hearing.

"Your shoulder," Kade said. "How does it feel? We should change the wraps."

He didn't answer.

"Dawlis."

Nothing.

"Dawlis, *wake up*."

Dawlis turned. He clenched his right fist down by his side, squeezed his lips together as though trying to hold something back, or force something out. He pointed to his mouth and shook his head.

Kade understood, but Kade didn't believe it. This was evasion. This was weakness that they couldn't afford right now. "You're saying you can' talk."

Dawlis nodded.

Or won', Kade thought.

From the sky, southwest, came a sound like air being sucked through a straw. Jackson barked. "Quiet," Kade snapped and cupped an ear. "Hydro engine. Guard ships run on cells. Usually."

Dawlis was suddenly dialed in.

"Could be a scout," Kade said. "Can't know for sure."

Dawlis started running.

"Wait!"

They ran out of the trees and into a river. The flyer was not guard. It zipped overhead, banked hard, and dropped down. Ayn pounded on the windshield. She was there in the door when it slid open. She saw something in the sky behind them, and her face dropped. A guard ship slipped over the trees.

9

Ayn paced the cell, considering which truths to tell and which to hold onto, what risks to take. She and Mays had witnessed the shutdown of the Rings, that curious momentary blackout of Qol's satellite defense system. They'd done it with flagrant disregard for the Code (hacked into one of those satellites, a rock buster) and then tried to sneak into a war zone (no thought put into *that* move, just shock, outrage, adrenaline, and a need to do *something*) and pull people out. But their transgression didn't put a scratch on their leverage, because their leverage was of a *new kind*. The question was whether Ayn could use it or if they'd just played themselves into the hands of whatever corrupt guard faction had helped MaGog shock the world.

So close, she thought.

Close enough to see the death all over Kade and Dawlis.

But the entire guard was not corrupt. The Rings had been cleared to fire at that meteor before being knocked out by the virus, and they took out nearly as many Gog ships as got through once they were back up and running. And the traitors, if their flawless execution so far was any indication, would not risk showing up at the scene of the crime.

The guard ship lurched, yanked by a magnet. A slam reverberated through the hull as another latched on.

Here we go.

She focused. She had one chance to play her first tile. Dawlis was the leverage. Gog came because they believed they were owed another world, but they also came for him. That would become clear to anyone willing to accept the simple facts of the targeted attack. Or to entertain the less tangible evidence of a street performer's prophecy.

Trailed by a great shadow.

And those weren't even her most valuable tiles.

Mind.

Earth. Another system. If Ayn could paint *that* picture for them, if she could get them to start doing some quick math in their heads, running a few searches, and wondering *what if*, they might trade a lot for the chance to confirm or disprove it. For the chance of finding a passage. That tile could blow minds and buy influence. But Ayn wouldn't play it on just any table with just any cast of players.

Footsteps in the hallway. She sat on the bunk and faced the door, crossed her legs, retied her hair, and straightened her back. The door slid open.

Well, she thought, *how about that?*

She wasn't sure whether her chances of getting them off this ship just got a lot better or a lot worse.

"Brava," she said in Korial, not trying to hide her surprise. "Maybe we can meet under different circumstances sometime."

She'd almost told Mays, as they were skirting the west coast of Nima in the flyer, to turn around. Dawlis and Kade would get picked up if they were alive, and she'd get to them the best way she knew how, through her network. And he would have been her first call. But it was different now. She'd expected to have to reach out. His showing up raised a lot of questions.

He sat in the cell's lone metal chair, laid his arm down on the half-circle, metal table molded to the wall, and tapped his wrist device. He didn't look at her. He breathed deeply through his ample nose. He'd not aged well in three turns. His light brown hair had retreated to the middle of his head, revealing a shallow dent above his left eye. The hair he'd lost had gone to his eyebrows. The lines in his brow, which Ayn had never once seen flatten in the time she'd spent helping him during his investigation of the second meteor, had deepened. His eyes, though, were exactly as she remembered: drab green, exhausted, and unsettled.

"What are you doing here, Ayn?" he asked. His pitch too was the same, high and worn out.

"The answer to that is very important," she replied.

"You'll have to provide it."

She shrugged. "There's an issue of trust here, Brava. The guard just let Gog in."

"Ko Brava," he said, scratching his nose. "I'm obligated to tell you."

"Ko Brava. Congratulations." She hid her disquiet this time. That was a big move up the ranks in three turns.

"Overseer of Uniques for Damarra," he added, compelled by regulation.

"This type of event is no longer unique."

"Ayn, why are you here?"

"Why has the guard let three meteors past the Rings in the last nineteen turns?"

"The Rings. What did you see in those cameras?"

So, they'd found out about the hack. She wasn't surprised, and it only added to her leverage. "Sure, I'll tell you. What did you find out three turns past?"

"All of Qol knows what we thought happened. A meteor got picked up by the Rings, but the computers said it would burn up, so the satellites didn't fire. We didn't know it came from Gog. Maybe it didn't."

Ayn smiled.

"See it from this side," he said in his strained soprano. "It's hard to imagine legitimate reasons for you and your friends being here. You hacked the Rings, and now you've been in proximity to two of the three events."

"Bombs? Experiments?"

"It's under investigation."

She looked straight into his troubled, tired, swampy eyes. "There are reasons I've been in proximity to two of the three events."

"Tell me."

"I want to see them first."

He surprised her again. "I have them standing by. Though not the, ah, groos." Then he rattled her. "You can speak to them in private. I turned off the camera when I sat down."

Her doubt about which side he was on just doubled. She tilted her head. "Why would you do that?"

"To gain your trust," he said. "I don't think you have anything to do with what happened."

Maybe because you know who does.

He stood and left. The door closed behind him.

Ayn shut her eyes and rubbed her temples.

Think.

The Brava she thought she knew from three turns past was a lifer agent just doing his job, assigned to the crash site because it was in his sleepy territory, relentlessly perturbed but for the right reasons: Qol had been hit by a meteor, and he had to make a report. But to rise from agent to Overseer of a continental department in three turns required no small amount of ambition, which she hadn't read in his character, and deep connections, which, based on her digging at the time, he didn't seem to have. So how, then? And why? Was he more calculating than she'd given him credit for? Was he a pawn? Was the camera really off? If so, which side did he not want listening?

The door opened again, and she saw him in pieces, one weathered, brown boot, one limp, weathered hand, blood-caked beard and bandaged nose, eyes that couldn't stick to her, couldn't stop moving. It blew her composure. She shot up from the bunk and pulled Kade into her arms. Dawlis, a circuited healing patch covering his left shoulder and collarbone, shuffled around them and sat on the floor. She reached for him but drew her hand back, afraid of the long-gone look in his eyes. He noticed her. He smiled on one side of his mouth, patted her foot, and looked up and away at the blank wall. She thought of Lorel and Shaw and felt like her chest was caving in.

Kade slipped from her hug and fell into the chair. "What now?" he asked in Korial. "We don't know who's who." His eyes darted like trapped animals.

Mays stood in the door, eyes wide and pale. "Sit," Ayn told him.

He stepped very carefully over Dawlis's legs and took a seat on the bunk as tight to the corner of the cell as possible.

Ayn closed the door, wiped her eyes. "Kade, I know the Ko running this investigation." But Kade had dropped his head onto his arms on the table and may have passed out. She switched to English. "Dawlis, wha can you tell me?" But Dawlis just stared at the wall like he was looking out a window.

Kade spoke muffled Korial into his arms: "He's not speaking."

Ayn didn't understand.

"Sticks on a beach," Kade said, his voice strange, higher.

"Kade?" She squeezed his hand. "Help me get us out of here."

She got what she asked for. He lifted his head. "The meteors were vessels," he said. His eyes quaked, as though from the impact. "The one that fell in Nima carried a warrior, their leader."

"No," she said. "That's impossible. That means—"

"Yes."

That the meteors weren't bombs, experiments, preparatory strikes? That there'd been a MaGog on Qol for nineteen turns and another for three? Waiting? Making ready? But how crude and clever! How terrifyingly determined! "We watched it, the third," she said in awe.

"What about the second?" Kade asked.

"Security was so tight then. I know what everyone else knows. But Kade, the Ko here led that investigation. He says we're not being recorded, but be mindful. What else? What happened?"

A great deal else had happened. Kade spoke fast like he was trying to rid himself of what they'd seen and done. He spewed his story and then laid his head down again. Ayn, who'd kneaded her chest throughout the brief and brutal telling and made no progress in easing the growing tension there, now looked at Dawlis and regretted it. Lorel screamed at her, 'Keep him safe while I make my way back!' Lorel, who'd tracked her lost child across two worlds over half of her life only to send him back to *this*. How miserably they'd failed her.

Breathe, Ayn told herself.

"Listen," she said.

'Keep him safe!'

Breathe. He's still alive.

She bit her fist. She decided where to draw the line with Brava. For now. "I'm going to call him in," she said in Korial. "Stay quiet unless I say." She knocked on the metal door. It slid open, and a guard stepped back. Brava was pacing the hall. "Ready," she said.

Kade was bent over the table, Dawlis was on the floor staring at his right hand, and Mays was on the bunk in the corner rubbing sweaty palms on the pants of his suit. Brava stepped inside, fingering the dent in his skull. It was too warm. It reeked of blood, sweat, and stress. Ayn took a seat beside Mays and held a palm out to Brava.

"I need to know who everyone is and why you're here," he said in Korial. "That's where we need to get to. You can dictate, to an extent, how we get there."

"English," she said in English and motioned to Dawlis. "He doesn' speak Korial."

Brava waited for an explanation, but Ayn didn't offer one. She'd started with a facedown tile that she had no intention of flipping this early in the negotiation and maybe not ever.

"English then," he said.

"We aren' being recorded?" she asked.

"There's corruption in the guard, and we haven' flushed it out yet," he explained. "I've been authorized to carry out this conversation in this way. There's a lot of this sort of thing happening right now. Is chaos."

That was either very honest or a very cold lie. Ayn's internal dial tilted toward the former, but that was just an initial read. "When did you figure out tha we'd hacked the satellite?"

"Not until after the attack. To your credit." He looked at Mays, who kept his eyes safely on his feet.

"We're suspec's then," Ayn said.

"Not in taking down the Rings."

"Who is?"

"I can' discuss that. I can tell you that Ki Nond has been relieved."

"Overseer of the Rings," Ayn said for Dawlis's benefit, though Dawlis gave no indication of knowing that there was a conversation going on around him. "You think it goes tha high?"

"I don' know, but it happened on Nond's watch."

A flutter in his inflection.

"Done?" he asked.

"Almos'. Did the guard know tha either of the firs' two meteors came from Gog?"

"No."

"Did the satellites orbiting Gog pick up the ships' launch?"

"No. A lightning storm took out the one tha had eyes on the hive at the time. They waited for tha, timed it perfectly. The only footage we have is from the next satellite, when it came around in its orbit, of a few silo caps closing. We assumed it was another test."

"Why didn' the Rings see them coming earlier? Mind, Brava, it must have taken them, wha, a hundred spins to get here?"

"You know part of the answer. The Rings watch Gog and track and analyze hundreds of thousands of objects and systems. We never saw a need to watch the space between planets as long as we kept a close enough eye on Gog's surface. A systemic mistake in hindsight. Plus, they came in from above a direct line of sight."

She shook her head in disgust. "How did the guard miss this so completely? I thought we were back at the table."

"How is it possible to keep a secret this big?" he asked as though asking himself and her and anyone who cared to offer up any ideas. "They've executed perfectly for a long time. They've kept us in the dark and strung us along. We thought their technology wasn' close. Negotiations always stall. I don' know the details. I know MaGog's demands are unreasonable, and we all know that there have been incidents along the way tha have damaged the relationship. We had no idea they had anyone inside the guard." His voice betrayed a perverse respect for what Gog had accomplished, however limited the scope of the attack. Ayn shared it. It was a relatively small thing that cast an enormous shadow of doubt on everything Qol thought they knew. It was an eclipse. But it was also self-destructive and thus insane. Gog had now played their tiles, and for what? To make a statement? To kill a boy? To strengthen their position at the table? They'd revealed their firepower and in doing so eviscerated their leverage. They'd taken their shot and spent their element of surprise. An armada ten times what they'd sent would amount to little but target practice for Ring satellites and Qol battleships alert and ready.

"Ayn, I need to know everything you saw and know. All of you. Tha's your path out of here."

She watched him closely and flipped a tile. "There was a man in the meteor that hit here."

His brow canyons were stone. "We know."

She expected that answer. They'd had plenty of time at this point to survey the crash site. She flipped another. "There was also one in the firs'."

He didn't flinch, but he hesitated. "Yes, tha's a possibility we now have to consider. But wha could you know about tha?"

What *did* she know? That a meteor came down in Fentum. That a foreigner was seen moving in and out of the villages near the crater, a bald woman with a limp. That the Fenti came after Dawlis not long after that. All of which was potentially very important. None of which was hard evidence of anything. Still, Ayn had more than facts to go on. Ayn was privy to a prophecy and to other, far stranger workings of the Mind. "Was there one in the second?" she asked, though she knew now that there was. Someone scouting and haunting Mon Teles, the place the boy was meant to return to. Someone roaming the halls of the Spire Yune, slipping into the bar where she'd had her nightly drink for four turns, slipping poison into the sap meant for her glass, and killing her young friend Ruve instead, her bartender, on the ninarc of Dawlis's arrival.

If Brava saw the heat in her face and the wet in her eyes, he didn't show it. "You know wha we found," he said. "A red-glowing, black pool of melted stone-metal."

Ayn gathered herself, breathed into the knife in her chest. "You know my background," she said. "You know when and why I came to Mon Teles."

"Yes," Brava said.

She looked down at Dawlis, who was looking out the window that wasn't there. He nodded. He *was* listening. He knew where she was going, and he gave his blessing.

"You know I was inspired by the death of a friend and her son."

"Yes."

"Tha's the son."

Brava stared at her. She stared right back. "The Fenti came after him when he had two turns," she said. "The Fenti have been involved the entire time."

Brava's eyes grew so slightly she almost didn't catch it. She flipped more tiles, pounded him with more truth. She told him that Lorel had killed the first Fenti and hid the boy and lost him. That they thought he was dead. That a friend of theirs said he was alive and gave the location and timing of his return. That he came back exactly there and then only to run into the Fenti again, this time with a guard escort. That he went straight from Mon Teles to see the prophet. "And where do you think the prophet lives?" she asked.

"Lived," Kade said, face still buried in his arms.

Dawlis looked around the room.

"He *lived* on tha island," Ayn said, accepting in that moment the past tense of Peis Ota.

She paused and gave Brava space to form his questions. His first was the one she had no intention of answering: "Where has he been this whole time?"

Dawlis muttered to himself. Or to someone else. He looked like he was staring straight into the eyes of someone not there.

"Different places," Ayn said and smiled at the enormity of her understatement.

"Where's his mother?"

"Died searching for him, as far as we know," she lied.

Dawlis stood and leaned against the wall.

"His father?" Brava asked.

"In the Gontomon for the las' fourteen turns."

"Where in the Gontomon?"

"Deep."

"I'll need more than tha if you want me to find him and bring him to his son."

"I doubt tha's necessary," Ayn said. "He's always known the timing. He's probably on his way."

"The Fenti and the guards on the Shole. Describe them. Tell me wha happened."

Kade didn't need to be prodded. He lifted his head off his arms and purged that portion of their nightmare once more. Brava processed. His brow lines were etched and indecipherable. "You're here because of a vision?"

"Yes," Ayn said and got the chills.

Dawlis placed his good hand on Kade's shoulder.

"They came here with no knowledge of the impending attack?"

"They didn' know," she said. "They fought. Dawlis nearly died."

Kade's eyes widened.

Brava rubbed his dent. "Tha's enough for now. You'll all have to go back to your cells. Nothing I can do about tha." He turned to go, but Dawlis grabbed him gently by the wrist and tapped his device.

"Turn it on," Ayn said. "He wan's to say something. Set it to English."

Brava turned on the device, took it off, and placed it on the table. Ayn stood up. Kade leaned back in his chair and eyed the screen suspiciously. Dawlis, brown eyes dark and calm and distant, typed with one finger:

-- They came for me. In part. You'll send ships to Gog? Kade and I should be on one. --

10

Radin soaked it in a moment longer: the warm wind on his face, the overflowing bloom of life all around, the overpowering bouquet of odors, the vast spectrum of grays promising a rainbow when his eyes adjusted and he could take off his goggles, the pillars of black smoke in the distance, the Qol vessel hovering and humming at his back, the light of Gorr warming his head and shoulders and not burning him from the inside and out. Qol was everything MaGog had dreamed of and so much more. It was worth another thousand rings of waiting, and he was delivering it.

But it was tainted. For now. It stung him again, his failure in phase one. He'd assume it until he saw Dawlis's body. Still, he could not deny the irony that the man he was sent across the void to kill, the man Oorroom foresaw killing *her*, had not only potentially survived, *again*, but had also separated Radin from his collar, his oath, his promise of forever loyalty to Koren. He could not ignore the feeling that it was a sign. Then this Rasmussa shows up speaking of *other* worlds.

And this Rasmussa, he did not look like these other Qols. He made the Dondarra sitting on either side of him inside the vessel look like Youth, his great long arms and legs draped in heavy brown cloth. He pointed at Radin with his crooked nose, smiled at him from small, dark eyes burrowed into his face behind strands of wet hair. He was not afraid, and *that* is what interested Radin most about him. Radin brushed past him, down the aisle and into the room at the back of the vessel.

He sat in one of two curved metal seats set around a thin, circular metal slab attached to the floor by a stem. The walls were close. He banged one with an elbow by accident, and a hole appeared. They were zipping over gray treetops. They crossed a shiny gray river. He tried to dip a finger into the hole and was repelled by the metal. It was still there; he was seeing through it. He laughed out loud. This technology. He ran a hand over the slab, smooth and luminous. He ran the other hand over his stone-metal scales and realized with a pang of nostalgia that they had lost their red glow. The memory was fresh and exquisite: watching the red mavzarra melt the meteor as the ash rained down, mindful of the radiation he was absorbing and not caring one little bit, marinating in that unique, corrosive death, taking on his father's hue and finding in it a next level of rage.

The guard stepped into the doorway. "Dondante," she said in awful trill-less Vrrgrrul, and placed a square piece of glass on the slab. "Call will come through here." She spoke in rote. She looked and sounded like she was following orders whispered to her by a voice in her head. Radin understood that that voice was somehow inside of this glass.

She left. The door slid closed. A bright gray dot blinked on and off in the glass. Radin let it. He took his time. He took a thick pull of dust from his vial and caressed the soft, worn handle of his sword laid across his lap. When he was good and high, he touched the circle.

A Qol head and broad shoulders appeared above the glass, floated there. Male or female, Radin couldn't tell. Thick, curly black hair. Wrinkled face. Fleshy mounds of skin surrounding active eyes. Fleshy lips. Hideous. "Bring Ravrada," Radin said in Vrrgrrul.

"Dondante, deeply sorry," the person said and removed the hair, revealing the slender MaGog skull.

Radin didn't react. He hadn't expected Ravrada to present in one of her disguises, but he was well aware of her methods and talents.

The eyes, they were convincing, trapped behind all that skin. They were revolting and very possibly not sane. But there was no denying what she'd accomplished and what he owed her. She'd cut the trail. And she'd failed too in phase one, twice, but Radin now shared that shame. "You've done well," he said. "MaGog is grateful."

"Dondante, thank you," she gushed, as though she'd been waiting all of her nineteen rings here for that affirmation. "All the wait means nothing now." Her trill was atrophied, flat. "All for MaGog. For *you*. You can't imagine only knowing you through stories and images, now meeting you."

Radin ascribed nothing to this show of respect. They had their roles, their ranks, and their orders, but it served him to assume that Ravrada had developed her own ideas about who was in charge here and who deserved what, and he wouldn't have blamed her. She'd sacrificed a great deal for a very long time.

"He's alive," Radin said.

"Dondante, I'm not positive yet."

But Radin was. Because *his* talent, *his* connection to the fabric was physical; and he'd always expected that when he killed Dawlis he'd feel some change, some beautifully violent vibration, some tearing of energy. Instead, what he felt was a tension, a live connection that pulled at him from a place deep down. And for all his guilt for not completing phase one—not yet—and all his worry about what it might mean for Koren, he was glad that it hadn't been so easy, that Dawlis had proven a nemesis. Radin would like to get to know him better. Perhaps they could talk first next time. "Where now?"

"Dondante, directly to Findo continent. We'll stay quiet, take time. Not too much. Just enough."

Radin's loins stirred. To see another new place, another lush ecosystem, here on the surface of Qol. And to *disturb* it.

"Dondante, to their *cradle*," Ravrada said and smiled. "I will meet you there. There are friends waiting. Eager to meet you and help."

Friends, Radin thought.

"How long?" he asked.

"Not long in this flyer, then an underwater vessel, then another flyer. Amazing the technology, yes, Dondante?! I have so much to show you."

Radin was trying to imagine what it was going to be like to slip through an ocean in an underwater vessel when something slipped into his mind. He looked at Ravrada calmly. She shrank. "Dondante, please forgive. It's hard for me to stop. I'm always working."

Radin peeled his lips back over his sharpened teeth. He allowed for the possibility that that had been an accident. It was plausible to him that Ravrada, connected to the fabric in *her* way, constantly probing for subjects, incepting ideas, and tuning others' minds to hers, would have difficulty turning it off. He empathized with the need to always feel one's connection and to control it. He also appreciated the test. His preparation was already paying off.

Good, Oorroom. You did well.

Oorroom, whose mental talents rivaled Ravrada's. Whose vision of his sister's demise nineteen rings by was the inspiration for all this adventure and the impetus for her cutting out his tongue. Who'd trained Radin in warding off inception in case there were Qols with that faculty or in case Ravrada's ambition had become overdeveloped. "No harm, Ravrada," Radin said. "You've made history and future with your gift."

Ravrada bowed her head. "Dondante, thank you, thank you."

"Where is Brrumida?" The second of their trio to crash into Qol, three rings by. Radin had gratitude to bestow and fear to instill in him as well.

Ravrada straightened up, and Radin noted her shoulders again. Artificial, perhaps, like her eyes and lips. Added skin or muscle. "Dondante, we met after he tried for the female, Ayn. He disappeared then. He doesn't abide. He comes and goes and is difficult to track."

Radin was well aware too of his other predecessor's talents and tendencies. It did not surprise him that Brrumida hadn't shown, and he didn't much care. Brrumida's role was played. He'd created the necessary vacancies in the guard and Council for Ravrada to fill with her subjects. He'd missed on that one, Ayn, but Radin had never fully understood the strategic imperative of killing her anyway. Brrumida had done well, and Brrumida no longer mattered.

Maybe none of you do, Radin thought, entertaining the fantasy, the impossibility that Rasmussa had said was possible. *Not even Koren*, he dared.

Ravrada cocked her head as though curious to know what her Dondante was thinking. But she made no second attempt to find out for herself. She'd learned her lesson. Radin smiled. "Ravrada, soon," he said. He pressed the light circle on the glass square, and Ravrada blinked out of existence.

What if? Radin mused. What if his destiny extended beyond the borders of these worlds and this conflict? What if the universe was calling to him, opening its doors through Rasmussa? It was a dreamscape worth exploring, for the fun of it if nothing else. He shouted to his Dondarra to send in the mutant.

The door opened, and Rasmussa entered, shoulders hunched and pressed up against the ceiling, hair hanging over his face, hands bound behind his back. The guard followed, picked up the square with a look of concentration dialed in from somewhere else, and tapped it in some pattern or code. She placed it back on the table and left. Rasmussa sat. His knees came up to the height of the slab. His bent nose was nearly as long as one of Radin's fingers. But his deformities seemed different now in this close space. Symmetrical. Intentional, as though he was not deformed at all but his own species.

"Why are you here?" Radin asked in Vrrgrrul. The words appeared above the glass and morphed into English.

Rasmussa read, smiled. His teeth, like his eyes, were too small for his face. "There are four planets in my system."

"Only four!" Radin exclaimed, not without sympathy. "A couple fell away?" This male was truly an unexpected and enjoyable entry into the fray.

"Eight in the system where Will Lark comes from," Rasmussa added.

"Eight in that one, sure. Will Lark?"

"The one we both came for, friend."

He meant Dawlis. Will Lark, it seemed, was a name he used on another world. One would have to be quite mad to make up such a story.

"Yes, friend," Rasmussa persisted. "Hard for you to believe me, I understand. I'll show you."

"Show me what?"

"There are holes in the worlds."

"Ha! Yes! You came here that way?"

"That's exactly how I came here and how I first traveled from my world to his."

"But you're wrong," Radin said, almost disappointed. "He comes from here."

Rasmussa shook his head. "I said it wrong. He comes from here. But he lived *there* most of his life."

This at least fit into reality. Dawlis had been missing for eighteen Qol rings.

"I've traveled the worlds," Rasmussa said.

"You say. Why?"

He frowned. "That's changed. I went there to kill him. I failed just like you. But see, when I came out of a hole again, I expected to be *home*."

"Why travel worlds to kill a man?"

"Why would *you*?"

There. *That* was it. *That* was why this could actually be real. "A seer on Gog," Radin said. "Saw into the fabric. Saw a threat to us."

Rasmussen's little eyes glimmered. "We were visited by a seer once."

Radin leaned in, indulging now, and why not? "Tell me."

The words floated between them, shifting back and forth between languages.

"Four hundred thirty-seven rings by on my world," Rasmussa said. "A young male crossed the desert into the oasis where I come from. Very few lived there then. There were small villages, sects, scattered hermits. He was found planting a seed beside a natural fountain in a garden belonging to a small and isolated order of priests who worshiped gravity. He told them that the seed was a nexus between worlds and that he'd come from another, sent by something called the Mind to plant it. That it would grow into a tree, which would form a deep knot, which would yield and shelter a bulb. That another man would come to harvest the bulb in four hundred thirty-seven rings."

"Harvest it why?"

"He said that this Mind was sick. Split between the worlds and seeking reconnection."

"What does it mean?"

"No one knows."

"Four hundred and thirty-seven rings?"

"It doesn't matter. It could have been any time. Time, apparently, means nothing to the Mind. Or it's lost in time. Listen, friend. The priests held onto their visitor. See, he was of a different race. Too small and straight-backed to be Awa like them, like me. Too large to be lassawa, the slave race. And what he said about the way he'd traveled there—what you know about how I'm here—it had to have something to do with gravity. He said that he would teach them how to find other passages leading back to the world he came from. They wanted to believe him. They had everything to gain. They thought it could be gravity speaking to them."

"Where he came from."

"Earth, friend. It's called Earth. But he may have only passed through there. See, the Mind is what they call it *here*. On Earth they call it God and other things. But *I* discovered this world and yours for mine. The visitor never mentioned this system. I thought I was coming home."

"Earf, Earf," Radin said, trying it out and struggling with the last sound, foreign to his MaGog tongue. "Did he do it? Tell them how to find holes?"

Rasmussa smiled from behind strands of dark, wet hair and nodded. "Science and art, friend. They align with constellations. He told them which one to follow and what to look for. He had a tool to do the geometry, the angles from stars to passages. And to detect their gravity when one gets close. They took it from him. I hold it in my pocket. They went hunting for anomalies and found them over time in a constellation surrounding our oasis. Each is guarded by people, secrets, culture, the land, an animal, a spirit, it depends."

"Guarded?"

"Agents of these energies."

"What happened then?"

"He escaped. Flew away with help from the lassawa. He was a bird, see. He identified as one. And the constellation? A bird. He was last seen on the other side of our world. And maybe he came back here, yes, friend? A different constellation. I understand that now. I discovered that for my world and yours, remember it. He left a note warning us never to touch the bulb, that it would die if touched by any but the man from the future. The tree sprouted not long after he left. The knot formed three hundred rings later. The order of priests grew an empire. We rule still. I am one. We hold the secret of the passages to Earth and the meaning of the tree. *I* hold the secret of *here.* There are twelve of us. There have always been twelve. One dies, another is initiated, sworn to protect the passages and the bulb and to wait."

"For the other man," Radin said.

"Yes."

"But you didn't wait."

Rasmussa shrugged his hunched shoulders as though his bucking of this alleged prophecy was hardly a decision. "Would you?"

"Making your own future," Radin said, and touched his collarless neck.

"That's just it! I decided I would see the other world, kill the person, then return and take my chances with the bulb. It budded just before I left. The visitor was right, it shrivels when touched! But I figured that if I traveled between worlds something might change, and the bulb might accept me. And if it died, it died. I'd have had an adventure and made, as you say, a different future. Anyway, the person is Will Lark."

Radin laughed. He felt for a moment as untethered as this Rasmussa had to be. He'd been concussed by Dawlis's blow. He was dreaming. He was falling for the delusions of a mutant Qol lunatic. But the mention of a seer had stuck him like a barb. For *they* were intermediaries of voices and creative forces unconfined by time or space, and those on Gog and Qol—Oorroom and Peis Ota—had so far *been right.* "How did you find me? Why did you come here, tell me this?"

The floating, glowing words morphed. Rasmussa frowned again.

"Good questions, friend. I hardly know the answers." He looked lost for a moment. His little eyes turned inward. Radin recognized the expression, registered it, but didn't put it together right away. "Luck had a part. He left a trail, Lark—a type of Earth bird, by the way—to a place called Mon Teles. You know it? I met a person near there. A strange person. And I look very strange in this world. Maybe that's why they stopped me. Maybe that's why I thought to tell them who I was looking for and what I meant to do to him. They told me about this place. I never got a name."

Radin was thrown. He felt penetrated, as though Ravrada had broken into his mind after all. He felt watched. She'd met Rasmussa? She'd sent him down here after finding out his intentions for Dawlis? As insurance in case Radin failed? Just to see what would happen? Was she playing games? Most importantly, did she *know?*

Sharp, clear anger sliced through his doubt and confusion. He calmed. He lifted his sword off his lap, placed it on the table, and leaned forward. "Did the person tell you I was coming?"

"No, friend. Just where to find him."

"Did you tell them what you told me?"

"No, don't worry. I don't go around telling it!"

But Radin couldn't trust that. If Ravrada had reached into Rasmussa's mind—the reason for that blank look on his face just now—it was possible that he'd revealed certain things without realizing it.

"But to come here and learn of these worlds," Rasmussa went on. "To learn that you too wanted him dead, and to see the lengths that you went to! *You* I find compelling. We're kindred, no? We both tried for him and failed. But I don't care anymore. I only want to travel. You don't understand, but you will. It changes you."

"How would I know? You could show me a hole and call it a passage. It could just be a hole."

"I told you, they align with constellations, and I have the tool. You'll know when it starts to point."

"Tell me how to find one."

"Nooo, friend. I won't just give it to you."

"You might. But I'll listen. What do you want?"

"Transport to your world."

"Ha! Why? What do you know about it?"

"Enough. I only want to travel, to see other worlds, and here's another at my fingertips. I'll see yours and then look for passages there to others. Or maybe return here, we'll see."

Radin smiled with his eyes behind his black lenses. If these holes existed on Gog, a people living underground for over a thousand rings would have found them. Besides, he had no way of securing transport back across the void. Maybe Ravrada could find a way, but going back was never part of the plan. But Rasmussa didn't have to know any of that. "If I agree, then what?"

"I find a passage to either world. Your choice. I contact you when I find it."

"You stay with my Dondarra," Radin countered. "Not too long. Just a couple of places I need to go. Then we search together."

"No. It will take time to find one. You'll only delay your chance. And don't assume I can't make life difficult for you. I've done things you're only dreaming of now. Though, how you came here, *that* was something. A small, attack, yes, friend? And not subtle. Interesting how we both failed. Makes you wonder."

This struck a nerve: Dawlis the subject of prophecies on two worlds—three?!—and Radin merely the one sent to sever them. But there might yet be twists in the fabric. Radin could very well be central. The evidence was mounting. It was feeling like less and less of a coincidence that he'd crossed paths with this Rasmussa. "How did the seer know it would be Dawlis, Will Lark, who came for the bulb?"

"The Mind showed the visitor an image of a bulb inside the belly of a woman. The bulb was her son. It showed her searching for him. It showed markers, including a red bridge, only one of its kind on Earth. Other things. I found the son by finding the bridge and then the mother and following her. I put a bullet in her knee, but she might be on her way here. None of it has been easy. They've made a believer out of me. And I told you, the bulb shrivels."

But what was there to believe in, really? Radin wanted to know. What had Dawlis accomplished yet other than to survive? How did that compare to what Radin had done and would soon do? Dawlis had earned his respect, but Dawlis had yet to convince him of anything, no matter what future any seer on any world might have glimpsed. "What is it called?" he asked.

"What?"

"Your world."

"Ashuwa."

"Find a hole to there."

"Arrange for my travel to Gog."

"Yes," Radin said and thought he might actually put some effort into fulfilling his end of the bargain. He was grateful, after all, for the emergence of this character, sane or not, in his unfolding epic. But exploring that fantasy any further would have to wait. There was still a great deal of fun to be had here on this very real world.

The ship slowed. Radin touched the wall, opened the window, and looked out on a watery horizon, water so blue he could sense the color through his goggles. Another vessel waited on the sand.

"What's next for you, friend?" Rasmussa asked. "'Places to go?'"

Radin warmed. "You'll see."

"How will I see?"

"Everyone will see."

The ship touched down. Radin left the room and ordered his Dondarra and the guard to give Rasmussa a communication device and to take him wherever he asked. He then walked down the ramp, crossed the sand, and stepped into an ocean for the first time. He spread his arms and bathed in its vastness and power. It was infinite and timeless, as *he* was timeless. *He* was the culminating history of MaGog. *He* was the creator of futures. *He*, not some bulb, was a nexus between worlds.

Gorr breached the clouds and cast a fat line of sparkling white light across the water straight to Radin, as though anointing him. The soft tide whispered to him and him alone. He kneeled, cupped his hands, and tasted the salty water.

11

Grugreera dipped his shovel into the lava, stared into its orange depths, and listened carefully to its sizzle, its voice. It told him that he was right, this was still their home. He lifted the shovel and poured the glowing ooze into a stone-metal box, filling it to the brim.

He closed the box, lifted it with his hand and stump, placed it on the cart, and pushed the cart down the track toward the storehouse, which was overflowing. It was their last box. Old Burdrr had gone to two forges requesting more, but they had yet to arrive.

"Rest," Burdrr said in Vrrgrrul, placing a hand on Grugreera's back. Dirra sat against a wall munching pulge.

"I'll go this time," Grugreera said.

"We don't need more. No runners come," Burdrr said. Not since the announcement three cycles by.

"They will."

"Maybe they have what they need."

"How could they?" Grugreera asked, and that was at least a couple of heavy questions in one. How could Zone 3 have all the lava coal it needed for rocket fuel when the migration had barely begun? How had Koren succeeded in launching the first wave a generation or more before anyone on Gog or Qol thought it remotely possible? And of course, the answers were evident: the maze, the system, everything she'd built over twenty-eight rings of rule, her limitless ambition and genius and foresight. Grugreera accepted it, the good and the deeply troubling. He understood why. If not for the system and the maze, Qol might have discovered MaGog's strength and been prepared. She was doing it. She was manifesting the destiny.

But the question that parched his skin every time he asked it of himself—and he couldn't stop asking it—was: How, if she loved them, could she have endured keeping her secret from them all this time? How had she lived like that? What else was she not telling them?

"They'll come eventually," Dirra said. "They'll need more for the next wave, then the next."

Burdrr hung his head. "I'm too old. You two could go."

"Could be," Dirra agreed with a bright trill.

"It will be slow," Grugreera reminded them, a simple, physical truth that most fellows willfully ignored. The migration of any meaningful portion of six hundred thousand fellows would take rings of time and be perilous. The Qol satellites were now on alert. The ships were on their way. Production of everything required for the building and supplying of rockets would ramp. Fellows would be redistributed in mass to the roles most critical to that effort and to protecting the hive. The population of able-bodied would decline as fellows left in waves or perished warding off the inevitable counterattack. Already they were losing small numbers to skirmishes with the emboldened resistance.

And these were merely the practical issues. Far more untenable, if not handled with care and empathy, were the psychological and cultural impacts of splitting their society in two, into fellows having or choosing to stay in the womb and fellows living only for their opportunity to leave. It meant balancing the hyper-present and the fast-approaching future with a past that demanded respect. Perhaps Koren, in all her wisdom and love and fierce dedication to fulfilling her promise had not fully accounted for these dynamics. Perhaps she could benefit from the ideas proliferating in Grugreera's mind about how to adapt the system to the new reality.

She *could.* The future came calling. A female from census walked into the depot, read Grugreera's name off a wafer, and told him he was going to meet the matriarch.

He composed his greeting as they sped through trroorra-lit tunnels. It should be concise, he thought. It should be expressive of his love, gratitude, and undying commitment to MaGog. It should include well-placed, brief, and confident allusions to his ideas. He drafted and redrafted.

They pulled into a station. The census female stepped out of the engine cart and led Grugreera to another track and another string, which was half full of fellows wearing many different colors of cloth. She approached the driver and flashed the wafer stamped with Grugreera's name and Koren's sigil, the two curved lines, the staff and blade of her scythe. The driver put up his hands, stepped away from the carts, and told the others to get out. The census female stepped into the engine cart and stoked the purple rreever. Grugreera got in a few carts back.

They rolled down a black tunnel. She stopped the carts and pointed to a crack in the wall that Grugreera or any fellow could have passed a million times and never seen. Someone moved behind a stone-metal gate. "Take it," the census female trilled to Grugreera, holding up the wafer. He took it and got out. She started up the carts and was gone.

"Here," said a tired male voice from behind the gate. A glome. A heat gun hung from the rope around his waist. Grugreera handed him the wafer. He struck a small trroorra flare, read the wafer, snuffed the flare. He opened the gate, closed it behind Grugreera, and started walking. Grugreera followed him into the crack.

They reached another gate with another glome waiting on the other side. The first passed the wafer through to the second, who lit a flare, read, snuffed, opened, closed, and led Grugreera down a thin, rounded tunnel toward a caged lift. Inside the lift, another glome read, slapped the wafer against her leg, and waved Grugreera in with her heat weapon.

She stared at him. She smelled off, dirty, angry, crazy. She cranked a squeaky wheel, and they rode up a silo to an intersection. She pumped a handle, and the cage rotated past one tunnel, two, then stopped in alignment with a third. She unlocked the cage and led Grugreera on.

His skin dried, and his life flashed before his eyes. He knew where they were. "Zone 3," he said aloud to himself. He was deeply confused. How could he help Koren from here? How could he aid in the restructuring of the hive if he wasn't out there with his fellows creating change and guiding them through it, lifting them up?

"No," said the glome. "Works the same maybe. She has other sites like this."

His heart dropped out of his throat. *Of course not!* he thought. His faith was restored.

They came into trroorra glow. Two Dondarra stood on either side of a stone-metal door leaning on the hilts of their curved, stone-metal swords. One pushed up on her chin above her stone-metal collar and popped a few vertebrae. The other took the wafer from the glome, who patted Grugreera on the back and left.

He stepped through the door into a wider tunnel lined with flares and small shapeless blobs connected by wires. Explosives, he guessed, and would be proven right. A muted, clickity-clack grew as he approached another door and another pair of Dondarra. He revised his greeting frantically. The Dondarra opened the door, and he passed into a square chamber. Three architects in light blue cloth sat together on one bench, two farmers in crimson on another, three diggers in the green that Grugreera had once worn on a third. Eight other fellows called to Koren.

He felt like a fool. He'd convinced himself that he would be the only one. But there was still hope of a private audience. He was the only lava handler. He took a seat on an empty bench and nodded half-heartedly to his fellows. One of the farmers nodded back.

A door opened on the far side of the chamber, and the clickity-clack machine chatter poured out. Two miners exited. A census male stood in the door and called the architects. They were not gone long. The census male came back with the architects and called the farmers. The diggers and Grugreera were called last. Grugreera tugged on his yellow cloth, politely pointing out the census fellow's mistake, but the fellow only told him to hurry up.

Census fellows in dark blue sat at machines punching wafers. Others stood over slabs reading, analyzing, and debating. This was a census station, a node in the nervous system of Koren's underworld. Grugreera had the odd sensation of being inside her brain.

A final door opened at the far end of the station, and she was there leaning over a slab, long, skeletal fingers splayed across it, ridged head and black-robed, mountain-peak shoulders pointing straight across the room at Grugreera and the other fellows approaching. Her scythe scraped the ceiling and scraped his spine. She stabbed whatever lay before her with a finger. A Dondarra on her left nodded. Maps of the hive hung from the walls, black webs drawn on thin, gray slices of wood, as rare on Gog as hospitable atmosphere. Glome marked the maps with purple chalk and spoke in low, tense trills.

She raised her head and black-hole eyes—and sucked Grugreera in. He went willingly. He could exist in there forever.

No, he needed to leave this place. He felt naked. She could read his every thought and emotion, his doubt in the system.

Koren, please! Hear me out! he pleaded in his captured mind.

The census male announced them as the diggers for 3-133.

Zone 3, no!

Koren unrolled her spine and stood to her full height, her head sliding just underneath the ceiling. Something shifted in her eyes, and Grugreera felt release. The diggers beside him exhaled. "Closer," she said, her stone-metal voice a razor. The cross scars on her protruding throat twitched. She took another map from behind the slab, laid it on top, and rapped it with a knuckle. "You know what this is."

"The maze," Grugreera said, hearing himself from far away.

"The maze," she confirmed. "You've been chosen."

Grugreera didn't feel chosen. He felt like his life was ending. This was the last reassignment he would ever receive.

"You know what's inside," she said. "Everything."

Not everything, Koren!

"Qol is coming for it. You will help prevent them from getting it."

Grugreera, like most fellows, had a general idea of how it worked. You were given a section to dig. You dug it and then were given another. Maybe you connected your work to the existing structure, maybe you didn't. You never knew exactly where you were. You never left your sections, nor did any fellows assigned to live and work there once the digging was done. Koren was the lone architect. Koren had drawn every section from the very start, for twenty-eight rings, nearly three generations, wrapping her secret in an ever-thickening cocoon of tunnels and rigid rule about who went where and who knew what. To great success. To the surprise of maybe every single human on two worlds.

Maybe Oorroom knew, Grugreera thought and wondered why he thought it. Then he saw the illurrur standing against the wall behind his sister. He was floating a stone-metal sphere over his right palm and smiling at Grugreera, open-mouthed and tongueless. No, there was no hiding here! Koren swallowing him with her eyes, and Oorroom reading his energy. To see either one in person, this close. But to see them *together,* the physical resemblance, and to *experience* their kindred abilities!

"You," she said to Grugreera. "I know."

Of course she knew! His concerns about her methods and MaGog's future. His selfish wonderings about his next, how many he'd made, where they were now. "Koren," he said, his voice cracking. It was all he could muster.

"Resilient MaGog," she said with a glance at his stump. "Brave. Handled that scavenger on the surface. We are grateful."

He could have died then. "For you. For MaGog." He tried to say something more, his greeting, but he'd forgotten every word.

"Grugreera is lead," she said. She rolled up the map and handed it to him. A series of dull pops sounded from the direction of the waiting chamber, quiet at first, then louder, then shaking the walls. Koren, Oorroom, and the Dondarra slipped through a door behind the slab. Glome gathered maps with speed and composure. The census male who'd escorted Grugreera and the diggers into the room told them to follow him back through the station; there was another way out. But Grugreera, map held up to show that he belonged, fell into the stream of glome following Koren. They ran down a tunnel rigged with more charges, climbed a ladder, passed through a door in the back of a hollow into an abandoned den, then through a common into a cart station with four tracks and four cart strings spewing purple rreever heat from their engines. Koren reviewed maps and fired orders. Glome and Dondarra nodded. All were steady and alert.

But Grugreera was not steady. "Koren, take me," he begged, approaching her.

Dondarra closed on him. She held up a hand. "Grugreera, don't you trust and love me? You think I call anyone lightly? I know your loyalty and digger skill. Go, do what MaGog asks."

He awoke to his surroundings. How did he end up here? It had all happened so fast, everything since Placement.

The carts pulled away in four directions. Tongueless Oorroom looked back over a shoulder and smiled at Grugreera. And they were gone. Koren was gone. It was over. They hadn't had the chance to discuss his ideas.

12

Droodroovid was dead. To be dead was to live in dreams and to know ecstasy and terror unlike anything he'd ever known. It was to see unbearably beautiful and horrific things and to go places he never knew existed, places in between places. It was to be spaceless and timeless or to be so compressed by space and time as to feel like a speck with the weight of all existence pressing down on him.

He remembered things from life. He could return there at times, if only to empathize with the living, to agonize with them in the moment: Qol was coming. The resistance needed him. What was he waiting for? Why did he just lie there? He slept for long periods of the strange time of death only to wake with gripping pains of hunger and thirst and longing into some other realm where he ate and drank and longed to no satisfaction. He walked through dripping, lush forests and metal cities on the surface of Gog before the meteor. Or on Qol, he was never sure. All was mixed together in death. It was vague and unreal or intensely lucid, depending on the realm.

He remembered a fellow, Hrulora. But when he saw her, it was less like a memory and more like she was visiting him in these spheres or dimensions. He was visited too by another, a *potential*, a male named Grugreera. Grugreera might pass him in a tunnel or be sitting alone on the far side of a common and not even notice Droodroovid but still never fail to remind him, by his presence alone, that if there was peace to be had for Droodroovid in this afterlife, it would only come after suffering for his mistakes. Droodroovid saw Grugreera more and more. He tossed and turned in shallower waters. He writhed in the manic tension of the time in which he'd left the worlds.

His dread and angst, in all their breadth and depth, were overcome by a bottomless sadness and hopelessness the moment he realized for sure that he was still alive. His face was on fire. Rings of fire burned around his stomach and lower back and left leg. He screamed and spasmed. He was tied to a slab. Caretakers held him down while others slathered ointment onto his burns. It cooled him some. He eased back down. He tried to settle into the pain, to accept it, at least. It was no less than he deserved.

He remembered now almost dying. He hadn't returned to the census node after Koren's announcement and execution of Obudud. There'd been no reason to. The resistance was finished. They thought they had time, a generation or more. But Koren had skipped time. She'd been slipping it past them for twenty-eight rings. They'd been duped, and Droodroovid had duped himself. He'd believed that he was doing good, that he could read his fellows in the dots and dashes of the wafers, that he could *know* them, that he could find those who would turn and set them free. But the markers were meaningless, and Grugreera was the prime example: his doubt in the system, his love for the Core, his connection to Obudud, his pining for Hrulora, whose role for the resistance had been precisely to stir such feelings, feelings none too gently discouraged by Koren's system on the grounds that they had been the root cause of so much pain for so long before she came to power. A fringe personality. A risk Droodroovid took, destroying two more lives.

So, he'd left the common where he'd watched Koren shock the underworld and flay Obudud and traveled in no direction, expecting to kill himself but putting no thought into how or where. He needn't have worried. The arrada worms obliged. It was like the stories one heard. The teeth that ran the length of their underbellies were so fine that you didn't feel them at first, just the dry squeeze. Then you started to itch unbearably, then to burn from the venom. You pounded on and pulled at their slick bodies, but they were already dug in; there was nothing you could do. It was quicker at least than he'd been led to believe.

But he'd survived. He'd been saved, it seemed, and he was eager to meet the fellow or fellows who'd saved him so that he could scream in their faces, "Why?!"

The sounds of remorseless reality were familiar. The moaning, screaming, shouting, and shushing. The smell of blood and burned flesh. Two rows of slabs covered in fellows. Caretakers mending and feeding and shushing. It was a scene Droodroovid had been seeing without really seeing it, blended into his delirium. MaGog of every color cloth slashed, battered, and bruised, worn down by the feverish pace of preparation, hungry to get patched up and get back out there. Glome with heat gun holes in their stomachs, arms, and legs and stories of their fights with the resistance. One, on a slab across from Droodroovid, a cloth-wrapped stump where his left foot used to be, looked at Droodroovid, at the teeth-mark tracks circling his face, and seemed grateful not to have it so bad.

Hrulora passed through the gate and down the aisle wearing the dark blue of census. She'd passed through the gate and down the aisle before. Those had been real memories. She crouched beside Droodroovid's slab. "You're still here," she said.

He turned his gnawed, festering face away from her. "Let me be."

"I have your reassignment," she pretended.

He smiled bitterly.

"Koren needs you. MaGog. Five cycles you're here. You can walk?"

"Where would I go?"

She eyed the stump-footed glome, leaned closer to Droodroovid, and whisper-trilled in his ear. "No time for this. No feeling bad for yourself. We need everyone. Get up."

He felt utterly repulsive inside and out. "Nothing we can do," he said. They were out of time. Qol was on its way. Koren would resist, and the blood would flow.

"We'll do what we can," Hrulora said.

"It won't matter."

She squeezed his hand. "Remember why."

"I don't."

"Because of how we *feel*. More than a mob."

He was back in one of his death dreams. "I keep thinking of one," he said.

"One?"

"The fellow who captured Obudud. Grugreera."

She released his hand.

"So unique," he said. "He seemed the type who could make a difference if we turned him. But we were blind."

Her eyes were distant, yearning. "I don't think we were wrong about him."

"You can't believe that."

She ran a hand slowly down her face. "The way he touched me and looked at me."

"I delivered his first placement."

She was taken aback. "You never said. I was there too, after, at the rip. I spoke to him."

Droodroovid swallowed a lump of hope, a sense that life was sometimes influenced by other than cause and effect and coincidence. But he resisted. "One of many mistakes."

"He wasn't ready. Most aren't. We didn't have the time, but we have Qol's ear."

"Too late."

"Get up," she snapped and grabbed his arm.

"Ah!" he cried.

"Enough rest. MaGog needs you. Look, he walks!"

A few fellows laughed.

In the tunnel, Hrulora handed him a wafer. "New safehouse. Send as many as you can. We have twenty cycles, maybe less."

Twenty cycles at most to find as many *potentials* as possible amidst a peaking wave of fanaticism. One thousand sixty-one rings of pent-up suffering and desire funneled into Koren's inescapable vision now butting heads with the advanced civilization she'd chosen to fire upon instead of reason with. It was hard to see anything but a massacre.

13

Kade was running through a tunnel in slightly reduced gravity when he smelled the sea and saw, for the first time since the guards snatched him and Dawlis out of Nima, sticks on a beach and the four-fingered green and copper stardust hand on its stardust mountain. The sticks stuck out of the sand and leaned against each other in a web of sorts, a net maybe, a maze perhaps.

His face felt strange. His heart pounded. He turned off the simulation and looked into the glass, expecting to see a woman's face reflected back—exhaled when he saw his own and saw Dawlis pumping his arms and legs in the box next to him.

He tapped the glass, read his vitals, restarted the simulation, and increased his speed. That was the trick. Keep moving, keep grinding. That was what Kade liked about the base, the nearly incessant physical and mental preparation, the accelerated schedule. It kept the *others* at bay. If they came, they came when he was still. They came in that flimsy, vulnerable space between waking life and sleep. At least, that had been their way during the first three spins at the base. The woman sliding her reality over his eyes in the middle of a workout was a development.

The tunnels and oxygen felt thinner on their walk to the Model. The weight of the quarter kel of dirt above them felt crushing. Dawlis led the way as always (Kade wanted him at all times where he could see him). They bore the usual stare-downs and sideways eyes, those looks of *Why are you here?* and *Watch your backs* that Kade was always, at any moment, prepared to wipe off the guards' faces. So far, they'd kept their hands to themselves.

They reached the line for the armory. Dawlis nodded to the guard ahead of him. He didn't nod back. Kade looked down and to his right so that the one behind him knew he knew she was there. The pair behind the counter tossed Kade and Dawlis their glasses and barrels with a little extra zip (they were not allowed their xims at the base), and Dawlis pulled Kade into the Theatre before he could say or do anything they'd all regret.

Dawlis chose the front row again. He'd been trying to engender trust in such ways. Kade found it reckless, their backs to a few dozen armed guards who didn't like them very much, but not useless. It sent a message of confidence, of deadliness even. The guards knew that Kade and Dawlis had fought, that they'd been *there*. It's all they knew, but Kade hoped it was enough to make anyone especially pissed off about sharing their ship with two civilians think twice about expressing their frustration.

The drill lead, a tall woman with thick legs, thick arms, and cold green eyes, stood beside the pillar waiting for the last guards to file in and take their seats. When they were settled, she touched the pillar and called up a holo map of the Model, a half-complete cave and tunnel network resembling what these good men and women could expect to find themselves fighting in on Gog. There was a Model under construction beneath each of the guard's four interplanetary bases. They'd been in no rush to complete them. They didn't expect to have to send troops in mass anytime soon. But it didn't matter. The guard was nimble, the guard was pissed, and the guard had Spire-sized, silver triangle ships capable of reaching Gog in nineteen spin-equivalents standing ready on platforms above three of the bases. The fourth ship was in orbit around Sid, farthest planet out from Nurin, waiting for the call. The entire interplanetary fleet pointing in one direction.

A red dot blinked inside a large dark hole in the middle of the holo map.

"Open cavern scenario," the lead said.

But Kade missed the briefing. He was covered in scales and thinking in a throaty, foreign language. He was outside, and it was so melting hot it felt like Nurin was too close or like there was more than one star beating down. He sensed something big, something in the blinding red light, or the orange one, or the ether behind them, some swelling force. Then Dawlis was squeezing his arm and looking at him with that infuriating calm. Everyone was filing out.

-- You good? Ready? -- Dawlis typed in English.

Kade read from his wrist device, rubbed his arm, his *skin*, nodded, and followed Dawlis to the Model.

The drill went smoothly. They'd run similar ones a couple of times already. Two scouts in sticky blender suits turned invisible, crawled in along the ceilings of separate tunnels, scanned the chamber, and sent the heat signature layout back to everyone else's glasses. They stormed in, the holo-MaGog fired first, and the guards cut them down with simulated blue lasers. Dawlis played along and took a few out. Kade stuck to his hip, head on a swivel, eyes on the guards. There were no issues except Lorel shouting in Kade's head, 'Keep him safe while I make my way back!'

It was not the first time she'd spoken up, and Kade did not begrudge her. She deserved to have her say, and Kade deserved to hear it, oh yes. He'd failed miserably so far in meeting his friend's plain and justifiable request, and he was now preparing to escort her boy across the void to more fighting and death. But Dawlis, see, he'd *already died. That* was why there was nothing Kade could do. Dawlis had gone somewhere in those moments on the boat. He'd *seen* something. And now he had to go *there*. That's what he said. There was no arguing with those experienced eyes, and there seemed a strange coherence to it all, a disturbing intelligence. There were forces. There was history. There were worlds colliding, and there were reasons for that, had to be, and Kade and Dawlis were going in search of them. That was Dawlis's hope. They didn't talk about it much, but they didn't have to.

Talk, if only. Dawlis still hadn't said a word. Couldn't or wouldn't. The medics were stumped, and Kade too had given up trying to understand. But Dawlis made up for it some by quickly becoming proficient with the holoball. They exchanged very few words during the grueling arcs of training, but Dawlis got to sharing when they were alone.

To that point in their short and miserable time together, Kade had spared Dawlis any questions about Earth. The boy had had enough trauma to process without diving into what he'd lost. But their first ninarc at the base, in the closet-sized bedroom that had been assigned to Dawlis and that Kade had insisted they share, glasses on, Dawlis lying on the bed and Kade lying on the floor, Kade asked him what it was like, and Dawlis started "talking." Kade didn't have to ask again the next ninarc or the next.

They were lying there now.

-- Where was I? -- Dawlis typed with the holoball.

He meant where was he when Kade had fallen asleep the previous ninarc. It hadn't taken long. Kade had slept well for three consecutive ninarcs for the first time in his adult life. He was exhausted, mind, body, and soul, but that wasn't it. He could have stayed awake if he had to. But for some reason, despite being trapped underground with a few hundred guards jacked up with adrenaline and the anticipation of murder, he felt safe in that little room with Dawlis. "Doesn't matter," he said. He didn't remember where Dawlis had left off and wouldn't have cared if the boy repeated anything. He only wanted to "listen." These were Kade's brief emotional oases. These were the times that helped keep him from splitting apart.

-- It's a confused place still. -- Dawlis wrote. -- Very beautiful for some, fine for most, terrible for too many. --

He tended to start with such musings.

-- Still a lot of space, but it's shrinking and abused. --

Seven and a half billion people to Qol's two, Kade recalled. Meaningfully more land mass, but that was still a big number.

-- Not all abuse it, and most of us who do, do it out of ignorance, not malice. There's just this mass misperception that we're separate from it and each other. Many feel the connection, a growing number maybe, but not enough, not yet. There's plenty of war still. In pockets usually, but there's always the threat of it getting bigger. If they had a common goal, like Qol did in reaching Gog, maybe they'd come together. --

He paused for a long time, and Kade was dozing off when this scrolled across his left lens:

-- They do. They just don't know it. --

Dawlis looked down at him then, smiled on one side of his mouth, and typed:

-- It all happened, and it's all happening. --

Kade shuddered.

Dawlis shifted directions, as he often did.

-- George took me to the Tetons once. --

Kade had heard a lot about George and the Ladies from the home for orphans, these people on another world who'd done their part, done what Lorel had asked Kade, Ayn, and Shaw to do, taken care of Dawlis. Kade loved them and was glad he'd never have to face them.

-- Just these incredibly high, sharp mountains. Bears, bison, eagles. We got lucky, saw a moose. And Jenny Lake, this incredible blue. Kind of like Nima. --

"Moose?" Kade asked, his eyes getting heavy again.

Dawlis described a tall, four-legged, big-horned, elusive animal, then turned to another familiar theme.

-- The music, man. --

He'd brought up music all four ninarcs now. Each time his breath caught. Each time Kade sensed the longing, the nostalgia, the *need* that invariably reminded him that Dawlis had yet to mention his woman. That's how Kade knew he was suffering, despite his calm and his quip: *It all happened, and it's all happening.*

Dawlis woke him again in the predawn. The crew was afforded two thin slivers of arc each spin, one straddling Nurin's rise and the other its fall, to do whatever they wanted. There was very little to do in an underground base surrounded up top by thorned thicket as far as the eye could see, but getting fresh air was an option, and Dawlis made sure that he and Kade got theirs.

Dawlis stared at his reflection in the silver wall of the lift as they rose. He nodded to himself and rolled his shoulder. The circuited wrap crinkled. It was the most by far that Kade had seen him move it, a step function improvement and ahead of schedule. It was alarming. It reminded Kade of Dawlis's training on the island, the speed of his progress, the urgency of it. It was like he'd sensed something coming and willed himself to be ready. And he'd woken up this fourth spin at the base with a different energy, some conviction brewing in his distant, focused eyes.

They walked out of the lift and out from under the platform. They looked back over their shoulders at the same time at the silver triangle monolith standing dull and dormant, waiting, pointing. The sky was rivers of blue-black in between the high, curved thicket walls. Stars winked out. A bird cried. Dawlis, who'd led them leisurely and aimlessly along these paths several times before, now took his turns with intention. He led them to one of the watchtowers in a corner of the high, black energy wall. A guard came out of the hut and looked down. Dawlis waved up at her and did what Kade feared he would, he started up the ladder.

"Dawlis," Kade warned him in English.

"You want to stop," the guard agreed in Korial.

Dawlis ignored them.

"Unarmed," Kade said, neck hairs up, blood pumping. They reached the top. The guard stood with her back against the hut and her arm barrel leveled, speaking into her glasses. A drone hovered over and extended its guns. Dawlis, unaware or uncaring, stepped to the rail and looked out at the ship as Nurin broke the horizon and filled the ship's silver belly with red light. He closed his eyes and nodded to himself again. That idea he was cooking. That conviction.

"What?" Kade asked him on their way back through the paths.

He didn't answer. He traced something in the air with his right pointer finger.

"*Dawlis.*"

Dawlis stopped. He looked up at the sky, looked at Kade, typed:

-- I am the butterfly and the squid. --

14

Jackson stood in the aisle between Ayn and Mays at the head of the flyer, gray-striped snout pointing out the windshield and sniffing the stale, pressurized air for signs of Dawlis. Orly lay between the rear pair of seats whimpering, his ringed eyes wet. Fred lay in the cargo closet in the back with his snout buried in his paws and his eyebrows expressive of deep concern for their situation or a hatred of flying.

The groos wanted out, but Ayn breathed a little deeper and a little easier the higher and further they got from the scene of her crime: seeing Lorel and Shaw's son off at an interplanetary guard base with a ticket to cross the void, a ticket she'd secured through Brava. She slumped in her chair and rubbed the knot in her chest. She sensed Mays struggling to say something, knew exactly what it was, knew she could squash it by simply not looking at him, but felt like she owed it to him to at least touch on the subject. "We've been split for six turns," she said in Korial.

"I know, but the way you've described him," he said, rubbing his stubbled jaw and running the other hand through his thick, unkempt brown hair. Full lips and pouty brown eyes. He was attractive when he was nervous.

"How have I?" She honestly couldn't remember, though she imagined she'd stretched the truth at times, times when she needed Mays's help, technologically or physically.

"A drunk. Jealous. A child in a man's body. For example."

She smiled. That sounded about right. "He'll want to know when I'm taking the girls back, where I've been, and what I know, in that order." She paused for effect. "Actually, when I'm taking the girls back, who *you* are, then the rest of it."

Mays shook his head. Ayn put a hand on his leg, looked out at the sharp, gray-green, white-capped peaks of Damarra's western range, and gifted herself a moment of cautious optimism. They were flying. They were putting long distance between themselves and Nima and that base and shrinking the distance between her and her daughters. Brava wasn't done with them, she wasn't done with him, and she was sorely missed in the small, serendipitously located city that she'd been elected to oversee. But that was all going to have to wait a little bit longer. She needed to see her girls first, needed it bad. She was maybe even looking forward to catching up with Tontine; and she was *definitely* looking forward to seeing the look on his face when she showed up with three groos and another man. "He's harmless," she said and smirked. "But best if I tell him about us up front and get it over with."

"Please don't do that," Mays said, color blooming in his cheeks. "Us" meant something very different to him than it did to her. She'd known that for a long time. He knew she knew, and he knew when he was being used. Still, she *had* felt something at times. She was feeling it now. Not love, not that strong, but a stirring, a seed that maybe they could water if there was ever a return to relative normalcy.

The flyer banked toward the serrated edge of the continent and slipped into a V-shaped valley. The ocean appeared at the bottom of it and filled it like a cup, filled Ayn's heart at the same time. Pink-hued beach fattened then transitioned into dark green marsh, which ended in steep, forested ridges. They turned north up the coast. The first Rivel village rolled over the horizon, a thin rectangle of dark wood that crossed the marsh and beach and extended out into the ocean.

Been too long, Ayn thought, and retrieved a memory, one of the best: flying here for the first time after buying their home, Mycah barely three turns old, forehead pressed against a window, oohing and aahing at the ocean; infant Maya sleeping soundly for once in Ayn's arms, two chubby fingers in her mouth; Tontine with a drink in his hand and a rare smile on his face. But this pleasant reminiscence was short-lived, for that memory triggered the one of their final, window-breaking blowup, of her telling him the next spin that he wasn't coming back with them to Mon Teles and him saying, "No problem." Which triggered another as magnificent as the first and as pathetic as the second, that of the window-breaking blow-up three turns later and the sexual relapse that yielded Zee.

Life, she thought. *Mind.*

The square village came into view as they passed over the rectangle and the pentagon as they passed over the square, each a collection of stilted, geometric, dark wood buildings, shacks-to-skyscrapers. The wave village appeared, and the knot in Ayn's chest tightened.

One crest and one trough, she thought.

She'd never really noticed it before. It was too common a thing. A lot of wave symbols had one crest and one trough. But she wasn't worried about a lot of them. She was worried about one floating inside an eye, inside a triangle, inside a square. The symbol of orange gems that Dawlis had found not long after passing back into this world. A Kyut symbol called Nuvium, which meant light map or light path, according to some old text Peis had found in his cave library. There was something there, something big and unresolved. Too big, maybe. Too much.

Orly whimpered, Fred stirred in his sleep, Jackson sniffed and sniffed, and Mays tried to ignore Ayn's sudden discomfort as they crossed over the wave and the oval appeared. She saw this one too for what it really was, an eye, one corner nestled into the base of the mountains, the other dipping into the sand on the other side of the marsh.

A wave, an eye.

She buried these thoughts. She focused on the profound but suddenly tenuous idea that she was about to see her girls. The flyer descended on a taught string between her heart and theirs. She searched desperately for their octagonal home and found it, but the deck was empty. She willed them to come outside and look up, but her view was blocked by a tower, her signal interrupted, her string cut. The landing strip lit up on the roof of the port.

The latest footage played on a holo in the lobby and on holos up and down the bazaar. Gog ships making holes in Nima. The gore-filled lake. Ayn and Mays had seen it all at the base. Ayn had watched it too many times. But these shoppers, diners, and drinkers seemed to be seeing it for the first time. They frowned, cried, and ground their teeth. They shook their heads, pounded revengeful fists, marveled at the interplanetary drama, debated what the Council would do.

"It's simple," Ayn overheard a woman say in Korial. She was sitting at a bar holding tight to a half-empty drink. "The ones that came, we find them and send them right back. We show force over there, keep a ship or two hovering, build more satellites. They'll never be able to do it again, now that we know."

A bleary-eyed man on the stool next to her shook his head, poured the last drops of his drink down his gullet, and nearly tipped over. "Hate to tell you. One choice, and that's to make them regret it. Deeply."

The woman threw back her drink, and they called for refills simultaneously.

Ayn picked up the pace. The walkways were empty. Everyone was somewhere watching. They cut through a pair of five-story trapezoids that were office buildings last time Ayn was there but were now clearly apartments: plants on decks, laundry hanging over railings, a guy with no shirt on and a bulging belly smoking and watching them. They passed the three-story hexagonal climbing space for kids that Ayn, Mycah, and Maya had frequented during the short time they'd enjoyed this place as a family. They turned left at the little triangle market with the best produce on the planet and walked around the circular patch of marsh and circular bench where she and her two eldest had shared many a juicy piece of fruit. She could hear the ocean now. And a rumbling over a walkway somewhere behind the market.

She stopped short and threw an arm across Mays's chest. Zee flew through the intersection on her board, face to the wind, thick, brown curls stretched out behind her. She disappeared behind the climbing space.

A skid. The rumbling again. She tore back and screeched to a halt. "Fia!" she screamed in Korial and jumped off her board. They ran to each other, and all the bad that ever was fell away. It was pure joy. It was perfect present. Ayn lifted up her youngest, her muscle-heavy runt, squeezed her and wet her purple, seashell-patterned suit with tears. Zee buried her head in the crook of Ayn's neck and laughed. Then lifted her head and saw the groos. "Fia, let me down!"

The boys stood shoulder to shoulder staring at the little, bouncing human. Orly wagged his tail and stepped forward.

Perfect match, Ayn thought, holding back the floodgates. "They need a place to stay for a while," she said.

Orly and Zee paused a few steps from each other, the tension thick and sweet as sap: two best friends who'd waited their whole lives to meet just dying to seal it. Orly closed the gap and covered Zee's face in kisses. She scrunched her shoulders and flapped her hands. "Tickles!" she squeaked but did nothing to stop it, and neither did Ayn. Zee froze, suddenly serious. Her violet eyes, one of the few genetic gifts Ayn had passed on to her daughters, were big O's. "What did you say?"

Ayn cocked her head, smiled. "Said when? Did I say something?"

Zee wrapped an arm around Orly's neck, a bit too tight, and jabbed her opposite pointer at her fia. "You said they needed a place to stay. You did. You said that."

"Oh yeah," Ayn replied, giving no more, dragging out this beautiful, innocent dawning of realization.

"Well, Fia, they'll stay with us," Zee said with authority, then waited like a coiled spring.

"I think that's a good idea, Zee."

"Fia!" she screamed and choked Orly with a hug. "This way, girl. You must be hungry. I'll show you our room. Let's go." She skipped back to where she'd left her board. "It's a beach room. Lots of things from the beach. Fia!" she yelled, as though she'd have to get Ayn's attention, but Ayn's was rapt.

"Yes, Zee?" Her jaw was starting to hurt from smiling.

"What is she?"

"It's a groo, baby. And it's a boy. Three brothers, actually."

Zee furrowed her brow and put a finger to her lips as though she was trying to figure a way around this little obstacle. Her brow flattened, and she shrugged. "Know what, Fia? Three brothers and three sisters."

"Know what? You're right."

"Let's go, you brothers!" She planted a foot on her board, bent her knees and elbows, nodded at Orly, and shoved off.

"Come on," Ayn said to Mays. "I want to see Tontine's reaction." Jackson led, Fred took the rear, and Mays stayed a few comfortable steps behind Ayn.

He was there where the walkway met the back of their home, leaning against the wall and scowling into his drink, wet black hair perfectly combed and freshly dyed, loose, white suit open wide at the neck, brown bottle of booze embroidered over his left breast. He looked like a caricature of himself.

"Surprise," she said in Korial.

"A little girl tells me these animals need a place to stay. Not here, obviously."

Zee popped her head around the corner. "Fia said!" she cried, tears welling in those big, violet eyes.

Ayn winked and waved her away.

"You got those hopes way up," Tontine said.

"I'm sorry, Tonti. It's temporary." She saw Maya in profile through the window, gawking at Fred and Jackson out front. Her flat black hair made a sharp line down her snow-white face past one dark, wide eye and her painted blue lips. The window was a picture frame. The moment it captured was an instant classic, and Ayn was painfully happy to be there.

"I guess I don't understand," Tontine said and took a slug off his drink. "You're back from wherever."

"I can't take them yet," she said, looking around for Mycah. "I'll have a lot of work to catch up on, and the guard might call on me. Mon Teles might not even be safe for them. I need a couple of spins to assess. Where's the tall one?"

"You can't just bring three groos here. I know you know that."

"Think of it as a favor if you want. You know I'm good for it."

"Didn't think to call ahead."

"I did. I liked the idea of surprising them. You should have seen Zee's face. Anyway, you'll be fine. There's four of you. Plus, I'm sure Gode will be happy to help out when he's around."

"There's two of *you*," he said, tipping his cup again and eying Mays over the top of it.

"Tontine, Mays. Mays, Tontine. Mays and I work together. We've been locked up in a guard facility for a few spins and could use a little respite. I'm going to go see our girls now. Give me some time with them, and then I'll answer your questions. You deserve it." She waited, pretending to care about getting his consent, which he happened to slip in—a nod—just before her window of patience shut. "They're very well-trained. One girl responsible for each. You'll be fine," she said and left the two men there to squirm around each other.

Orly's and Zee's backsides were sticking out of the fence on the front deck, their heads between the wood rails. Zee was pointing down at something in the marsh. Orly's tail whipped. Maya stood frozen in the open glass door. "Maya, girl. What do you think?" Ayn asked, then shut up and watched. Maya's eyes were the only part of her that moved as Fred gave her a passing sniff and Jackson a thorough once over, leaving wet marks on the paintbrushes lining the legs of her deep blue suit.

"They're friendly," Ayn said.

Jackson walked around back, scouting. Maya tiptoed up behind him, stopped dead when he looked back. He wagged his tail in invitation, then continued his work. Maya stalked.

A pan banged on the kitchen counter. Mycah disappeared beneath it, rumbled around in the cabinets, then popped up with a wooden bowl in her hands and a huff in her movements. Her face was flushed and her nest of black hair (another bit of Ayn passed down) was tied haphazardly on top of her head. She looked older than her turns, hassled, and absolutely gorgeous. Ayn stepped inside, and Mycah stomped off down the hall toward the bedrooms. Ayn gave her space and took a moment to look around. With the exception of things being clean—gleaming counters, empty sink, chairs pushed in around the table, doors and windows smudge-less, all the signs of Mycah being in charge—nothing had changed. Same chipped, red wood table in the lounge, same beat-up chairs, same constellation of small paintings they'd bought from a local artist during that first trip. It was like Ayn was looking at a picture taken on her way out five turns past, after the beautiful mistake of Zee's conception.

Ah, but there was something new. The back corner storage space had been turned into an art station. Painted rocks and shells garnished with feathers, flowers, reeds, and Zee's initials covered a triangle glass table. Maya's work hung askew on the walls, the cuts and strokes and violent color cocktails as compelling and unintelligible to Ayn as ever. The precise organization of the dyes, brushes, and sponges could only be Mycah's contribution. It was hard when seeing such things to understand how war could exist. But it did, and so did bad mothers and angry daughters. Ayn straightened her spine and braved the walk to Mycah's room.

She put her ear to the door. A holo game zipped, zapped, and whooshed behind it. She lifted her hand, stuck out a knuckle, and knocked. No response. "Come on," she said. "I'm here now."

The game cut out, and Mycah expelled a sigh expressive of never in her life having been more rudely interrupted or offended. She had every right to be upset with Ayn for sending them down here without explanation early in the arc that Ayn and Mays had rushed off to Nima, that Gog had attacked, but Ayn sensed something else going on here. Mycah's displeasure with her had intensified over the last few phases, dating back to before meteors crashing and lost boys returning.

The door slid open. Mycah sat at her holo station in the corner, arms crossed, eyes burning. She shrugged like she was confused as to why Ayn was there, like she couldn't think of a single thing they needed to talk about.

"You deserve to be angry," Ayn said.

Mycah's face turned a combination of reds. "I bled."

It hit Ayn like *déjà vu* and a punch in the gut. The signs were all there in hindsight. "Oh, Mycah, I'm so sorry."

"Don't worry, Ayn. I figured out what to do."

As though life wasn't insane enough right now. And who did Mycah need more than anyone, more than ever? And who hadn't even noticed?

"When?" Ayn asked.

"Three phases past."

"You could have told me."

Mycah cut her with a laugh. "Sure, Ayn."

"I've been busy and distracted. I'm sorry."

"Problem is, I don't believe you *are* sorry."

Ayn breathed. "There's a lot you don't understand."

"Yes!" Mycah yelled, leaning forward now, shaking. "Of course, we don't understand! We're in the dark and on our own!"

"You're not wrong."

"Well, thanks!"

"Stop," Ayn said with a note of hysteria in her voice that surprised them both. She shoved her fists into her eyes and watched the explosions behind her lids. "You want to know why I've been absent? What I know?" She opened her eyes to pulsing, fading stars.

Mycah hesitated. Ayn was offering to flip a tile, one Mycah had been waiting to see for most of her life. The thing Ayn had been hiding from her and her sisters. The thing she seemed to care about more than them.

"Think you can calm down and handle it?" Ayn asked.

That was enough for Mycah, that challenge from her fia. "Go ahead, Ayn," she said.

"Stop calling me that. Listen."

Ayn let her have it. The reasons for the life she'd forced upon her daughters. The inconceivable. The friend Lorel and her son, the street performer, the long wait, the return, and the island. Mycah stared at Ayn throughout, searching her face for tells. Ayn had passed her eyes to Zee, her long neck and lack of blind acceptance of anything to Maya, and her hair and ability to read people to Mycah. It was why they'd struggled so much to get along. Ayn had been keeping secrets from them their entire lives, and Mycah had known it from an early age.

Mycah asked a single question. *The* question. "Where was he?"

Where was Dawlis all this time.

"I'm impressed," Ayn said. "But that's one thing I can't tell you, not yet."

Mycah didn't argue, and that impressed her even more.

"Thanks," her daughter said. As in thanks for confiding in her finally, for treating her like the woman she'd become while Ayn was buried in work and waiting on a prophecy. She seemed to accept the truth despite the implausibility of it and Ayn's track record. She would have known if Ayn was lying anyway. "I guess I kind of get it now," she said, "why you were obsessed."

Ayn rubbed her temples. It was the right word.

"But it doesn't change, you know, that it's been hard."

"I know. When this is done—" But Ayn stopped herself from making promises. She swallowed the rock in her throat. "I'd like to, anyway. Take a break. Spend more time."

Mycah nodded. She seemed to believe at least that Ayn wanted to try. She sympathized. They were two women.

<h1 style="text-align:center">15</h1>

Time was acting strange, Ayn realized, as she stepped out of Mycah's room and down the hall. Had been since she got there. She looked at the family photos on the wall and felt like she was still there while also being here, like the past was part of one big moment running forever. She looked ahead too, out the glass door toward the future and the ocean without expectation and with a sense that she was swimming in some even bigger ocean and always had been. Might be some rough waters, Mind, but if they stuck together . . .

The men were out on the deck. Tontine was leaning against the railing and holding another mostly empty drink. Ayn smiled at him, feeling an echo of the good times. He frowned like he wasn't sure what to make if it. She smiled at Mays too and thought, *Yes, maybe there's something there.* Gode was riding high in the seat of his chair, fixing at the edge of the roof. The pole beneath him wobbled. Gode, that old piece of good luck.

They hadn't finished unpacking the first box when he rolled up to their deck, puffy eyes scanning the house as though hunting for something to do, gray hair sticking out every which way, stumps for legs, chair made of spare parts, tool belt hanging from a hook on one side. He asked in a raspy drawl if he could help unpack, and Ayn declined gracefully (rule number one: never accept a favor before giving one) and told him that they were excited to do it as a family. He looked at infant Maya asleep in the pouch slung across Ayn's belly like she was some other species, at toddler Mycah climbing on the rail like she was yet another, and said fine, he was called Gode. He'd had a place here for some time. He came and went. He knew this house. There were a few things that needed tuning, he could come by. She said why don't they start with a meal after they got settled. He said fine. So, she satisfied rule number one, but it wouldn't amount to much. It was Gode piling up the favor currency before long.

He'd roll by whenever he was around, which wasn't often but happened to coincide with their own stays a handful of times those first couple of turns. He'd say he got to thinking about the heat panels or water filter or railing, how it had been a while, they might need tuning. He made things worse about as often as he fixed them, but that was entirely beside the point, and Ayn never once tried to stop him. She offered him real compensation for his first repair but knew he wouldn't accept it. She asked him about his legs that time too, and he told her the story with a distant look of trying to understand the world.

They had meals. He never said much, never smiled, though he seemed a gentle soul. The girls baffled him with their giggling and screaming and throwing food. Ayn got her kicks goading Mycah into climbing his chair or dropping Maya into his lap and telling him he better be careful. She belly-laughed every damn time. She laughed now, looking up at him tending the roof like he knew what he was doing, and maybe he did.

"What is it?" he said in Korial and rubbed his face like he was worried he might have sauce on it or something.

"How have you been?" she asked.

He turned those puffy eyes up to the sky. "Well."

Ayn sympathized, but she had zero interest in talking about Gog right now. "How about otherwise?"

"Fine, Ayn, but what is that?" He pointed down at Fred, who was napping on the deck.

"They're here to liven things up for a while."

"They?"

The rumbling started up on cue. It warmed Ayn's heart to the point of burning. Zee flew around the corner on her board, and Orly, Jackson, and Maya came running up behind her. Mycah stepped out of the house and smiled with wonder at the groos, smiled like a kid. She held her hand out to Fred, who was suddenly awake. His eyebrows shot up. He stood and sniffed her like she was some kind of discovery. If groos could blush!

"Let's go to the beach," Ayn declared.

"The beach!" Zee echoed and took off west, Orly hot on her heels.

"All of us," Ayn said to the men.

"Ayn, I'm nearly done here," drawled Gode.

"Quiet. Come on, you two," she said to Mays and Tontine. "It'll be worth it."

She was right. The groos discovered sand and surf, and that was a sight to see. The girls rediscovered it alongside them, splashing and spinning like it was the first time. Tontine stared at them, eyes glistening. Mays stared too with a serious look on his face like he was wondering if maybe he wouldn't make a decent fium. Gode nodded to himself from time to time as though thinking that life was okay after all, everything was fine, things worked out.

To Ayn, it was like they'd passed through some invisible membrane into a different time-space. It was the girls' laughter and unencumbered joy. It was every human and groo having an experience. It was the salty ocean smell. It was Nurin casting a flickering line of fire across the interminable rippling sea and hanging over it, taking its time, giving them more. Had it stopped sinking? Were they timeless?

They could be, Ayn thought. For moments. She'd known that once when she was younger, but she'd forgotten it. She'd been watching a clock for eighteen turns, waiting to find out if Peis was right, and he *had* been. So what did that say about time?

That it didn't work quite the way you thought. Not always. You could climb or stumble into some other realm. Or love your way into it.

It got dark without anyone noticing. The groos were dashing white ghosts, the girls jumping shadows against the grainy, blue-black sea-sky. "Well," Ayn said, as much to herself as to Tontine, Mays, and Gode. "Maybe, we …" She yawned. She stretched a delicious stretch. She whistled to the groos in the way Dawlis had taught her, three slurred notes, up-down-up, and waved to the girls. All came without protest. It was time.

Ayn hardly ate. She was too distracted, too happy. She was huddled with her girls at one end of the table peppering them with questions just to hear them talk. It was a song, noisy in spots, harmonized and syncopated in others, perfectly imperfect. The men kept up a conversation at the other end, about what, Ayn didn't care. The groos circled the table for scraps and scratches behind their ears.

There was a single mark on that otherwise perfect spin: Mycah mindlessly and playfully tracing a curve on the wall as she led her sisters and Ayn back to the bedrooms. One crest and one trough. It summoned the feeling of timelessness again but then twisted it into anxiety about what now. Ayn felt small and out of control, like she was part of something too big and too powerful, like she was flotsam on an ocean. She slept it off.

The parting was hard. They hugged tight. They sighed and sniffled and whimpered, respectively.

Ayn kissed Mays on the flyer. They talked about their childhoods. They pointed things out to each other in the landscapes and the sky. They watched the news about the imminent launch of the three ships and the fourth on its way from Sid, then turned it off and didn't speak of it. They rested.

The flyer dropped out of the clouds and skimmed the snow-covered trees. The pastel, glass tips of the Spires pierced the forested horizon and slid toward them. Blue tracks lit up beside the river. The flyer landed and slid into the hangar.

The same hangar from which Kade had rented a flyer and then taken off for the Shole to find Dawlis. The flyer that had been sabotaged. Ayn wished she hadn't thought of that and wished they'd gone to another hangar. She didn't like the attendant's blank eyes. She didn't like the way he said, "Serve well" in deadpan like he was speaking for a voice in his head.

"Ayn," Mays said.

"Hold on," she said, watching the attendant walk away, smelling something.

"Ayn?"

It was the hole in Mays's stomach, smoking.

A man laughed from a door in the corner of the hangar. A trilled laugh. A gangly man in a polished green suit and brown, round-brimmed hat. A man who'd put poison in the sap meant for Ayn's drink on the ninarc of Dawlis's return to Mon Teles and killed her young friend Ruve. A man who later met the person with the white mask and glowing green eyes. He lifted his hat for Ayn to see, for the first time, his smiling, over-sized MaGog eyes. He left through the door as Mays collapsed.

PART THREE
HEIST *and* SPIRAL

16

Grugreera drove his pick into the dark arra. Lighting fired up his arm and into his shoulder. He relished the feeling, *interpreted* it. He hit the arra again and barely scratched it but learned more about it by the strength and feel of the recoil.

To be born when I was, he thought, a thought that used to fill him with an almost unbearable happiness and gratitude. Born early enough to make a sustained contribution to the final push and eventually see the destiny unfold. Born late enough that he would be too old to go. Perfectly placed in MaGog history. Impossibly lucky.

He remembered this feeling darkening into anxiety in the cycles leading up to Placement. He remembered it peaking as he sat in his hollow staring at his curtain, waiting for census to deliver his future. Census did. That male, that forgettable male who Grugreera would never forget. The same who would later, by long odds, deliver Grugreera's brief and fateful reassignment to the surface. Back when all fellows knew that the rockets were more than a generation from being ready. Back when Grugreera was on the cusp of a long, inspired career as a digger with a hand in the final push. Well, he was a digger again.

To be born when I was.

It meant something very different now.

But what an honor, he told himself as he struck the arra again and again, harder and harder. An honor to have been given this place-ment by Koren herself. And maybe it *wasn't* his last. Everything was upside-down now. The migration and fighting would start soon. Koren might very well call him again, might seek his counsel regarding the restructuring of life in the underworld. It seemed very odd and very unlikely that a fellow of his loyalty and ambition would remain stuck inside the maze of Zone 3 at a time like this.

The arra was his outlet. He'd found this small deposit during his second cycle here and had returned to it before and after every shift of boring tunnels and hollows since. Because *that* was bone-rattling, brain-rattling, ear-splitting work. The bore brutalized the nerve endings, eroded the senses. *This* was Grugreera's way of building them back up. One had to feel the cracking or repelling of stone and mineral to truly know them. One had to hear the distinct musical tones that each sang when struck by a pick.

Arra's existence was unassuming. It was rare, inert, and colorless. It had no industrial use. It was not made into pendants for the females. It had no value in the system. But value was subjective, and arra had strength one had to respect and depth if one looked closely.

Grugreera struck it and was struck by an image of Hrulora. He held the image and attacked the lighter stone around the arra, exposing more of its surface. He uncovered a thin, darker vein and came down on it over and over.

A fellow called out from behind him: "Grugreera?"

He hit the arra once more, turned. "Fellow," he said in Vrrgrrul, then recited the eight-number code he'd received from the last runner. The fellow dropped a sack of food on the floor, handed Grugreera a new section of map, then walked off. Grugreera asked his usual questions: How much time? Where will the attacks come? Where are the glome gathering? Are you for leaving or staying, fellow? But he was talking to the fellow's back.

He unrolled the map. Another small tangle of tunnels and another spoked intersection. More maze to dig to make it just a bit more impenetrable.

He passed through Verderr's intersection on his way to wake his team. She was leaning against a wall, fiddling with her heat weapon, and staring at the ground. Grugreera had seen her do little else over the last nine cycles.

"Have a sip, fellow," Grugreera said in Vrrgrrul, offering his canteen.

"Where are the rest?" she asked.

"Asleep. I just received the next assignment."

"No one told me."

"Didn't see the runner?" Grugreera asked, and frowned. Another leak in the system? He'd help patch it.

"Oh, maybe," Verderr said.

"Any news?"

"News? Yes."

"Tell, fellow."

"Tell?"

"The news!"

"Oh. You know, it's hard to believe."

"It all is, fellow. How much time? Where are the glome gathering?"

"You know, I wonder where we are," she said, still staring at the ground.

Grugreera put his hand on her shoulder. "Fellow, stay strong. It will go bad for the Qols, and you'll get in line for the rockets or die protecting them. Or stay in a new underworld. I have ideas. You'll see."

"Rockets?"

"Think of these tunnels lined with glome and Dondarra. Imagine the Qols trying to make their way through!"

"You think they'll come here?" she asked and raised her eyes finally. They were lost.

"Of course," Grugreera assured her.

She looked around. She came off the wall and whispered in his ear. Her breath was foul. "I never told a fellow. I don't think we're in the maze."

Grugreera patted her back. "Hold on. MaGog needs you. I'll come back next cycle. We'll talk again."

"Wait. You want the news? Hard to believe. Dondante."

"Dondante?"

"What he did."

"Yes, what he did!"

"No. The second phase."

"A second phase?!"

Grugreera did not wake his team. He returned to the arra exhilarated, proud, unsure, and freshly betrayed. Another Dondante strike. Another secret Koren had kept from them. She'd had to, of course. *Had* to. She couldn't risk Qol spies finding out. But oh, this corroding trust in his breast! What else was she hiding from devoted MaGog? What good could he do for his fellows stuck inside this maze?

He struck the arra vein with everything he had and for everything he cared about. Two small chunks fell to the floor. He picked them up, turned them over in his hand, and dreamed of Hrulora. Where was she now? What was she doing? What was she thinking and feeling? Was she for leaving or staying? He knew the answer to that last. He imagined their next looking up at him with her mother's eyes, eyes that believed in him. He could find his way out of here, out through a leak. He could find them and gift them each an arra necklace. They could make a difference, together.

17

Droodroovid's eyeballs ached. The wafer he held split into two transparent wholes and drifted apart like square planets sliding out of phase. His mouth was parched. He searched the blurred piles of wafers on his slab for his water bowl, stumbled into it with his hand, found it empty, and found no motivation to go fill it. The two halves of the wafer came back together, and he saw something different. This reassignment was not for Zone 3. It called for thirty-five fellows to be made glome and sent to a site on the edge of 16, an edge of the hive.

That's where she expects the Qols to come in, he thought, and shivered.

An analyst dropped another stack of wafers on his slab and stared at his scars. He waved her away. He grabbed a few wafers off the top and skimmed them. It was back to the gushing flow of reassignments of able-bodied to Zone 3. Off to defend the destiny or get in line for the rockets, sure. What pathetic number would actually make it to Qol? A few thousand? A few hundred? How many MaGog-full rockets would get carved up by Qol ships and satellites out in the void or before they even breached the silo rims? How many fellows in Zone 3 would perish in the rubble? The more that gathered in one place, the larger the hunk of MaGog flesh, hope, and will that Qol could lop off with a single swipe.

Koren knew that, of course. It was part of her plan, had to be. Create pain. Force the Qols into mass murder. Sacrifice MaGog in order to build greater anger and determination. It was not a rational tactic, but nothing about this ever was. This was always a vendetta, Koren's, implanted in them. That's the only way it made any sense. The scars that crossed her neck: she'd been bloodied, and she needed blood. She was unaccepting and unforgiving of this life. She meant to create a new one, and she meant to do it her way.

Droodroovid could not stem the flood. He could only dig a small trench at its edge and redirect a trickle. It was meaningless, but he kept going because there was nothing else for him to do and because he did not have the courage or energy to attempt to kill himself again. He scanned the dots and dashes too fast. He leaned on his gut, which he didn't trust. He enjoyed little conviction that the fellows he chose would defect, especially now. They might just as easily run screaming for glome to come burn the traitors.

A runner brought the news of Dondante's stunt. Droodroovid laughed out loud. How sad, the resistance and the Qols! How utterly in the dark. The other analysts danced and hollered and spit at imaginary Qols lying dead on the floor. Droodroovid wiped his tears and picked another wafer.

18

Radin enjoyed a night walk through the bush. The air was thick and hot. The fanned, waxy leaves brushed against his chest and arms and cooled him some. Stars blinked on and off in little holes and slivers in the canopy.

A caldera hissed nearby. He went to it, stood by its edge, and sucked its burning, putrid odor in through his nostrils. He stared through the darkened rainbow iris into the black hole pupil. A large bubble formed, grew, popped. He looked up at the stars, found Gog floating alone in its pool of space, and thought, *Not long now.*

He climbed his favorite hill, came to the ledge, and peered through the leaves. The canyon was a dark cleave in the distance filled with floating lights, lit windows in the flowing, marble towers. Flying vessels circled, circled, watching the canyon and the forest above, obsessed over the safety of their Council. So nervous all the time! This view never failed to amuse and inspire.

He followed the stream through the bush, down into the valley, and into the cave in the marble wall. He dressed in the Qol suit and climbed the wall several times, up and down. He didn't need the suit here, but he would there, and he wanted it to feel like a second skin by the time it was time. It already did. He still felt the extra gravity, but it was a ghost of itself, and he missed it. It had been a unique struggle, that. But it was also a novel and fascinating sensation to lighten over time. All these new experiences, and he was just getting started.

He stretched in the cave, drank from the stream, pulled liberally on the Qol dust that Ravrada had provided (weak but serviceable at high doses), and turned on his wrist device. There were no new messages from Rasmussa, just the last one growing stale and becoming the final words of a trick played by a psychotic, mutant Qol, not some traveler from a world called Ashuwa. Translated to Vrrgrrul from English, that language allegedly shared between Qol and a fourth world, Earth, it read: "I'm here on Gala continent. Now the real work begins. Have patience."

Gala was the continent furthest west and south. Rasmussa had said that when he'd passed through a hole from Ashuwa into Earth he'd come out on a land mass very far from Dawlis and the red bridge and the passage leading to Qol. He'd also said that the visitor to Ashuwa, the seer who, four hundred and thirty-seven rings by on that world, planted the seed that would become the tree that would yield the bulb that Dawlis was meant to harvest, had come out on one end of their world and disappeared on the other. And Dawlis had come out on Qol, from Earth, on the continent Damarra to the north and east. What this was all supposed to mean was that a passage from Qol to Ashuwa, Radin's chosen first destination in this alleged system of solar systems (he would like, eventually, to see where Dawlis had lived his life, but this concept of the bulb was intoxicating) would be found at the other end of Qol's continent cluster. It was rather simple, this proposed celestial design. Any lunatic could have invented it. But Radin bore no risk in letting this go on. And besides, one thing before another. He still had history to make right here.

He watched Qol news, always good for a smile: another inspiring update on the crossing of the mighty Qol fleet (*yes*, Radin thought, *very mighty, all together, and far away*); developments in the pursuit of Radin's force in Nima (*two more captured, good fellows, build that hope!*); new footage of the attack (*yes, watch it over and over!*); comforting reminders that MaGog had left but a tiny wound in a remote region. Still blinded by the false confidence propped up by their slick ships, lasers, and satellites. Still so unaware, even as Radin roamed the very hills and swam in the very same hot springs as the earliest known Qol humans.

Hello, he thought. *Here I am.*

In their cradle, Cinda, where their diggers and historians had found the first tools and this artifact, this cup they held so dearly. He couldn't wait to pluck it and shatter anew their fragile, rebuilding sense of security.

He dozed.

He awoke to the sound of Ravrada's broken gait and a near-silent, barefoot tread. Both stopped in the bush across the stream.

"Dondante, I'll approach?" Ravrada asked in thin, flat Vrrgrrul.

"Yes," Radin said, stepping out of the cave. Starlight coated the bush and shimmered in the stream. Ravrada hobbled out of the leaves, stood on the bank, and bowed. She wore the disguise reserved for these native Cinda Qols, the half mask, the flowing clothes, the pale, thick hair. Disgusting. Mad. Radin regretted the need for this make-believe. He ached to cut the false skin from around that left eye, rip off the mask, and treat the other eye the same. Yet he wouldn't be here without her. Her skill and execution were uncanny and undeniable. "Time, Ravrada?"

She shifted back and forth from her good leg to bad, both unseen beneath her skirts. "Yes, Dondante."

Radin's blood warmed. He rolled his neck. He'd enjoyed the waiting and the process of adapting (he still had to wear his goggles for much of the light part of every cycle, but he'd soon be free of this final restraint). It had pleased him to live quietly under their noses in this ancient place. But it would please him too to make more noise.

"But Dondante, there is something," Ravrada said.

"Speak."

"Dawlis is gone. On one of the ships."

Radin laughed involuntarily. There was so much to unpack from that statement, he hardly knew where to begin. "You're sure?"

"Yes, Dondante."

"Ravrada, last launch was several cycles by. Why am I only learning now?"

Ravrada hung her head. "Dondante, forgive. I'd been searching. Information is harder to obtain now. The guard is paranoid. I only confirmed this cycle."

It had to be true. Ravrada would not have withheld this information. She, a fellow shepherd of the destiny, had as much to gain from Dawlis being dead as Radin did. But though she knew that Dawlis was a threat to the destiny, she didn't know *how*. She knew every detail of Oorroom's vision except the one that mattered most. Oorroom had heeded his sister's warning and kept that secret between them. He'd lost his tongue and chosen not to risk losing anything else. But he'd told one.

Radin would never forget their meeting on the eve of his launch. The shock and searing rage he felt upon reading the note that Oorroom passed him. It enflamed him still. His violent love for Koren and his determination to deliver the destiny for MaGog burned stronger in his breast knowing what was at stake for her. But he wondered now, for the first time, about Oorroom's motivation. Had he told Radin to fuel him or to *free* him? For, the violent end of the illurrur's vision would now certainly be realized. What other outcome could there be? Oorroom had seen clearly into the fabric. Dawlis would kill Koren.

But Radin, collarless, was already beginning to make his peace. He felt moved, delighted even, by this chance Dawlis had taken, this jump into the prophetic current. Dawlis was not afraid. Dawlis was a true survivor and a true nemesis, more potent and dynamic than Koren or Oorroom or Ravrada could begin to realize. Only Radin truly knew him. Only Radin had fought him, and only Radin knew where he'd been during the long gap between attempts on his life. *Might* have been, of course!

But for all his travels and trouble, what difference could Dawlis really make? The destiny was all but assured, whether Koren lived to see it or not. Everything was poised. Everything was now in Radin's hands, and Dawlis had gone in the wrong direction if he wanted to have any say in it. Let him have his piece of history. Radin would have more than his share.

"Dondante?" Ravrada inquired. Smirking? Grimacing? Did she know of other worlds? Had she reached into Rasmussa's mind and found his treasure or forced him to tell? It couldn't be. She'd told him where to find Dawlis, directed him down into Nima. She never would have let him out of her sight if she'd heard the strange tale of his origins. She would have held tightly to such knowledge, just as she held from Radin the secret of having met Rasmussa. Just as Radin held the secrets of his own meeting with the mutant and his knowledge of hers. Perhaps she did suspect *something more*. Rasmussa was too odd and timely an entrant into their drama to pass off. And he didn't *look of this world*. She sent him, perhaps, to learn more about him, to see it play out. But she would have kept him close if she knew.

Her strained left eye betrayed her ignorance. She was hungry for Radin's thoughts and holding herself back from trying to reach in and grab them. Oh, the things she would have found!

"I'm ready," Radin said.

She bowed again. She let it go, wisely. "Yes, Dondante. But quickly, Brrumida."

Radin bristled at this waste of time. He'd spared little thought on their rogue assassin during his time in Cinda and wasn't interested in sparing any now.

"Dondante, he missed the female Ayn a second time. She helped Dawlis onto the ship."

The implications were not lost on Radin. As the only one other than Oorroom who knew the full prophecy, he understood them better than Ravrada. Brrumida had failed in his attempts on Ayn, Ayn had secured Dawlis a trip across the void, and now Dawlis would get his chance at Koren. But Radin was feeling less and less troubled by the whole idea.

"Dondante, he intended to miss. Killed the male she traveled with instead. Playing games."

"Being himself," Radin said and was done with this subject and done with Ravrada's horrid accent. "Ready."

"Yes, Dondante. I have someone to take you."

Had someone.

Ravrada called for the Qol, who stepped out of the bush with animal quiet, dressed in animal skins. It was one of the many idiosyncrasies of this world that Radin found remarkable, the extent of the Qol technology and the fact that some lived entirely without it. And tall, these Qol females.

Ravrada put a hand on her shoulder and smiled. "Dondante, this is Syda."

Syda wrung her hands and spoke in Korial. Radin's wrist device translated: "Dondante, I'll take you," she said with flat passion, as though she felt it fully but didn't quite know where it stemmed from. Her eyes were little dark holes in her white face.

Ravrada stood up on her toes, took Syda's face gently in both hands, and whispered in her ear. *Tuned* her.

Radin walked into the cave, picked up the harpoon, and held it to his belt, which grabbed it with a magnet. He did the same with the laser, then the box. He kissed his sword, sheathed it, put the strap over his head, and walked back out. The stream gurgled. Ravrada scratched at the fake hair above her left ear. "Dondante, shock them again," she said. "You have no equal. MaGog thanks you."

He looked to Syda, who pointed into the bush and started off. He followed. Ravrada walked off in broken steps in the opposite direction.

Syda led in silence at a strong pace, deeply honed to her task. She proved her worth. What might have taken Radin most of the dark half of the cycle took much less, leaving him plenty of time before Gorr's rise. He smelled it first, then heard the soft sizzle, then felt the heat and saw it through the trees and the metal fence, the lake-sized caldera, the vat of boiling minerals.

This world is not so different, he thought.

Not in its essence. It was heat and water and dirt and rock and life. But *so much life*, and *so much space*, afforded by a sustained atmosphere. By not being destroyed by a meteor. By Gog taking the hit. But MaGog made their own luck and brought their own meteoric retribution. It was strolling right now through the oldest part of Qol humanity.

The station across the caldera matched Ravrada's description, a fusion of metal-framed, green glass domes and cylinders. Wide metal pipes extended from the base, elbowed down, and dipped into the broiling pool. Radin and Syda took a path along the fence and came to a marble boulder. A male Qol stepped out from behind it wearing a suit with a small square of red light on one breast and a symbol on the other, a replica of the station.

"Mindo," said Syda, and they embraced, the tall, pale, native female in animal skins and the small, dark male in a suit that bragged of Gog's technology. Two races from two times, it seemed, nothing in common except for incepted love for Radin and a cause antithetical to their very being.

Syda turned to Radin. "Dondante, thank—"

He took off her head. Mindo watched it roll away, concerned in some part of himself that he was unable to reach at the moment. "Dondante, I'll take you," he said. Radin smiled and motioned for him to lead.

Further down the path was the gate and the booth on the other side. Mindo stopped and held up a hand, then closed three fingers. Ravrada had told Radin to expect two or three. He crouched in the bush, as Mindo called out in Korial. The gate opened and shut. Two guards came, and Radin thought of his father as he stood and swiped once, twice, opening their necks. They stumbled and fell, shocked and dumb. The gargle, it always brought him back.

Mindo held the light on the breast of his suit to a dark square set into the gate, and the gate opened. He did the same at the booth. Inside was the hatch in the floor. They climbed down a ladder into darkness. Lights flicked on as Mindo's feet touched down. They walked along a curved tunnel of green stone, circling the caldera toward the station. They passed through another door into a long room through which ran a channel of the scalding, rainbow mineral soup. At the far end of the room was a wall of blinking lights beside another door. All, so far, consistent with Ravrada's intelligence.

They went up a ladder, down a tunnel, through another door, and into the room with the thick pipes that crisscrossed the ceiling. Mindo looked up as they walked, his lips moving, counting the pipes silently. He stopped, pointed up, and turned. Ravrada's sway over him broke as Radin's sword entered his chest. He held an amusing look of not being quite sure where he was or what he had done. Then he dropped.

And oh, the flowery, metallic smell of fresh Qol blood!

Radin jumped and pulled himself up onto the pipe. He straddled it, took the laser off his belt, and cut a circle wide enough for his slender-strong MaGog shoulders. The putrid gas poured out. Radin dipped a gloved hand inside, felt the flow but not the scalding heat. The Qol suit, thinner than MaGog cloth, was impregnable. He pulled the goggled hood over his head and face and took a few breaths, testing the manu-factured air, stale but perfectly breathable. He slipped into the pipe.

It was tighter than he expected, the flow against him stronger, but he was happy for the extra work. He dragged himself forward with his forearms, pushed with his toes. He laughed at the thought of the Coun-cil Members sleeping soundly inside their canyon perimeter beneath the watchful eyes of their ships and satellites. As he crawled through their intestines.

He crawled and crawled and reached the elbow. He stood up in it, typed the code into his wrist device to activate his suit's camouflage, then took the laser off his belt again. He'd been very much looking forward to this part, and he was not disappointed. The looks on the faces of the two guards and two station workers were priceless. They stared dumbly at the circle of pipe rattling on the floor, then up at the opening and the blur coming out, which might have been the hot gas except for the way it moved. Radin jumped down and did them all in a quick, lovely flurry. He took a moment to appreciate where he was, when, and who. He then cut the light out of one of the worker's suits, opened the door, climbed the ladder, and stepped out of the building into fresh air.

Masses of gray-green marble, frozen worms and globules, thick and thin, oozed and wiggled up into starlit space. Some were exactly as they'd been for several hundred thousand rings. Some were carved-out buildings with circle, square, and triangle windows, all dark now except a few. And there, in a lighted circle, halfway up a twisting tower, the silhouette of a sleepless Qol.

A writhing, swollen body to Radin's left burst from the ground and split into two appendages, which thrashed away from each other and came together again, forming a melted oval frame for monoliths, arches, and waves flowing down the canyon. Blue lights blinked on the tips of a triangle vessel sliding overhead. Radin waited for it to pass and then removed a glove. He was now a floating white hand. He ran his fingers over the marble, the subtle grain, unsmoothed by time. It touched him back. It had proven itself the alpha element, like the stone-metal of Gog. It had survived an epoch-defining eruption of the sizzling mineral brew, which had eaten the trees and dirt and other stone and made this canyon. And Radin was just a hand feeling around several hundred thousand rings later, ha. He put the glove back on.

The ground was soft, moss or lichen. A Qol crossed his path, a native Cinda out for a walk. Trouble sleeping perhaps. A bad dream. A splinter in the back of her mind. A shadow stalking the collective Mind. An itch they couldn't scratch. A feeling while walking in a dream or waking in a dark room that someone was there or something was off. It was pure bliss for Radin, to be there and to know that they could sense him.

There were many guards, tired and tense. The ships circled. Radin took care, took his time through the city, enjoyed it while it lasted. He passed an immense droplet, two squirming towers, a rising swell, and a braided twist. He saw it emerge in parallax, his target, a smooth, sinuous worm curving gently back and forth, up and up and spilling over in a flat hook above a nob. The window on the outside of the hook threw off a rectangle of light at the height of the canyon rim. Inside was the artifact.

Four guards flanked the lone entry. Others kept watch from across the paths. There'd be plenty more inside, here where the Council met, here where at least two of them slept. They took no risks at this building. But one could not account for risks that one did not consider.

Radin simply walked around to the other side of the worm, waiting for a guard to turn away in her anxious pacing, and started climbing. The first section was windowless and convex, and Radin climbed without the aid of the suit. He turned it on to crawl up a backward sweeping curve, his hands, toes, and knees sticking and unsticking with silent static electricity. He craned his neck, looked down, and smiled. He moved on steadily, methodically, not rushing, relishing the early acid buildup in his muscles and the literal increasing gravity of his situation. He turned off the bond coming over a hump, turned it on again as the wall went vertical. He came to a lit window. A guard sat in a chair at the end of a hall, and Radin had a funny idea. He knew he shouldn't. He knew it was an unnecessary risk. But he was enjoying himself.

He crawled above the window and rotated his body so that his head was pointing down at the ground and his feet were pointing up at the stars. He pulled his sword and tapped on the glass. The window slid open. The guard stuck his head out and looked in all directions but up. Radin stifled a laugh. It was too good, the head just hanging there, the very picture of Qol naivety. He tapped the wall, the guard looked up, and Radin split his face in two. The body went limp and hung over the ledge.

He climbed faster now, giving the Qols at least that much credit. Several dead at this point—they'd figure it out eventually. He used the bond to climb up the back of another curve, then free-climbed over a twisting hump. He stopped at a dark, square window that looked into a room with nine glass seats set around a large glass table. One seat for each of Qol's island continents. This was the very room where the Council deliberated, debated, planned, guessed, clawed blindly, panicked. Radin took the laser and burned three lines into the window ledge, then circled the middle one: a clue for them to wrestle with in the bitterness of hindsight if they had the wherewithal to find it: three phases to shake them from their arrogance and complacence, this the second.

Above him was the nob, the tumor-like growth that circled the neck of the worm. He climbed up from under it, stood on top, shook out his arms and legs, and took in the view. Magnificent, the canyon of ancient, ossified flows, the rolling hills where he'd lived and roamed, the circling vessels looking in all the wrong directions.

He climbed up and then down the inside of the hook. The window was on the outside and was protected by the best cameras and scanners that Qol had to offer. The underside was protected by nothing, for who would think to come this way?

Two feet and one hand on the marble, Radin took the laser and carved a hole. He pushed the chunk through, and it smashed onto the floor. White light poured out of the hole. He crawled inside, stood up, and froze. Hovid stood before the artifact, staring with useless, cloudy eyes in Radin's general direction. His wrinkled jaw dropped open, snapped shut, opened again. "It's you," he said in Korial.

Radin read the Vrrgrrul from his wrist device. "Yes, Hovid," he answered and watched the old man closely. *This* had not been part of the plan. *This* might very well be Ravrada trying to throw him off and gain some leverage. But he was more intrigued than anything. It was a nice surprise to meet their Council Member.

Hovid muttered to himself and backed away. Radin stepped up to the column, rapped a knuckle on the glass triangle case, and shook his head. Inside was a cracked clay cup covered in symbols carved by an unsteady hand, some whole, some chipped, all worn down by time, none bearing any obvious relation to any of the others. No color, no symmetry, no art. Radin set his wrist device to audible translation. "A sad relic, Hovid," he said. The sadder for how highly they valued it.

The device liaised aloud in an electric-tinged version of Radin's trilled Korial. Hovid tilted his head. His face jiggled with anger. He jabbed his walking stick at a wall, dead eyes locked on a target that wasn't there. "What we can no longer do is sit around this table and debate. We've been through it. We have to decide. You know where I stand. Full show of force, but we lead with the emissaries. Let's vote."

Spewing incepted thoughts? How interesting! He looked confused again, frightened. The spell seemed to flicker. Radin's understanding was that Ravrada had to retune her subjects from time to time, an inconvenience to do with the mind's strong desire not to be controlled, to be itself and think its own thoughts. It accounted for Ravrada's constant travel. But perhaps she'd been unable to reach this particularly well-positioned and well-guarded pawn of late.

"Here to kill us?" Hovid asked. "It won't matter. The ships are launched."

Radin smiled. "Yes, they voted with you."

Hovid frowned, gone or half-gone again, sad, plagued by guilt he didn't know the source of. "It was useless, your attack. Suicide." But he didn't seem convinced of that or anything at the moment.

"*Our* attack, Hovid. But no, I'm here for this."

Hovid started. "For the cup?"

"Yes," Radin said and thought he should probably get to it.

"The symbols. Do they mean anything to you?" The clouds in his eyes seemed to part and let some light through.

"Nothing," Radin said, though he wondered at the question.

"I only thought—" Hovid said, cutting himself off and stomping his walking stick. "Full show of force!"

"Thought what?"

His lip quivered. "I've studied it."

Radin stepped closer to him. There was something trying to get out of that mixed-up mind. "Why?"

"Looks like babble to you? It's far more. There are celestial elements. Look. The other side."

Radin walked around the column. "Where? What?"

"The symbols. They're all different attempts at expressing the same thing. A mad brainstorm. You!" he cried, as though noticing Radin there for the first time. "You," he whispered and lowered his head. "The broken lip. The symbol with the stars around it."

Radin noticed the corner of an ellipse inside the corner of a triangle inside the corner of a square, surrounded by stars. The rest was gone, lost, a fossil somewhere in the dank, Cinda forest.

"A wave inside an eye inside a triangle inside a square," Hovid explained. "*That* version endured. It's been found in far corners of Qol."

"Why has it endured? What is it?"

"It claims other worlds."

Radin felt a tingling through his core, out to his limbs, and over his scalp. "How many?" he asked.

Hovid leaned forward over his stick. "Three stars—the triangle. Four worlds—the square. What do you know?"

"What else?" Radin demanded and rapped his sword against the stone column.

Hovid raised his stick in defense. "I told you it's been found it in different places. Old texts. A cave. Here too! The one who designed this room. She obsessed over it. I've read everything there is to know about her. I've found documents no one else has bothered to read or take seriously. Look out at the viewing spot! Think!"

He meant the platform on the canyon rim where people came to look at the artifact, always in the dark half. They saw it through the square window and the triangle case with the stars above.

"The artifact represents the eye," Ravrada said.

Worlds were born. Rasmussa was from one called Ashuwa. Dawlis had lived his life on a fourth called Earth. The cup proved nothing, but Radin didn't need hard evidence. He felt the truth. It was walking up his spine. Some ancient Qol mystic had known it all along. Some raving Qol builder had discovered it too. Now Hovid and Radin knew. But no one else could know.

An alarm sounded. Hovid shook his head violently as though trying to rid himself of the voice inside it. "You've served well, Hovid," Radin said and showed him the mercy and respect of a quick death. They'd shared, after all, this historic moment.

He shattered the triangle with his sword. More alarms screamed. He sheathed the sword, placed the artifact in the cushioned box on his belt, then turned on his camouflage and crawled out through the hole and around to the outside of the hook. He took the harpoon off his belt and fired. The wire whistled. The spear hit the canyon rim with a quiet thud. The spool reversed and pulled the wire taut. Then Radin, the Dondante, wrapped his hands around the barrel, pushed off the hook, and slid across the canyon beneath the stars.

19

Will awoke on his back on the fifth "morning" and stared up at the
dark-blue metal ceiling. He mused. He hadn't dreamt since ... He supposed it was nerves. He was moving on in his research this morning

from what Gog had to how it was all lost. They were four-plus spin equivalents out from Qol.

He sat up and peeled the circuited wrap off his shoulder. Rolled the shoulder. The pain was deep and dull. His wound was down to a thin, seeping cleave, and his collarbone was nearly fully healed. A marvel, this technology on this world where he was born.

He stepped over Kade, grabbed a fresh wrap from the bin in the wall, applied it, and turned it on. He then grabbed a meal bite, filled his cup with water from the spout, and sat down at the holo station in the corner. Kade stirred in his nest on the floor, muttered, and rolled over.

Nerves indeed. Will's chest was tight. Mavardarum: he wasn't quite ready to abandon it to its fate. It was once a shining metal city on the eastern continent, a melting pot, a cultural and technological center with stone streets, green parks, and internal combustion of some sort. It had tolerance and contentment. It was a beacon and role model for the rest of Gog in an age of progress. It melted within a fraction of a second of the first Rhode Island-sized meteor fragment crashing into Gog.

Will procrastinated. He sipped his water and reviewed his notes from the first four mornings. He'd started on day one with three papers on "peak Mavardarum" written by three different Qol academics. From there, he'd gone backward and spread out, plucking times and places at random from the vast and patchy forest of Qol's archives ('Littered with trash,' Kade had warned him) on their neighbor. He'd found Gog's ancient history to be far less violent than Earth's, an attribute it shared with Qol. He'd scoured the journals and textbooks for potential reasons why and found none but came up with his own theory on the third morning: that the particular light of Nurin, a couple of shades lighter than the sun, made particular physical, chemical, mental, and emotional soups. He had not a shred of evidence to back this up, but it resonated, nonetheless.

He'd dabbled in pre-meteor Gog religions, which he interpreted to be decidedly less diverse but more organic and grounded than Earth's, less psychical than Qol's. He'd sampled cultures, art, politics. These histories were incomplete, passed down over centuries by the few survivors of an apocalypse and subject to the biases of the Qol academics and journalists. But they were chock full of telltale signs of humanity.

He'd enjoyed this reading very much. What wasn't there for a boy to love about studying an ancient, alien civilization? He could forget at times that almost everything had died. He wanted to forget it now. It could wait. One more session on the time before would be beneficial. A bit more context. But he'd put it off too long already. The clock was ticking. Fifteen more "days," all filled to the brim with grunt work, and he had a lot of research ground to cover. The least he could do for MaGog was attempt to understand where they were coming from.

He took the plunge, and it might have broken his heart could he have fathomed the scale of physical and psychological loss.

Slowed the spin of the planet, Jesus.

Time slipped. A half-hour? An hour? He was terrified and enthralled. He was a kid watching a trainwreck in slow motion. Or a slasher film. Or the skinning of an animal.

Beep-beep-beep.

The ship alarm snapped him out of the other world.

"Around the edges," Kade mumbled in a feminine voice, coming out of a dream.

Still with the voices, Will observed, shutting off the holo.

Some sort of escape. Some retreat into characters, maybe other personalities split off by the trauma. Will tried to speak to them at times, but they never stuck around long enough for him to get a word in.

Kade sat up against the wall and shoved his mat and blanket under Will's bunk. "So?" he asked in English, in his own voice, in his something-European accent that of course wasn't. He insisted on knowing everything Will read each morning and the sources.

Will put on his glasses, palmed the invisible holoball with his left hand, and typed:

--The event. Let's talk in Korial. --

He was learning the basics of both Korial and Vrrgrrul. He had no expectation of ever being able to toss away the translator crutch (even if he had the time, his brain sucked at languages; he'd gotten straight Cs in Spanish in high school), but he wanted to show an effort to the guards and eventually to MaGog. Kade, who knew enough of a dozen languages to get by in the dozens of places he'd gone searching for Will over the years (turns) and was himself immersed in advanced Vrrgrrul, was a good if not a distracted teacher.

"Who?" Kade asked in Korial.

Will took their suits out of the closet and dropped Kade's into his lap.

--Mostly Masa ma ra Hyda. Also Kama ton yu Nunti. --

"Nunti knows how to conduct research," Kade said, putting one leg into his suit and then the other. "You know how I feel about Hyda."

--We'll cover it at lunch. --

Will reached down with his good arm, pulled Kade up, and threw the arm around Kade's shoulder.

--Come on, I have mouths to feed. --

Pots banged. Grills sizzled. The cook trio hustled. Just another "day" on the silver triangle spaceship crossing the void between planet Qol and planet Gog.

--Wow, smells good. -- Will projected in Korial over his wrist device as he popped into the kitchen. Mina scowled, Deva turned her back to him, and Yu ignored him, their typical responses to his attempts at engagement. Not surprised and never discouraged, he whistled a tune from another world, *Karma Police*, and started loading dishes into the dishwasher. It looked a lot like the ones in the restaurants he'd worked in back on Earth, though this one did its job in under five seconds. Honto walked in, winked at Will like he had something to tell him, then rolled the rack of plates, bowls, and cutlery out into the cafeteria and started setting the tables.

The crew came in bunches, all coiled energy and controlled aggression, waking up and ready to feed and get to work. Two hundred-plus infantry, a dozen or so ambassadorial staff, and two dozen engineers, ninety-percent of everyone on board (Kade was among the ten percent holding down the fort), never together in one room except for breakfast. And Will got to be in the thick of it. He got to see just about every face every day (a rainbow of skin tones, the most diverse space he'd ever been in; in his life). He got to make eye contact as he passed them their food from behind the counter. He maintained a deferent smile. He stretched it for those with choice words for him. There were a few of those this morning. There were always a few. But another meal passed without incident.

Cleaning time, and Will was sweeping up when Honto slid over to him like an eel and started wiping down a red metal table that Will had already wiped to a gleam. Tall as a female, skinny as a MaGog fellow, he watched with hooded eyes as the last happy customers filed out. He kept his voice low. "Emissaries are butting heads," he said in Korial. The English streamed behind Will's right lens. "Can't settle on a strategy. Captain's getting impatient. Starting to *exert his influence*. Similar thing happening on the other ships. Don't ask me where I heard it." Will never did, but Honto always said that.

"That guy, Ijooma, gave you a hard time just now?" Honto whispered, moving on from the ships' shifting political sands, which Will knew he knew nothing about. "*Killed* someone. I mean before the guard. You didn't hear that from me."

Will stashed this away. Honto was sick. He was running a fever like that satellite operator Ayn had watched in the days leading up to the attack. But he always seemed to wax coherent when it came to guard gossip, and he'd proven himself knowledgeable in that field already:

skeletons in closets and little embarrassments that Will had used a couple of times to wipe the smirks off the faces of extra zealous guards mouthing off at him or Kade. And he had something on Nopa that he was holding onto.

-- How about me? -- Will asked.

Honto read the Korial on his wrist device. "How about you what?"

-- Your sources say anything about me? --

Honto's eyes glazed over. He started wiping another clean table. "Nothing about you," he said. "Tell you something, though . . ." But he didn't finish, just trailed off and winked at his own dull reflection in the red metal.

Will thought about walking him down to the infirmary, thought that would probably be best for everyone. But he decided he wasn't ready to give up his informant. He pointed to the clock on the wall.

-- See you tomorrow. --

Honto wiped.

Will took a ladder down a silver tube nice and easy. He was still acclimating to the simulated lower gravity, which the captain had turned on the moment they broke out of Qol's. Going up was fun. You felt extra fast and strong. Going down you reached each rung a split second too late and always felt like you might have missed it and were about to fall.

He cut through the infantry quarters, a cross-hatched triangle of tight, odorless, dark-blue metal corridors, all empty and quiet now. In the middle was the locker room, also a triangle and also empty, but not at all odorless. There were four long rows of cubbies, ten suction toilets, and ten "showers," booths where you got sprayed with a citrus-smelling sanitizer and then dried by infrared heat. Will's second job every day, a job he took seriously, was to tidy this entire space. He wanted things spotless and spruced up for the guards when they returned from their long hours of workouts, war games, and strategy sessions, all of which Will and Kade had so far been excluded from. They knew who was cleaning up after them, and so they made an effort to keep things raunchy. For example, someone left Will a present each day, a shit on the floor of one of the showers. Today was no exception, but Will didn't blink an eye. He whistled while he worked. He looked up at the cameras and smiled. On his way out, he left his daily message on the digital board like a hotel maid might. In Korial: "Have a good day."

He had a few rus to kill before lunch with Kade, so he took the scenic route past the common rooms on the port side. He stepped into one and looked out the wall-sized window at the mist of stars in black infinity, the billions of incomprehensibly large and powerful balls of fire all light years away from each other. It blew his mind every time, the scale that made a mockery of human existence, the fact that the ship could be traveling somewhere between the speed of sound and the speed of light, and it could still seem like they were standing still. Will could understand why some historically stable minds might struggle with all that.

Someone had left a holo on tuned to a game of spiral. Not the Tiralee version but the one Will had seen projected from the wall of the pill station on the way to Peis Ota's island. Normal-sized Qols wearing suits and fins instead of translucent, rubber skin. No webbed hands. No aquadynamic heads. They threw a metal spiral instead of a wooden one. They maneuvered through groves of artificial reef inside a giant oval fish tank surrounded by bleachers packed with fans instead of through tendril trees in a lake surrounded by nets covered in Nimar breathing through reeds as the Tiralee circled and bellowed rally songs. Will thought of Vinson and Piper and everyone. He thought of Peis as a ball of light and didn't know why, except that maybe that was what happened to people when they died.

He reached the stern and climbed a ladder as fast as he could in his lighter body. He gained the top floor as the alarm went *beep-beep-beep* and the guards started spilling out of conference rooms and training facilities. He hugged the wall, moving against the grain, nodding and smiling. Some noticed him. Some pretended not to. One guy threw a shoulder, and he turned sideways without breaking stride and patted the guy on the back as the guy flew into the woman in front of him. His friends busted his balls, and everyone walked away.

Kade stood outside the room where he took his Vrrgrrul lessons, back to the wall, eyes fixed, peripheral dialed. Will knew how much he hated these times between shifts, these tight, packed hallways. He reminded Will constantly that a shoulder could just as easily be a laser.

-- Ready, sir? -- Will typed.

Kade nodded and fell in behind him. He insisted on covering Will's rear wherever they went.

There were two other people in the cafeteria, both sitting alone. The kitchen was empty. The leftovers from breakfast and a bowl of meal bites were out on the counter. There was no such thing as lunch on the ship, or on Qol for that matter, as far as Will could tell. Qols (of which he was one, he sometimes had to remind himself) ate a big breakfast and more or less grazed the rest of the day. But he'd instituted a brief midday meal in this small, shared gap in his and Kade's schedules. It served as a touch point and a taste-of-Earth ritual. They spent the time each day reviewing Will's morning readings.

He put on his glasses and blinked at the blue square in his right lens. The holoball filled his left palm and purred, said Hi, what can I do for you? It was more and more a part of him. Like his xim, it was getting to know him, intuiting him, helping him learn. He played it like an instrument, tapping, squeezing, rolling.

He paraphrased his readings from that morning, written by journalist Masa ma ra Hyda and academic Kama ton yu Nunti. He "spoke" like he was thinking aloud, studying for a test, committing things to memory. Because he was. These sessions were as much about reinforcing what he'd learned as they were about soliciting Kade's feedback.

But Kade was quiet today. There wasn't much for him to comment on. There were many loud voices and strong opinions when it came to Gog's history and motivation, but there was limited controversy surrounding the event and the aftermath.

Two continents on one side of Gog. The western one looked like Russia stood up on its end. The eastern one was a shapeless blob just as big. They were connected by a thick, mountainous land bridge to the south and a thin, flat, wavy one to the north. Between them was a rough-edged, bean-shaped sea. The largest of the three meteor fragments came down near Mavardarum in the center of the blob, leaving a crater the size of Hellas on Mars. The second one boiled the sea down to scattered puddles. The third hit a plain on the western continent, shattered its brittle rock foundation, and made a web of radiating canyons a few hundred miles in diameter. This third also woke the three volcanos on the west coast, the ones Gideon would see through his telescope roughly seven hundred Qol years (turns) later.

--Sound right so far?-- Will asked.

Kade picked at his food. "More or less." He looked like he was nursing a headache. Or arguing with the voices. Will thought maybe they should quit now and pick it up tomorrow. Or even just skip right over this particular subject matter. But Kade sensed his hesitation and probably the reason for it and waved him on.

Ash collected on the underside of the blanket atmosphere that had kept Gog hospitable to life for something like a billion years that far from Nurin. The planet darkened and choked. The gray seeped up into the white over Gog years (rings), corroded it, fed on it until there was nothing left, then faded away from starvation, leaving not a wisp of cloud to block the solar or cosmic radiation. The few survivors on the western continent and the greater number on the distorted star-shaped continent on the far side of the planet (spared the initial devastation but not this slower, certain death) all eventually retreated underground.

The first three hundred rings were brutally straightforward: survive and rebuild the race. They had help. Gog had prepared for this eventuality. That, at least, was the metaphysical conclusion reached by one thrown-together tribe, the MaGog ancestors. It was the foundational belief of a new religion. These lucky few found their underground full of water. They found themselves in a nexus between filtered, tidal flow from the ocean to the west and runoff from a space-piercing mountain to the south. They found several species of fungi, algae, and lichen, a modest animal kingdom of worms and critters, and a great diversity of minerals. The first generations met with many small plagues as their guts adjusted to the bacteria in their planet's guts. But, as it goes, the strong passed on their genes.

Beep-beep-beep.

Will turned off the holoball and stretched his fingers. Kade gave him the names of two other experts on the event, and they went their separate ways.

Will jogged. He would not be late for Nopa, never again. He'd been on time for his first shift, then late on purpose for his second. He'd done it to solicit a reaction, which he'd received: wrath. He'd done it because of the way she tried not to look at him that first day and because of the door behind her. Since then, he'd shown her how he could be better. He was the first to arrive today.

-- Hi boss. --

She ignored him. Her calloused, mocha-colored hands flew around inside her holomap of the warehouse, plucking at neon objects, moving them around. The tip of her tongue poked out of the left corner of her mouth. Blue eyes tracked her targets.

Kavano and Loli showed up together, second time in as many days (spins, cycles)—not a pattern yet, but curious. Maybe they also had a little free time between shifts. Will smiled at them and nodded. Loli looked off into the stacks. Kavano nodded back. He was one of the small few on board who seemed more interested in Will than resentful of him.

"Put them on," Nopa ordered in Korial.

They put on their glasses. Will blinked open the file in his right lens—freezer again—then the map in his left. A red dot marked a stack of crates of that surprisingly good ship-grown spud that made the base of most meals here, including the meal bites. Three drones hovered over with their pincher-fingered snake arms coiled and at rest on their flat backs.

"Get going," Nopa said.

--OK boss.--

"Stop calling me that, mute!"

Will winked at Loli, who'd been eyeing him and thought he hadn't noticed. She seemed to regret it. He hustled off, trailing his drone.

Fifth day on the job, third in food, second in the freezer, and Will pretty much had it down. This wasn't his first rodeo in a warehouse. He'd worked for a printing company one summer in high school lugging fifty-pound boxes of pamphlets, drug bottle inserts, and whatever else. Back then, he had his bare hands, his back, a pen and paper, a dolly, and a shitty truck to work with. Here he had a drone that followed Nopa's pre-programed instructions and did all the heavy lifting. All he had to do was make sure the numbers on the crates matched the numbers in the order, open the crates to double-check the contents, then tap a four-digit code into his wrist device authorizing the drones to go make the delivery. Easy peasy. Will banged through his orders in an hour or so and returned to Nopa for more.

She sighed very deeply as he approached, like she could not for the life of her understand how certain people could be so dense. "We have to go through this again?" she asked in Korial. "Just message me." She fished around in her holo. "You'll have to wait."

Will read the English words in his glasses but didn't really have to. He knew a few of the Korial ones, and the tone translated just fine.

-- I forgot. No problem. --

He hadn't forgotten. He rocked heel to toe, looked around, snuck a glance at her and made sure to get caught. He didn't have to feign interest, not with that blue eye and chocolate skin combo, those long legs, that thick, dark, carelessly tied-back hair, that no-nonsense scowl.

-- Cold in there. -- he typed and faked a shiver.

She closed her eyes and breathed. Opened them, reached over the counter, and grabbed his wrist. "Watch closely, yes?" she said like she was talking to a toddler and doing everything in her power to maintain serenity. She tapped the code into his device, and his suit's heating software popped up in his left lens.

-- Right, thanks. --

He already knew how to control his suit temperature and had been perfectly comfortable in the freezer. She turned back to her holo. He tested Honto's nugget.

-- What do you think about those two? --

"Those who?"

-- Loli and Kavano. --

"What's the question, mute?"

-- You think they're …? --

"They're what? I just sent the orders. Go."

-- I think they are. --

He drew a smiley face with the holoball and sent it.

She finally got it. The tips of her brown ears turned crimson. Somewhere a virgin radar was flashing like a strobe light. Honto had a fever, but he also had his moments of clarity, and, apparently, his sources.

-- Anyway, see you. --

She stared into her holo and didn't say a thing.

He was done long before the *beep-beep-beep,* but he hung back and made sure he was last in line to close out. Nopa had recovered her pride.

She reviewed his files with the air of the boss, then dismissed him. "Go free."

-- See you tomorrow. --

He took a single step, then turned back.

-- Actually, I have a question. --

She kept it nonplussed. She pretended to be annoyed at his lingering.

-- What do they say about us? --

He looked past her at the metal door leading to the other half of the warehouse and wondered if this was a good idea. But he suspected that he was going to need her.

"Us?" She looked mortified.

-- No one wants us here. I get it. I'm just interested in what people think they know. --

She exhaled. 'Us' meant Will and Kade, the John Does, not her and Will, of course!

"What we've been told is that you're here because you were *there*. You fought them. You have some knowledge. Makes sense, I guess."

-- Most disagree. --

"Most around here don't think. They're angry about what happened."

-- I understand. --

And he did, truly. He remembered anger and hate. He remembered the ground-shaking thunder of the Gog ships, the burning forest and columns of smoke, the churning black and red stew. How badly he'd wanted to kill Radin. How hard he'd tried.

"Will you answer one?" she asked.

-- If I can. --

"*Why* were you there?"

He took another chance.

-- Not a coincidence. --

"What does that mean?"

He looked at her like he wanted to tell her something, to open up, he just didn't know how or where to start.

-- Hard for me to explain. Hard to talk about. --

This captured her, this intrigue and vulnerability. Her face softened. "There's one story floating around."

-- What story? --

"That you were missing most of your life. Not just living outside the Cooperative."

'Living outside the Cooperative.' The party line, written by Brava.

Will made hurt, introspective eyes.

-- Better told over a drink. --

A guard walked up. The drone behind him bore a single crate.

Nopa cleared her throat and looked at her map. "Go ahead."

"Sticky blenders," the guard said.

Will had an idea then. The start of one. He put it aside for now. He looked at the time on his wrist device.

-- See you, boss. --

She didn't answer.

Ninety percent of everyone on board (including Kade in this case) got forty rus (about an hour, in Will's estimation) to themselves before lights out. He and Kade started each of these periods of free time the same way, by walking to the nose of the ship, requesting an audience with the captain, and being denied. Kade considered this a waste of time and made a habit of letting Will know it. But Will respectfully disagreed. He didn't necessarily expect to be admitted, and he didn't care. He would go every night and insist on Kade being there. He would smile at the guards flanking the door, nod respectfully, and ask them to pass along his and Kade's offer to provide their unique perspective on the situation. It was the thought that counted. It was a reputation they were building.

They went again on this fifth night. They were denied. They went to the gym and worked the climbing wall, which was only eight feet high but which streamed like sheet music in one of those old-timey, self-playing pianos, so you could climb and climb. They climbed as though their lives depended on it. Will's shoulder hurt like a bitch, and his motion was still somewhat limited, but everything was coming along nicely beneath the circuited wrap, all things considered.

They did their ten, fifteen minutes on the wall, then huffed it to the artillery, where they signed out their xims and sparred, under supervision in a room locked from the outside, like savages, just went at it for another ten, fifteen. Then they made the short walk to their sanctuary.

It was a large office-turned-receptacle for compost barrels. They knew about it because Kade worked the farm during his third shift every day. It offered privacy and a window, both priceless on a spaceship. It also offered the smell of rot, earthy and grounding, a comfort out there in the void.

Kade took his place at the desk in the corner, turned on his glasses, and reviewed his Vrrgrrul lessons, mouthing the guttural words. Will sat on the floor beneath the window and between two barrels, looked up into star-dusted space, crossed his legs, closed his eyes, and tuned in.

He didn't need to set his intention. He'd already set it, though he couldn't remember when. Sometime before the launch, during their time at the base; or on the muddy shore, as the shattered Nimar and Tiralee cried for their lost loved ones; or before any of that; or after it, he didn't know. It felt like a memory, only different. It felt like remembering the future.

It was the moment, and he was in it. He was inside a sub-subatomic particle sea of consciousness that challenged the absolute black between the stars. Proved it wrong. There was nothing empty anywhere. It was all absolutely teeming.

Will watched the pixels swirl like galaxies behind his lids. He let the images come and go. He waited for ideas. The magnet of his intention drew things, like the MaGog apocalypse, which he could barely comprehend but to which he committed every spirit-ounce of his sympathy; Honto, delirious, telling him about sources; the Shole and his own delirium; the roof of 1449 Washington Street and a swell on the horizon, out there beyond the red bridge, a tidal wave; Raider, a dog he loved.

The wave crashed and settled. Debris bobbed on the surface: sticky blenders, those suits that the guard scouts had worn during the attack drills in the fake Gog tunnels beneath the launch base; three emissaries whispering to each other; a swarm of foot-long Gog worms eating a MaGog fellow's arm; other mental scraps. He let them go. He clung to nothing. It all spiraled down.

He'd been seeing this spiral since launch. He'd been observing its silent, sucking power. Nothing escaped, not a pixel. Nothing wanted to. Seeing it now, Will formed a question, which at once began to obsess him.

What's on the other side?

He was humming, he was deep, when he saw, for the first time, something hovering above the hole at the bottom of the spiral. But it was vague, he couldn't make it out.

He opened his eyes and thought, *the sticky blenders and the emissaries.*

Kade was standing behind the desk with his glasses off, rubbing the back of his hand and looking at it as though he didn't recognize it. Will stood up, walked to him, and squeezed his shoulder. "What is it?" he asked.

Will had kept his intention to himself to that point. Kade had had enough on his mental plate to deal with. He'd been brutalized by what they'd seen and done, and he'd formed, like so many others on this ship and on both worlds, in his split head and battered heart, a simple, bloody forecast of what would happen once the armada reached Gog. But sparing him had been a mistake, Will realized now. Reaching him and helping him claw his way out of hell required more than hugs and sleeping in the same room. It required engaging him and making him co-creator of a new inevitability.

Will grabbed him by the back of his neck, as he had done to Will in the everbluegreen-blanketed hills beyond the Shole after Will had killed for the first time. Kade had told him then, 'You'll never be rid of it,' and Will had known it to be true. He knew it then, and he knew it now. But he was determined to make something of their pain.

He typed: -- We're going to save them. --

Kade's eyes started shaking. "What do you mean?"

-- I don't know yet. --

That was mostly true. He took Kade by the arm and led him out of the sanctuary. Back in their room, Kade made his nest on the floor and soon passed out. Will read papers on the event written by the two academics Kade had recommended.

20

Kade lay on her depleted stomach peering over the edge of the cliff, miserable with unrequited love. She listened with a growing, calming apathy to the waves crashing beneath the mist. She dropped a stone that fell and fell and then was simply gone, swallowed by the mist and the roar.

It will be soft and perfect, she thought.

She would become the mist and float away.

The smell of the ocean. The oppression of the wooden fortress on the hill behind her. The sense of infinity in the slight curve of the horizon.

He was stalking a herd of namid. He was carrying a carcass over one shoulder back to the village, back to his woman and their two girls, back to love. Warm blood dripped down his chest. Then they were dead, and he was digging up their graves with his bare hands and screaming.

He was pacing his cell, muttering in English in a strange accent. He was telling the walls that the Mind had lost its mind. Cracked mirror, mate.

He was covered in scales, and there were two red suns.

She was a hoverbird.

She was a woman giant on a beach beneath the stars. The stars were speaking to her, and she was arranging the sticks according to their message.

These were not memories, of course. Kade had never been a young girl or a father. He'd never been to prison. He'd never had wings or scales. The sticks, though, the sticks.

He plucked and planted, plucked and planted. How much time left in the shift? How many shifts had he worked in the farm? How many spin-equivalents had they been out there? He checked the date in his glasses. Seven! Was that possible? He supposed it was. Could have been more, though. Could have been less. Time on the ship was different. But the countdown clock read seven spins with twelve to go, and Kade had to assume it was right. Certainly, he wasn't going to ask any of the other farmers if they too suspected it of being off. He plucked and planted.

He knew he was sick. He knew he was hiding and compartmental-izing. But he was managing it. He actually didn't mind the slips of place and time. He sometimes preferred the confusion of the illusions to the confusion of reality.

Dawlis didn't know he was sick. Dawlis was busy in his own world, distracting himself in other ways, convincing himself that the answers to his questions lay somewhere, somehow, in MaGog history. Kade went along. It was something to "talk" about, at least.

But one thing Dawlis had "said" a long time ago frightened Kade. Or maybe it hadn't been very long ago at all. 'I am the butterfly and the squid.' No, no, not that. Well, yes, that, but something else. What was it? And why was Kade giving himself a headache trying to remember it as they speed-walked to the gym?

Dawlis didn't climb today. He paced, staring into his glasses and working his holoball, his lips pressed together. Kade came down off the wall and grabbed his wrist. "What is it?"

Dawlis sent a file to Kade's glasses. A drawing. A creature with tenta-cles and a single, large eye floating in negative space between two curvy wings. Inside the eye was a wave with one peak and one trough.

-- A butterfly-squid. -- Dawlis explained.

Mind, Kade thought. Dawlis was losing it too. He was coping in his own way, creating his own chimeras.

-- We're going to save them. --

That was it. The other thing he'd said. And he'd just said it again. He wasn't letting it go.

"How?"

-- By reminding them that they can choose. --

Kade's head throbbed. "How from this ship?" Dawlis knew as well as he did that the captain would never let them off. The captain had gritted his teeth, followed the orders issued through Brava, and taken them along. But they were a long way from his superiors, and he was in charge out there.

-- We'll find a way. --

Kade was a giant. He was himself. He followed Dawlis out of the gym.

21

Will turned on the holo, chewed a fingernail, and typed in his search: "renaissance." Kade moaned in his sleep.

It began in earnest amongst the MaGog ancestors three hundred rings after the event. The weak had been weaned out. Disease was no longer a constant threat. The strong had survived and were now relearning how to *live*. They'd long ago given up the fantasy of returning to the barren surface—there were no green shoots—but they'd come to appreciate what they had and to worship what had given it to them. It was not the light of Nurin that stewed life in the underworld. It was the warmth of the Core. They kissed the rock floors in prayer to it. Art returned in homage. They dug deeper and wider and crafted their dens and sites with greater pride and purpose. On these generalities, the Qol scholars and journalists largely agreed.

An intrepid few migrated several hundred miles south to the headwaters beneath a mountain that scraped space, a singular apex, two thick-tendoned arms melded together and culminating in twelve sharp fingers that pointed up (the *praying hands*, Will named them). But here is where the braid of consensus started to loosen and fray. Here, rational, learned people could disagree on how to interpret the same facts. The accused "spiritualists" and "novelists" of Qol journalism and academia saw this mountain as yet another example of the planet's resilience and unwillingness to abandon life, of a Gog Gaia. In the earliest rings after the meteor, the snow and ice that tipped the fingers, laced the arms, and capped the rolling shoulders melted under the suffocating blanket of ash, flooded the underworld, and combined with the tidal flow from the ocean to the west to create a cradle of lakes and rivers. The arms reached violently further into the sky, driven higher every few rings by massive earthquakes. Eventually, the fingers pierced the ash and started its recession. They went dormant for decades of cloudless sky, then burst higher in a final fit of creative destruction. They were the hands of a human being buried in a gray waste, a human begging to be seen and heard. It was a poetic narrative with more than its fair share of doubters.

Whatever the case, by natural or supernatural forces, the fingers penetrated blue-black space, and it bled on them an island atmosphere. The cycles of snow, freeze, thaw, and burn became daily. Those who'd gone south proved prescient and industrious. They took economic ownership of the runoff and manipulated it with dams and channels. To this day, Koren's hive maintained a tenuous trading relationship with its neighbor, exchanging wealth in minerals and derivative products (mainly drugs and fuel) and the threat of war for reliable water flow. Not much about those particular atmospheric, geological, or political fundamentals had changed in seven hundred rings.

One thing *did* change, however, and this change was enshrined in a myth that all Qol pundits agreed was nothing but. One hundred rings after the expedition south, six hundred rings ago, a female named Arrarra, living in a deep corner of the northern hive, climbed to the surface to kill herself and saw a cloud on the horizon as Gorr was rising. The cloud blocked Gorr, giving Arrarra more time. It rose and fell with Gorr, protecting her for all the light half of the cycle. Gorr's warmth lingered into the dark half, and Arrarra saw, floating between two of Gog's moons, the blue star. She was the first to see it for what it was, a heaven. This was the Pramma, the Vision, the moment when this pocket of Gog humanity began to believe again in a future on the surface and an afterlife on the blue star.

At first, those looking up and looking forward were the minority, and their beliefs were unwelcome. The Core religion balked at this misguided soul distraction. They snapped their fingers to wake the dreamers. Then slapped them. Then lost their patience and came down harder.

The establishment was right and wrong. The paltry atmosphere did nothing to protect anyone from the elements. But this did not discourage the obsession. It did not stop hundreds, then thousands, then tens of thousands from signing up to die, by heat, cold, or radiation, to place a few blocks of the pyramids, or to join in the fight against the Core religion missionaries. With those noble traditionalists attacking from the sides and below and Gorr attacking from above (equally by its presence as by its absence), it took more than one hundred and fifty rings to build the pyramids. But they did it, this pseudo-scientific faction born of the parable of Arrarra. Then the whole movement died off from exhaustion. Or nearly. It left a legacy. It gave birth on its deathbed to a single cell that wiggled and pulsed. A cell with foresight, aspiration, and a reborn interest in technology.

Human curiosity took over. The cell divided and multiplied into a brain, and the dark heart of religion was forced to adapt. The engineers rediscovered controlled combustion, but this time they had more than their version of coal. They had minerals that burned at relatively low temperatures and with minimal emissions. They crafted basic engines. They dug and laid the first rail system. They consumed the underworld's resources at a greater rate and fought over the right to consume. They divided into trading groups led by alpha merchants, who were constantly making deals with each other for goods and territory and deploying their youth to take what they wanted if they didn't like the terms. These were the Marradar, the *fat cats*, as Will thought of them. They made the rules and remade them. Exploitation and murder were accepted tools of their economy. Technology advanced, but slowly, because of the Marradars' certifiable inability to cooperate. One would take a step forward and three others would try for the formula and rather see it burn than remain in a competitor's hands. Income inequality widened to an uncrossable chasm. The great majority had few economic opportunities other than to join one of these gangs, and the fat cats had many wives and many children. This was the societal structure, give or take, for roughly four long Gog centuries, all the way up to the time of Koren. It was what she dismantled.

Beep-beep-beep.

Will jumped in his seat, and Kade jerked out of his troubled sleep.

Cleaning time. It happened fast. Honto screamed something garbled as though his brain had misfired, and lunged. Will turned his shoulders (the blue laser-blade slid past his chest in slow motion), cupped the back of Honto's head, slammed it on a table, and laid him gently on the floor, all in more or less one motion.

Will was not surprised in hindsight. Honto had been running a serious fever. But it didn't feel quite settled. Honto had always seemed less mentally infirm or delusional to Will and more like a piece of hardware running on software that skipped on him sometimes. Like maybe his connection was spotty. But connection to what?

Most saw the incident as confirmation that bringing Will and Kade along had been a mistake. But Will got more eye contact after that, and no one left shits on the locker room floor anymore. The captain responded by reminding the crew, over the speaker that night, that they had a responsibility to get their asses down to the infirmary if they ever felt a fever coming on. And his door seemed more closed to Will and Kade than ever.

On the Ninth morning, Will dove deeper into the Core religion, finding in it a great deal of humanity: hope, love, comfort, dogma, intolerance, and brutality.

-- It's more like certain religions on Earth than on Qol in those respects. -- he later said to Kade. They were eating lunch.

-- More pain, more heart, less Mind. --

It was a question really. This similarity between Earth and Qol and this difference between Qol and Gog dealt a blow to his theory that Nurin's and the sun's particular light waves made particular flavors of psycho-spiritual soup. Kade did not attempt an answer.

A female guard, red-faced and seething, walked into the cafeteria and told Will, Kade, and the three other guards there about Radin's heist. Will slumped in his chair, floored, blown away. Such an elegant job. Such a smart move. So unexpected and deeply troubling. The Qols had believed thus far—*had* to in order to salvage their pride and sanity in those early stages of adapting to the new epoch—that MaGog had taken their best shot in Nima. They'd left a mark and implanted a small force. They'd gained a bit of leverage at the negotiating table and maybe earned a say in the terms of a migration. Maybe. But it was ridiculous really. The technology gap was a century wide. What were they planning to do against four battleships?

Yet this warrior, his range of ability. One day making craters and the next slipping into what may as well have been the bedrooms of the Council Members. One day a sledgehammer, the next a ghost.

Hearing the death toll (non-zero), Will shook his head at his nemesis, his shadow, and doubted his decision to cross the void and leave Qol to fend for itself. But the four guards banging their fists on the tables and hissing about the swift and total retribution that the Qol armada would bring reminded Will why he was there.

On the tenth morning of nineteen, Will learned that the pyramids were more than a release of claustrophobia and a desperate expression of the dream of living on the surface again and ascending in death to a blue star heaven. He learned that a cottage techno-religion had been born a couple of centuries after the completion of the pyramids; among the descendants of the architects and suicide volunteers, a sect that believed that the blue star was not a star at all but another world and that it was only a matter of technological generations before they would propel themselves to their new home.

This was the birth of the manifest destiny. It was loosely supported by advancements in astronomy and chemistry. Engineers began to play with larger-scale propulsion using different combinations of minerals. It was a niche effort with a passionate but only modest following, for the ideas were still too farfetched for the average fellow. That is, until a century later when the first Qol satellite appeared in their sky.

Beep-beep-beep.

The Marradar, Will discovered on the eleventh morning, managed to cooperate not long after that first Self-shattering indirect contact seventy-three turns past, forty-four rings by. They built the rocket lab and manufacturing facility in a central location, currently Zone 3 of Koren's system. Even the fat cats most strategically resourced to approach the science-fiction problem of spaceflight knew that they could never tackle it alone. Still, they all plotted to be the one with their name emblazoned on the nose of the first ship. They bribed and assassinated the engineers contributed to the facility by their rivals, sabotaged when they didn't feel sufficiently represented, blacked out chunks of institutional knowledge.

Will did a great deal of cross-referencing. Eventually:

Beep-beep-beep.

Morning twelve, and he uncovered a controversial theory that Koren was the daughter of a fat cat. He asked Kade what he knew about it at lunch and ran into one of his personalities. They'd been quiet for a few spins, and Will had hoped that they might be sinking back into his unconscious, a sign of recovery. No such luck.

"No one bloody wants to know," he said in the voice that always made Will think of a black-lunged, British coal miner, a la Dickens.

-- Know what? -- he asked casually.

"The Mind's lost its mind. Cracked mirror, mate. Cracked mirror. Keep me locked up? Makes 'em feel bet'a. They'll see."

-- See what? --

"What?" Kade asked in his own voice.

-- Nothing. --

This episode stirred Will in more ways than one. It was a wake-up call. Seven more spin-equivalents to go, and they'd yet to gain an audience with the captain or be included in a single landing drill. Still, there was no panic in him. He had his intention, and he had his ideas cooking on their fires in the back of his mind.

Middle of his shift at the warehouse, Will peeked through the stacks and saw Nopa alone at her counter working her holo. He walked over with his drone and reported that the contents of one of his crates didn't match his order, which implied that she'd made a mistake, which she didn't like very much. He stepped around the counter uninvited and stood by her side as she troubleshot. He leaned in, brushed against her, backed up, typed, -- Sorry, boss. -- He felt the heat coming off her reddening ears.

It turned out there was nothing wrong with his order after all. He'd just looked in the wrong crate. He apologized again and went back to work.

He was meditating in the sanctuary beneath the window between two barrels of compost. He was seeing the object at the bottom of the spiral, and it had taken shape for the first time. It was a column, a monolith, a skyscraper, or a two-by-four. He remembered standing on the island with Peis Ota throwing rocks at the buoy. He remembered Peis saying, 'The more you feel your connection, the more you are interacting with the universe. But harnessing it is a different thing. It cannot be gained by reaching, only by letting go.' He didn't know why that memory popped. He simply acknowledged that it did.

Thirteenth morning. Kade was mumbling in his sleep, eyes roving behind his lids like searchlights, and Will was digging through the archives for anything he could find on Koren as a child. Anything at all. He came up empty. From what he could tell, she didn't appear in Gog's history until the age of eight rings (roughly thirteen Qol turns, sixteen Earth years), in the records of one Marradar, who credited her with killing four of his bodyguards in a failed attempt on his life. This was shortly after Qol's first ship arrived, which epoch-defining event, fifty-four turns past, thirty-three rings by, happened to take place above this Marradar's dominion. That was it, the first impression, a topic that plucked more than a few very sensitive nerves among the Qol academic and journalistic communities. Will's entry into it was fortuitous. He stumbled upon the writings of one Monte lo ara Bige, a fringe, isolated academic who Will would come to know as a contrarian on virtually every debated point of Qol-Gog relations. The Qol crew were agitated, Bige noted. No surprise, they'd had a long journey and then got lost in the tunnels. They were exhausted and disoriented. The first shot may have been an accident, fired by an overwrought guard with an itchy trigger finger. It didn't matter. What mattered was that Qol fired first. The Marradar and his minions had been defending themselves.

But that was not at all how it happened, according to every Qol scholar of any credibility. The Marradar's people closest to the surface saw or heard or felt the landing and spied the small, ambassadorial Qol crew working its way down. The Marradar waited until the crew was good and lost on his home turf. Then he rescued them and welcomed them. Then he killed them neatly. A second Qol expedition, larger and more heavily armed, crawled down after a tense Gog cycle of not having heard from the first. A small army of the Marradar's men and boys was waiting. Another small army climbed up and stormed the ship. Then the Marradar, with every man, woman, and child at his disposal, dug a wide tunnel down from the surface, dug a garage, dragged the ship down, and prepared for war with his rivals.

But no, shouted Bige. That revisionist, ethnocentric perspective was symptomatic of everything wrong with how Qol had approached the Gog problem from the very start. Those Marradar records were not without holes, he admitted, but it was clear, to anyone who didn't use the holes as escape hatches, who was responsible for putting the two planets on a collision course instead of at the negotiating table. His complete dismissal in a few vague words of Qol's sustained military restraint since then and its many documented attempts at diplomacy did nothing good for his already suspect reputation. But Will valued this side of the story. He was sure that there was some truth to it. He was sure that MaGog had been just as scared as the visiting Qols.

What was not disputed was the bloody muck that followed first contact. The fat cats did exactly what was expected of them. They scratched and clawed over the golden chariot and its technologies. Nothing came of it but self-mutilation. They thinned each other's reluctant, ragtag armies. The gaps were filled by youth raised in even greater poverty and fear, trying to develop identities under impossible circumstances. Koren was one of them. Koren felt her people's boiling hatred and confusion. And Koren had the courage to disrupt this life of madness.

She worked alone at first, picking off Marradar. She was a physical freak, and she was bewitching. She developed a cult following but did not engage with it. There was safety in stealth and power in myth. The Marradar were sluggish in their response but eventually grew wise. They caught her before long, and she ended up like every other uprising they'd squashed under their heels over four hundred rings: a reminder.

But she survived. She reemerged in the annals with a cross of scars on her neck and a whirring, metallic voice, which she used as expertly as her new weapon, her scythe.

Beep-beep-beep.

That night Will dreamed of a Grendel squeezing a screaming woman to a pulp. He awoke in a cold sweat with a physical need to learn more about Koren's childhood. He dug and dug and found a single, rabidly disputed article by Bige claiming that she was the daughter of the very Marradar who'd stolen the ship, and that she was a patricide. As far as Will could tell, Bige did not respond to his colleagues' calls for evidence.

Will decided later that morning, as he was dolling out breakfast, that he was going to do whatever it took to see her. He did not mention this to Kade right away.

On the fifteenth morning, Will got swept up in the groundswell of Koren's revolution. How happily the oppressed came together behind this fearless, enormous young female, who told them that they *could* and that they *should* and that she loved them. How swiftly and energetically they plowed over the bumbling fat cats. But the cats came together once more. Backed up into a handful of dens surrounding the rocket site, which now included among its assets the stripped Qol ship, they decided that if they couldn't have it, then she couldn't either. They blew the site and set the program back by generations.

But here, once again, Bige was forced to interject: it was *she* who blew the site. And once again, he did not respond to his critics' irate demands to describe in detail his method of arriving at such a conclusion.

———————

Will stalked Nopa from the stacks. She was leaning over her desk, her face lit faintly from below by the light of a blue pen laser. She was carving something into a metal plate, and Will felt things falling into place. He walked over. She turned red on her ears and put the plate and laser under her counter.

-- I draw too. You're much better. -- he typed, then sent his drawing of the butterfly-squid to her holo. Then told her about Peis Ota's vision.

"I don't know what you just said, but I wish you hadn't," she said in Korial.

-- All it means is I have some role to play. --

"Good for you."

-- Radin came for me. --

She laughed. She was very uncomfortable.

-- I saw Radin in a dream, and it came true. --

"Please go away."

-- What do you think is going to happen? --

"What do you mean?"

-- More fighting and death. --

"The emissaries are along for a reason," she said, and scratched her nose.

-- I'm going to help. I need to try. --

"Good luck."

-- I need two sticky blenders, two sleeper guns, and one of those lasers. --

She wasn't laughing anymore. "You shouldn't have come to me like this." She turned, held her eyes to the scanner in the wall, and walked through the door into the other half of the warehouse.

On the sixteenth morning, Will took a detour in his research and regretted it. He made a particular inquiry that he realized only then he'd been avoiding. He asked the archives how humans could exist on two planets in the same solar system. The answer was that no one knew for certain but humans on both worlds share 99.9 percent of the same genes. It was just such a gaping hole.

He woke up extra early on the seventeenth morning and read nothing, just lay in his bunk letting his thoughts swirl and coagulate and fly apart. He didn't climb or spar that day. He worked his jobs, meditated, and paced.

On the eighteenth morning, he learned why Qol never saw the Gog launch. The lonely patch of atmosphere above the southern mountains fired lightning down onto the praying hands.

Reach out and touch, he thought, and the hairs stood up on the back of his neck.

These storms were relatively new phenomena, several years old maybe, signs of the atmosphere's continued slow and apathetic healing. The stronger ones were sufficiently electromagnetic to fry a few circuits in the Qol satellites if one happened to fly by at the wrong time. But this latest one, which struck only about a hundred Gog cycles ago, completely blacked a satellite out. The next came around in its orbit just in time to observe, somewhere in the field of stone-metal silo caps above Zone 3, a few of the caps closing. The guard had thought little about it then—they'd seen MaGog test the caps before. They were thinking a lot about it now. The academics and journalists spared no ink shaming the guard and marveling at how easy it had been in the end for Koren to slip her armada past them. She'd simply taken what the planet had given her, just as Gog peoples had been doing for a millennium. She put her soldiers in position, waited for a break, a big enough surge, and jumped on it. Done. Gone. Three dozen stone-metal ships, one carrying a stone-metal meteor, fired up through the wake of the knocked-out satellite.

But Bige could only throw his hands up at his peers and at any Qol who took a syllable of what they said as anything but self-delusion at best, smokescreen at worst. He pointed out the obvious truth without need of supporting evidence that the lightning was a weapon and that Koren had harnessed it.

Will was very sure that it mattered who was right. He was just as sure that he would not learn the truth from the bickering pundits. Besides, he was just about out of research time.

He led Kade to the nose of the ship. He knew the captain would not invite them in or assign them to a dropship, but he wished to keep up appearances.

They skipped climbing and sparring. Instead, they took a walk and got lost near the docks. They turned around with apologies to the guards, got lost again, walked to the docks from a different direction, apologized again, then went to their sanctuary.

Kade sat at the desk. Will paced.

"Missed the signs," Kade said in Korial in another man's soul-weary voice. "Thought they would not tread. Did not sniff the raid. Should never have left them."

This was the hunter-gatherer father who had lost his woman and two daughters. Will had met him twice before.

-- There's nothing you could have done. -- Will offered, trying once again to connect with one of these others, but the father was already gone.

"Wha's your plan?" Kade asked in English.

-- I'm working on getting us two sticky blenders. We sneak on if we have to. --

Kade's eyes darted.

Will sat down beneath the window between two barrels, crossed his legs, straightened his back, typed: -- For now, we remember the intention. --

"What intention?"

-- Zero casualties. --

"Sorry, Dawlis."

-- I know it's not possible, but it has to be the goal. We don't fight fire with fire. We fight it with rain. Kade? --

"Yes."

-- Don't be afraid of the voices. Maybe they're trying to tell you something. --

He seemed shocked that Will knew. That was how lost he'd been.

Will closed his eyes and sent the intention out onto the pixel sea.

The captain came on the speaker. In Korial: "Finish up. Get a bite, get some rest. You're here, and you're ready."

The alarm was dull, reverbed, and urgent in the dream, sharp and coldly routine in waking life: *beep-beep-beep, beep-beep-beep.* The captain again: "Get moving. Get focused. Thirty rus. Trust each other."

Kade was already awake and dressed. It was the first time he'd woken up before Will since they started sharing a room at the base, twenty-something spins past. Will's suit hung over the back of the chair.

"We were assigned landing seats," Kade said in English. "Here, on this ship."

Will checked his wrist device and saw the order. He put on his suit, hoping he'd be swapping it for another very soon.

The door slid open. A male guard, big sucker, stepped back and motioned down the hall with the laser barrel extending from his arm. An escort in case they got any ideas. The captain wasn't taking chances. Will put on the face of someone just happy to be there and see it all go down. He projected over his wrist:

-- Exciting, huh? --

But he was officially worried. He genuinely did not expect to be in this position. He thought an opportunity would manifest. He thought Nopa would come through. Now what, knock this guy out and hope the other guards rushing about didn't notice or didn't care?

Nopa turned the corner trailing two drones stacked with crates. She looked at Will like she'd come for his head, and all was right in the universe.

"Sleep in?" she snapped in Korial. "I *told you* there'd be last-second orders. I *told you* I needed you early. Here." She banged her fingers on her wrist device and sent Will an order and the location of a second, smaller warehouse on the lower level not far from the docks. She aimed a finger at the bridge of the guard's nose. "I need them," she said with the authority of someone overworked and underpaid. "I'll have them in their seats on time."

"Can't happen," he said.

"You're welcome to come. In fact, you're welcome to help. I've got nine orders left and no time. I've got backup suits and weapons for you and the rest about to drop onto a hostile planet. You want to get in the way?"

Maybe she convinced him. Or maybe he didn't like the way that Kade was looking at him in this tight hallway starting to empty out.

"Let's go," Nopa said, her voice catching but her feet moving. Will turned and followed the drones. Kade took the rear.

Nopa's counterpart in the other warehouse was a short male with a barrel chest, buck teeth, and big black eyes. He stood behind his counter watching his holo and nibbling on a meal bite like a kid at the movies. Space was a floating black basketball, Gog a dull gray dime in the center. He looked up at them as they walked in, then back at his holo, then back at them. He saw the crates and seemed to come to the harsh realization that he had something to do other than watch the approach.

Nopa finger-drummed her device. "Sent you the order," she said to the guy. "Last-second adjustments. Don't ask, I don't know. I'm filling this stack from here and taking it to the docks. You've got the other."

He took a last sad look at his holo, cursed, then walked out with the drone. Nopa closed the door. Will opened the top crate of the stack floating between them. Inside were two sticky blenders, two sleeper guns, and one pen-sized laser. He and Kade stripped and put on the blenders.

"What was that thing anyway?" Nopa asked in Korial.

-- What was what? --

He held a black-gloved hand up to his face, rotated it this way and that. Gossamer circuitry glistened under the electric lights.

"That terrible drawing you showed me."

He smiled. He felt an energy like things happening.

-- It's a symbol. --

"Of what?"

-- It's a combination of two animals from where I lived. Outside the Cooperative. --

He winked. He made oozing tentacles with his fingers, then fluttering wings with his hands.

She raised her eyebrows. "Must be good stuff you're on."

-- It means we get to choose who we want to be. --

Gog was a dilating gray pupil consuming the black cornea of space. There were no stars around it. It was all alone.

Not alone, Will thought.

-- You chose, Nopa. Thank you. --

"If I get caught, you stole those."

He presented his mind to her. She shook her head and got the hell out of there.

Gog swelled inside the holo and took on curved and cragged contours: a massive, shapeless, corpse-gray continent in the center; a dull gray-blue ocean to the east; a black-gray, bean-shaped chasm, the dried sea, to the west. Inside the continent, just east and south of center, shaded as though with a graphite pencil, was the crater. You could fit Massachusetts inside. You could put Mount Everest on the bottom and its peak would just break the plane. It was one thing for Will to read about it and see static images. This was another. He felt like that astronaut whose life was changed by seeing Earth in its wholeness from space. He was smacked in the head with intuition.

The Chief, he knew.

Eamon, the Kyut leader whose vision was the symbol of orange gems. The triangle. Will knew what it meant now. It seemed obvious in hindsight, but he supposed that sometimes one had to see things in a certain light from a certain angle at a certain time. Three worlds, Gog, Qol, and Earth, joined in some cross-system constellation and connected by invisible energy unimpeded by space and unbounded by time, energy that accounted for things like prophecy. The wave or the eye or both represented the energy. He knew it in his cells. But the square?

"Wha now," Kade said, his voice ice-cold.

--Our xims.--

"Five rus until atmosphere," the captain announced.

Will pulled the goggled hood of his suit down over his head and face. Kade did the same and launched his camo software first. Disappeared. He moved, and the wall behind him wavered. Will launched his, and Kade became a sharp-edged, black-eyed, neon-purple phantasm. Still, fearful, formidable.

Will looked at his hands. They were purple too. He picked up his sleeper gun and *it* turned purple. Anything the suits touched.

--Let's go.--

They were running through the empty cafeteria when the captain said two rus. They were climbing down a ladder when he said one, strap in. Kade said in a feminine voice, "Find flight on the edge."

Will stopped.

-- What's your name? --

But no one answered.

The ship shook.

"Hang on," Kade said.

They wrapped their arms around rungs of the ladder and rode it out.

"You're here and you're ready," the captain said.

Ready, Will said to himself.

Kindo, pensive dude, quietly curious about Will and Kade from the start, never an asshole, was sitting at his desk outside the artillery watching his holo and chewing a nail. The eastern continent rolled under the ship, and the dried sea panned into view. Will took his sleeper gun off his belt and crept in. "Made it," Kindo said to no one and dipped his hand into the holo. Two silver triangles, two of Qol's four interplanetary ships (the fourth was still on its way from Sid) hovered over a splintered, gray wasteland, the western continent. Their ship dropped down and slotted in between the other two. Seventy-five percent of Qol's interplanetary fleet was now poised on the doorstep, noses pointed west in the direction of the hive, somewhere over the horizon.

Will lifted his sleeper gun. Kindo squinted at the holo as though he thought he saw something.

The captain yelled, "Brace for impact!"

Will flew sideways, hit the wall, smashed his head, and hit the floor. His vision went blurry, then steadied. He rolled his shoulder, tested his limbs. No permanent damage, not yet. He looked up at the holo. The other two ships were peeling off and firing thick blue lasers down at the surface in a strobed panic. Theirs was falling out of the sky.

Will cried inside for the lost souls. They were the reason he was here, the dead, the broken families.

The ship lurched, tried to pick itself up. The captain: "Dropships and lifeboats!"

Kade lowered a hand. Will took it and stood.

-- You here? You with me? --

"Yes."

-- Help me. --

Kindo was knocked out. They each grabbed an arm, lifted him up, and held his face to the scanner beside the artillery door. Kade threw him over a shoulder as Will ran in and got their xims. They hustled to the docks.

-- Suits off but hoods stay on. --

They fell into the organized chaos, handed Kindo off to a pair of medics outside a lifeboat, then walked onto a dropship like they belonged there and took seats beside a trio of emissaries.

PART FOUR

THE RANDOM
and the
PURPOSE

22

Ayn watched with the rest of the nineteenth-floor inmates, all squeezed together in front of the wall screen. No shoving, no jostling for position. Just grinding teeth, fuming eyes, clenched fists.

There's no way, she kept thinking. *No way.*

Silver triangle battleships fired lasers into cracked, gray hills and plains. One went down. They watched it over and over.

No way Dawlis and Kade were on that one.

Simply impossible that she'd helped Lorel's son get on that ship—*Keep him safe while I make my way back, Ayn!*—only for him to die the moment he arrived.

The names of the dead scrolled, and her heart attacked, a warning shot, a suicide bomb ready to blow if "Dawlis lo sha" came up.

Keep him safe!

No Dawlis. No Kade ru sy Bhomik. Ayn clutched her chest and shoved her way out of the crowd. She stumbled up to the call room and slapped her hand on the counter. "Need a holo, Henna," she said in Korial.

"Used your time today," Henna replied from behind the glass wall, eyes glued to his hollow, snarling and shaking his head, picking at a scab on his pockmarked face. "Rodents. Going to pay now."

"Open up. I need to check on my girls."

"I wish I was there so bad."

"Henna, look at me." She snapped her fingers.

"Ayn, you know I can't just—"

"I know you will."

He caught on. He swallowed. She knew things about him like she knew things about an unhealthy number of guards and inmates in this glass tower in the middle of nowhere. Some were acquaintances she'd exchanged favors with over the turns. Some she'd been digging into since being thrown in here twenty-two spins past for the murder of Mays. Henna belonged to the former group. He lowered his voice. "Listen, you said—"

"Henna, it's between us. Just do the right thing. Extenuating circumstances."

He keyed the door open, turned back to his holo, and mumbled threats to MaGog.

Tontine picked up, half-empty drink in his hand, eyes wide and unbelieving. "Ayn, what?"

"How do I know? How are they? Have they seen it? Tell me Zee hasn't."

He finished the drink. "It's on every holo everywhere."

"I need to see them."

"Any word on your case?"

Her heart was on a hair trigger. "Tontine, I'm starting to believe—"

Zee jumped onto his lap. Her violet eyes were wet, her brown curls listless. "Fia, I'm scared."

"I know, little girl. It's all very far away."

"I thought maybe they'd be nice."

"Oh, most of them probably are. There are just some bad ones too."

"That's not what everyone is saying," Maya said, edging into the holo, one big, dark eye wide like she was still seeing it, like she was never going to unsee it, the other hiding behind her waterfall of black hair.

"Don't listen to everyone," Ayn offered weakly.

Mycah appeared over Tontine's left shoulder. "Fia, what do we do?" she asked. She had the swollen, stoic eyes of a sleepless mother.

Ayn was painfully proud of her. Ayn dug her nails into her palms and fought back the tears. "There's nothing to do, just take care of each other. It's fine to be scared. None of this has ever happened before."

"When are you coming home?"

"Soon," she lied.

"When is soon?"

"Try not to worry. You're perfectly safe. Keep busy. Go have fun. Maybe Gode has some jobs you can help with."

"He hasn't been around," Maya said.

"Help your fium then. Help each other. Wait, how are the brothers? I hope you're taking care of them."

"We are, Fia!" Zee said, brightening.

Maya moved aside so Ayn could see Jackson out on the deck, snout pointed up at the sky. "Good," she said. "Time to go. See you next spin. Just stick together."

They nodded.

She choked up. "Bye."

"Bye, Fia!"

There's no way, she thought again as she marched back through the common room. Everyone was still there watching the same clips, feeding on the crumbs of information thrown to them by the journalists, getting hungrier and angrier with every little bite.

No way.

Of course they'd be fine. Of course she'd see her daughters again. Of course she wouldn't be held here forever for a crime she didn't commit.

The rain poured in gray sheets outside the glass box balcony. The wind whipped. The Wolla was a desolate place on the clearest of arcs, black earth, green mud lakes, and white-trunked, red-leaved trees to the horizon in all directions. Not a speck of civilization. Not a single blinking light. But this was a deeper loneliness, a colorless infinity.

Maybe she wasn't getting out, after all. The quick and quiet way she'd been arraigned and dropped here. The deafening silence on her case since. Twenty-two spins, and Brava's assurances were growing very stale. How deep was he? How high did his influence go? What did he want? Why put his career and maybe his life on the line to get Kade and Dawlis on that ship and then stand back and let Ayn take this fall? Was he behind Mays's murder? Did he know who was? And why Mays? Why was she still alive?

The assassin had *laughed*. He'd found it all very funny. He'd clearly missed her on purpose, but it didn't make sense, because he'd try to kill her before. Ruve was supposed to be collateral damage. Ruve had drank her own drink but also one meant for Ayn, the same cocktail they'd sipped together every ninarc of their lives for the last four turns. *Every single one.* Except the ninarc that Dawlis fulfilled a prophecy by showing up in Mon Teles. The ninarc that Ruve told Ayn about a dream she had about dying.

Ruve, I'll take it straight tonight.

Dumb luck? Mind, no. There was something else going on here. There were subtle workings. There was *intent* or some cousin of it. And Ayn wasn't dead yet. This tower of hackers, swindlers, and monsters was fertile ground for the game of favors, and she was still playing.

She'd let a couple of rumors slip out about where she'd gone after the meteor and who she'd been with. Anyone here who knew anything about her—more anyones than she'd care to admit in polite company— and had a sense for the depth and breadth of her network probably found it plausible that she was wrapped up in this somehow. It was all the leverage she needed to get a few inquiries out the door on supply flyers in exchange for the promise of tapping that network and returning the favors once she got out. She didn't have Mays or the web, but some information lived only in dark, human pools.

She caught a break right then. That very moment. She heard a heavy tread and turned. Daga lumbered toward the balcony. But which thread had she asked Daga to pull on?

Oh. Yes.

The assassin's estranged colleague. The person with the white mask and glowing green eyes.

Daga stepped onto the balcony and leaned against a glass wall. Ayn had to crane her neck to meet the woman's eyes, which were too small for her head, which was too small for her frame. Her hair was cropped and fire-red. It had always impressed Ayn how a woman so tall and awkward had become such an effective infiltrator of human circles. You would think that one would see her coming.

"This weather," Ayn said in Korial.

"Been watching?" Daga asked. That squeaky voice too, so pathetic and memorable. But maybe that was it. You almost felt bad for her. You let her hang around because you assumed she was harmless. Until she harmed you. But Ayn blamed herself for allowing that to happen.

"I saw," Ayn said. "Everyone's so shocked."

"You're not?"

Ayn shrugged. Maybe she was privy to certain things.

"I assume I don't need to repeat our terms," Daga said.

"No, thank you."

"I found him. Or her."

"Daga, that's outdoing yourself," Ayn said, and she meant it. She and Mays, in the time between Ruve's death and the attack, had scoured the web, Mon Teles's security footage, and both of their networks and found exactly nothing on the person with the mask.

"It wasn't easy. You've run up a tab," Daga said.

"Are you asking if I'm good for it?"

"My contacts say this person is a ghost."

"Oh?"

"What I mean is that anyone who has encountered him or her—and there aren't many—doesn't remember him or her."

"Then how do your contacts know they encountered him or her?"

And how could they forget that face? Ayn thought. She could still see it through May's goggles zoomed in through the terub window. The assassin on the other side of the table.

"They remember the mask and eyes very well," Daga squeaked. "They just have no idea who the person is, where they were when they met them, what they did, what they talked about."

"Drugged?"

"Maybe. It's like someone tried to wipe their memories of the meetings clean and just about succeeded."

"Who are these people?"

"Just people."

"Where?"

"In villages forming a rough semi-circle around Mon Teles."

"What do they say?"

"There's only one thing they *all* say. That he or she saw inside them."

"What?" But Ayn knew what she'd heard. Had she felt the same while watching through the window? Did she feel it now? "What else?"

"That's it."

"That can't be it."

"That's it. Except—"

"Except what? Come on."

"One mentioned a metal leg."

Ayn wracked her brain. "A metal leg?"

"A metal leg. Why?"

Some faint bell tolling. Some ship or lighthouse out there in the gray. "Daga, I need to know who this person is. It doesn't matter what it costs."

"I'm changing the terms. I want the truth."

Ayn was prepared for this exact eventuality. She'd chosen Daga precisely because of their history. She knew Daga would see this job as an opportunity to learn who sold her out. And now that she was of value to Ayn, she asked it straight: "Was it you?"

Ayn wouldn't have put it that way. She would have said that she'd suggested something to an interested party, who'd done some digging and then done the selling out. But Ayn harbored little sympathy for Daga. Daga had done good work for her during her campaign for Overseer, had dug up some nice white skeletons on her opponents. But then she'd gone and rummaged around in Ayn's past too, and she should have known better. Ayn had her answer ready. "No. I'll give you the name when this is done."

Daga stared. But Ayn, if she was a master of anything, was a master of eye contact. "Give me a few spins," Daga said, and left.

The wind shifted. The rain pounded the glass. There was a lull, and a beam of light broke through the clouds as Henna stepped onto the balcony. "You have a call," he said.

Ayn turned on the holo. There was an empty chair in the center of a windowless room. Brava walked in and stood in a back corner. Shaw walked in and sat down.

Shaw?

Was it Shaw?

It was Shaw with hollow cheeks, a brown, weathered face, thinning gray hair, and brown eyes heavy with time and loss. It was Dawlis with twenty more turns of hard life. A rock formed in Ayn's throat. Her hands shook. She hated herself. She wasn't ready for this. She couldn't tell him.

"It's OK, Ayn, I know," he said, in Korial. He knew where his son was. Eighteen turns of waiting to see him, and he was gone again, across the void.

"Shaw, it seemed right."

"Maybe it was."

She couldn't look at him.

"I understand you were there when he came back," he said. "Thank you."

Came back. From Earth.

She wiped her eyes on the red sleeve of her Wolla Tower inmate suit, wiped her sweaty palms on her pants. She pulled herself together. Brava was *right there*. They were in the game. "Shaw, it's been a long time. It's hard to believe."

"It all is."

"Where are you?"

He looked at a blank wall. "Back home on Damarra, Ayn. A guard base. Not sure where exactly. Safe, as far as I can tell."

"Brava, why is he being held?"

Brava looked up from his wrist device, frowned.

Shaw answered. "He lifted me out of the Gontomon. His people. I was attacked, Ayn. That's what took me so long."

"No. Shaw, what happened?"

"I left with the Pymm well before Trimus. I made it to the port and hired a pilot. She said she could take me as far as Findo. But she didn't have a flyer. She had questions. About me. My life. The village. The Ursi. I guess my answers weren't sufficient. She flipped." He unzipped his suit from his throat down to his belly. A circuited healing patch covered his left ribs. "Laser blade. I was in a clinic at the port for most of a phase, in and out of consciousness. I woke up three spins past and learned about everything. The attack. The meteor." He paused, breathed. Like everyone else on Qol, he was having to come to grips with the reality of the Gog attack and the current state of the worlds. *Unlike* everyone else, he was having to reconcile all of that with his son's timely fulfillment of a prophecy. "A man came," he said quietly. "Recently. Tall, very tall. Big, hunched shoulders, huge nose, little eyes. He also asked me about the Ursi."

"Ursi?"

"Lives in a cave, Ayn."

Ayn's flesh crawled. She changed directions. Brava was watching. She flipped a tile. "Shaw, Lorel is alive."

Brava shifted in his corner.

Shaw winced. "Oh," he said. "Yes? Yes."

Did he know? *What* did he know? He'd guided her to that passage. *"She found him,"* Ayn said.

Tears streamed down his cheeks.

"You won't believe what she went through. And what *he* did, Shaw, to get here. How he fought. He's changed. He's a change agent. You'll see it in his eyes, in his… confidence and calm and connection. And Kade with him every step."

"Kade," Shaw said. "With Dawlis."

"Every step. Shaw, you were instrumental too. Lorel wrote us a letter. I'll read it for you, but not here. Except, Shaw, she said you led her to Dawlis. What you taught her about the stars."

"The stars," Shaw said, and looked down at his hands. "The Ursi lives in a cave, Ayn. Dawlis was lost in one."

"Shaw, let's stop here." They'd gone far enough. They were now hinting at tiles best left face down.

But Shaw was distracted, pensive. "Lorel too? A different constellation. The man with the hunched shoulders, he knew."

"Shaw. Friend. Look at me. I want to do this in person."

He looked up and caught her warning. Fresh tears dripped down his creased, leathery cheeks. He looked twice his age. Eighteen turns without his son. Fourteen without his woman. "Can I see her?" he asked.

"Not yet," Ayn said. "Brava," she snapped. "Get me out of here."

His perennial brow lines deepened. "Time's up," he said.

23

The dropship stank of sweat, hatred, and adrenaline. The guards slapped their laser barrels against their palms and banged them against the metal walls. Their knees bounced. They wanted into those tunnels bad.

But they weren't going, not this lot, not yet anyway. Plans had changed. Their ship had emergency landed closer to the oasis than to the hive. Half their crew was back there repairing and guarding the ship. Half, including this hungry, bitter pack of wolves, was headed to the oasis to rendezvous with the Gog resistance and await orders.

Someone punched a wall. Someone else spit on the floor. The three emissaries were huddled in a corner trying to think. Will observed it all with a straight back and a hand on Kade's shoulder. He saw through their masks of anger to their creeping doubt. They were finally starting to admit to themselves that the underdog had bite. Ground-to-air firepower of that magnitude that far outside of the hive was just the latest example of Qol not knowing what it was dealing with. The guards had that look in their eyes. The heavily favored northern spiral team had had the same look during Fast Tomit's comeback in those final rus of that final game around Peis Ota's island. They were asking themselves and each other, without daring to say the words out loud: These guys can't beat us, right?

All very human, Will thought. They were making the same old mistakes. But they were also experiencing real pain and loss. It was hard. Will felt it too. He stroked the electric gossamer leg of his sticky blender suit.

Word came that the other two battleships that had made the trip from Qol were in position above the field of black, stone-metal lids that capped the launch silos of Zone 3. The fourth had started its deceleration after its breakneck trip from Sid. They were holding fire for now. Orders from the Council. The emissaries from all ships were to meet virtually and amend negotiation tactics in light of recent developments. The ships were to cast shadows over Zone 3 and pour thick, hot lasers into any hole that opened up.

The pack waxed optimistic. They might get in there in time after all. They might get to cut up some MaGog and have a hand in putting this sorry excuse for a civilization out of its misery. They slapped each other's backs, looked in each other's eyes, and nodded with the seriousness of death.

Will took his laser off his belt, set it to a shallow burn, rested his forearms on his thighs, and started carving the left wing of his symbol into the metal floor. Guard boots retreated. The two women directly across the aisle from him and Kade said the rough equivalent of "What the fuck" in Korial at the exact same time (they'd said the same earlier when he and Kade had stepped onto the dropship and removed their hoods). The emissaries stopped deliberating and looked over. He carved the right wing, then ten wavy tentacles (squids actually had eight arms and two tentacles, a factoid he'd picked up somewhere along the way in a former life, but he figured those details would be lost on these Qols at this current moment in history). Between the wings, he carved the eye with the wave inside. He had everyone's attention now.

Kade sat forward with his hand on his xim. Will placed the laser back on his belt, looked around and made uncomfortable eye contact with a few guards, then typed and projected over his wrist in English that rearranged itself into Korial: -- You know that we were on the island. Our friends died too. --

Silence. Bared teeth. Bouncing knees.

--MaGog, they're no different. They're scared and angry and following orders. --

"Coward," a guard said casually. He was standing in the corner opposite the emissaries. He patted his weapon. "What would your friends say?"

Will pointed down at the symbol.

--In a place I used to live, there's a winged insect that comes in a thousand different colored patterns. It flies like this. Floats kind of. Beautiful. --

Will demonstrated with his hands to thirty or so knitted brows.

--There's another. --

He made pulsing, wavy motions with his fingers.

--A one-eyed giant that lives deep in the ocean where there's no light. Boneless. Oozing. Bottomless belly. Hunting incessantly. Shoving whatever it can find into its beaked mouth hole. Forever in that place. There will be moments when you get to choose. These moments will impact futures, including yours. They will seed your misery or your pride. --

The guard in the corner yawned. "*They* made choices."

--I won't let other's choices determine mine. --

The dropship dipped a wing, and the guards' attention was drawn through the portholes to Gog's cragged surface, an endless web of splinter canyons. Somewhere far away, in the center, was a crater the size of the Great Salt Lake. Somewhere nearby was an oasis, a place host to emerging, primordial life. Will had read a bit about it.

The ship slowed, hovered, then lowered into a canyon. Beamless spotlights flitted over barren gray walls. Sparkling, icy mist drifted across the portholes.

"Helmets," ordered the pilot over the intercom. "Crank your heat."

Helmets were donned. Suits were cranked. Weapons were checked and rechecked. A couple of guards glanced over at Will, then down at the butterfly-squid. One emissary, a middle-aged female with pale green eyes, six-foot-three easy, stared at him.

The ship scraped a wall and landed hard.

"Go," said the pilot.

They marched in two lines in slightly lower gravity through an off-gassing, dry ice-coated crack in the ground a quarter mile deep. Visibility was a few feet. An insect the size of a tarantula, black exoskeleton and double the legs, crawled over Will's foot (snug inside the circuited, spider web-strong, gel-soled bootie woven into his suit) and disappeared into a crack in the ice. Will searched for Kade with his left hand and found him immediately on his flank.

They slid down a slope a hundred yards long into a pool of shimmering, crystalizing air spilling out of knee-high coned geysers; down another slope into a larger, deeper pool where dew collected on helmets and goggles and quickly froze; into a crevasse where they snaked single-file through a cold dank gloom, a gloaming. Armored, gray inch worms bored into the ice and fed on gray-green moss. It was a spartan, prehistoric world. It was a world trying to live again, a world in its second infancy, one thousand sixty-one rings old and just getting started.

They passed into a misty boulder garden. Two caves were black eyes in the far wall. A trilled voice called out in Vrrgrrul, and a guard responded in the same. Two lithe humans in Qol suits, their narrow, pale heads ghostly inside their helmets, stepped out of one of the caves. The guard met them at the center of the garden beside a leafless tree the size of a bonsai.

Contact, Will thought. *Jesus Christ, I'm here.*

The fellows waved everyone into the cave. They spiraled down a tunnel into a diffuse green glow (trroorra-green, Will knew from his studies, somewhere between jade and sea) and into an underground, human-alien world. The coals lining the walls emitted no halos. The light was a *presence.* It smelled faintly of sulfur and sunlight. Water trickled somewhere. MaGog chatter spilled from the end of the tunnel, a tense, multi-voiced vibrato.

Two dozen guards, three emissaries, and two stowaways filed into a green-lit chamber, and all the chatter ceased. MaGog stood in threes and fours around gray-brown, live-edged, stone tables littered with square metal plates the size of napkins. They stared. Their eyes were the size and color of baby plumbs, their skin colorless and hairless, their bodies thin, their muscles like rope. They wore the cloth of their race, hemp-like, each sleeveless shirt and pair of shorts dyed a single color. The two MaGog fellows in Qol suits walked toward a holo in the center of the chamber. The suits and holo were evidence of the pre-existing relation-ship between the guard and the resistance. But it had been a slow and measured courtship. They never expected to be thrown into a shotgun wedding.

Four guards joined the fellows at the holo. The rest of the Qol force spread out along the walls and eyed their allies with undisguised dis-trust, daring them to try something. MaGog went back to reading and discussing their heaps of metal squares, their documents, written in dots and dashes. Will stood in the mouth of the tunnel with Kade on his left flank. He removed his hood and scanned the room with his eyes, ears, nose, and the hairs on his arms. For what, he didn't know. Openings. Exits. Opportunity.

A female fellow in red cloth not ten feet away was staring at him. He stared back, and she kept on staring. He approached her. She stepped forward, essence of trroorra-green in her all-pupil eyes. She reached out and touched Will's matted hair. His body tingled.

Contact. Touch.

He smiled and ran his fingers down her slender, root-strong arm. Her skin was dry. That meant she was scared or nervous.

-- I'm called Will --

The words morphed into Vrrgrrul above his wrist.

"Hrulora," she replied.

It was love at first sight. He saw her, knew her. She was beautiful and fierce. She was battling through this unfathomable time. She was *human*. *That's* what he saw. *That's* what he loved.

--What can we do?--

A fellow called for her from the growing crowd around the holo. She backed away, still gawking at his hair.

Nice to meet you, Hrulora.

She squeezed into the crowd, as an emissary squeezed out. The tall, green-eyed one who'd been staring at Will on the dropship. She paced and chewed a nail. Will and Kade were waiting for her when she turned on her heels.

--What's next?-- Will wrote.

She pulled up, kept her distance. "Waiting on orders," she replied in Korial.

--But what do you think?--

"I think they've given us little choice."

Voices rose on cue, strained Qol ones, hoarse MaGog trills. The sounds of growing ferment.

--Maybe that's by design. Maybe it's a trap. You emissaries will lead?--

"That's still the plan for now."

--Buy as much time as you can.--

She took a single step closer, looked around to see if anyone was listening. "What will you do?"

He knew what. He knew it for the first time. He just didn't know how.

--Disrupt this sentiment. Sneak around and get in the way. Be unexpected.--

That was all he knew and all he needed to know for now. His plan was waking up in little bits.

"The Council is split on turning it over to the guard. It won't take much."

-- Do what you can. We'll give them something to think about. --

She tunneled back into the lathering crowd as Hrulora tunneled out, rubbing her bowed, narrow head, her lithe shoulders slumped. She walked to a wall, leaned her back against it, and slid down to a seat. Will followed and sat down beside her. Kade stood where he could see them and the rest of the room.

-- What are they saying? -- Will asked.

She read the words over his device. Her baby-plumb eyes watered. She spoke in broken Korial, good enough for Will's translator: "Thought we had time."

-- Time for what? --

"Turn more from Koren. Get them safe. She was always going to fight."

-- Why? -- he asked. It was rhetorical. He'd read enough of Koren's history to know how difficult a question that was. But Hrulora had an answer.

"Mad," she said. Her strong, thin hands, the hands of an eightieth- or ninetieth-generation cave-dwelling climber, were shaking. Her skin cracked in places. Will could see it happening. She was draining of hope, as though she was just now waking up to the full implication of her own one-word response: the futility of the resistance's efforts, the impossibility of going head-to-head with well-resourced insanity and megalomania.

Will took his laser off his belt and carved his symbol into the stone between her left leg and his right. She didn't flinch. She traced every curved line with her eyes as he cut them. She asked him what it was. He told her. She looked at him as if he'd jogged a memory but one out of reach. Or as though she suddenly recognized him but couldn't recall from where or when.

-- Where do you send them? --

"Who?"

-- The ones you save. --

"The trail. Leads here. Or abandoned dens in the hive."

-- We need to get in. Point us in the direction. --

"No. They found the trail. Glome, Dondarra. We were rushed, careless. There is fighting."

Will squeezed his eyes shut. Fighting already. Tunnel warfare. Hell on Gog. He opened his eyes and took Hrulora's hand in both of his.

She said it before he could ask: "The surface."

-- How? --

"Rovers. Here. But guarded."

-- They won't see us. --

He tapped his chest, his suit.

Her ivory brow wrinkled. "Not enough time before Gorr."

Before Gorr rose and baked the surface.

-- You're sure? --

"Never done it. Only rode once. Never drove."

-- You can do it. --

She was deciding whether she believed him, whether she had it in her. She was beautiful and fierce. She was battling through this unfathomable time. "Won't see you?"

He tapped his chest.

-- Where's the bathroom? --

She watched them go in. She didn't see them come out. She jumped when Will squeezed her wrist, then settled herself and led them along the wall into a dark tunnel. The night vision in their goggles brightened automatically, coating the stone walls and their guide, their friend, their fellow, in a light blue tinge. It faded out again, yielding to trroorra glow. Ahead was a black lattice gate. Stone-metal, Will assumed. The crown jewel of Gog's underground riches, ubiquitous, invaluable, and nearly indestructible. Nearly. MaGog's ability to mine it, melt it, and mold it through controlled application of its single weakness, the red, radiating, corrosive mavzarra, was the greatest strength of their geologic technology and engineering. It was their pride. It was the ships and meteors that had crashed into Qol. It would bother MaGog on a deep level, Will suspected, to find out that there was another substance capable of destroying it, the one Will had used to shatter their Dondante's collar. It would hurt, this truth. But Will decided that they would benefit from hearing it.

He decided something else too. These things were coming to him as they came. He blinked open a file in his goggles, then another, then another. He was sure he'd seen it at some point. Yes, there, a camera. What better way to gain trust but through transparency? What better way for the Qols to see what and who it was they were so confused about?

He hit play as a fellow in black cloth, heat weapon in his right hand, a black barrel loaded with incendiary, red rocks, opened the gate and let Hrulora in. The fellow rubbed his eyes as Will and Kade passed, as though his vision was blurred, as though the sleepless nights and the merciless, incessant motion of this exploding new age were starting to get to him. Will took the sleeper gun off his belt, fired a sharp puff of chemical mist into the male's face, and gave him some much-needed rest. Will caught him, laid him gently on his back, then burned the butterfly-squid into the floor. The Qols would see it all through Will's goggles. He would send clips to Nopa when he found a signal and implore her to risk her career and maybe her life by leaking them. And maybe she could, and maybe she would.

Neon-purple Kade pointed two fingers at two glome leaning against a mini-van-sized, dull gray, metal-plated worm with six spiked wheels and a cannon on its back. Will nodded and looked up. They were at the bottom of a silo. A ramp spiraled up the inside of it toward a large gate beneath the ceiling a hundred yards up. There were two other rovers. The stone floor was perforated with holes from their wheels. Hrulora stayed put as Will and Kade tip-toed up to the two glome, who were trilling away in Vrrgrrul and unaware that their fellow had gone down for a nap. They thought they heard something. Or thought they saw the air move. They looked at each other and then went to sleep.

Trust us, Will thought. They'd wake in an hour or so with headaches and fuzzy memories of phantoms blowing cold, minty breath in their faces and catching them as they fell. They'd assume it was a dream. Then someone would tell them what happened, and they'd have to decide how they felt about it.

Hrulora slid open the door of the nearest rover.

Will turned off his suit. -- Ready? -- he projected in English that rearranged into Vrrgrrul.

"Never drove. Only rode once," she reminded him in quaking Korial. Her skin was parched.

-- Maybe you were born to. --

She jumped in before she could change her mind. Kade appeared on Will's left flank. Will looked him square in the tinted goggles.

-- We have to. --

"I know."

They lowered their heads and stepped in. They could stand hunched over. There was a metal ladder built into the floor beneath a hatch, beneath the cannon. Two benches behind the ladder. Two narrow, flat-backed seats up front before two round windshield eyes. Hrulora sat in the seat on the right and fidgeted with a grove of knobbed levers poking up from the floor in between her legs. She was trying to remember, it seemed. Getting the feel. Will took the seat next to her. She yanked a lever, and nothing happened. Yanked another, and warm air hissed out of vents in the floor. Shoved one forward, and they were off taxiing, the spiked wheels crunching the stone floor. She palmed a knob on her left hip, eased it to the right, and they turned. She backhanded another, and the rover threw a cone of trroorra light onto the rising, curving, silo thread. Kade stepped into the tail of the worm and looked out the only other window. "Here they come," he said.

Hrulora dropped the throttle. They climbed. The second rover ground into action, then the third. A laser cut a blue line across their front windows. Chunks of stone exploded out of the wall and fell under their wheels. They went up on two, slammed back down, hugged the wall, saw the gate. Hrulora yelled something in Vrrgrrul, yanked a lever, and the rover screamed to a stop. She turned on Will, eyes dialed, exhilarated, terrified. "You don't know how to open it."

-- We'll cover you. -- he wrote, then jumped out of his seat, blinked on his invisibility, ripped open the rover door, checked his goggles to make sure he was still rolling, and took his xim. Purple Kade was on his left. They stood on the edge of the ramp looking down into a trroorra swamp where little shadowed figures scurried. Neon-blue lasers crisscrossed over their heads and dropped chunks of rock onto the rover. The other two rovers spiraled up the ramp behind green headlights.

-- Shields. -- Will typed

He pressed the handle of his xim with his thumb three times and held it. The xim enveloped his hand and emitted its him-sized, concave, blue-green shield. Kade threw his up. The rovers stopped twenty yards away. Guards and MaGog jumped out and screamed in their respective languages to throw down weapons and all that. Will poked his left hand out from behind his shield and projected from his wrist:

-- We're making up our own minds. You also get to choose. --

They chose lasers and red-hot mineral balls. Will knew they would. He didn't fault them. They were too startled by this move, too wacked-out on anger and adrenaline to think of this as anything but treason. It would be up to him to convince them. It would be *his* failure if this two-world dumpster fire spread.

He and Kade leaned into the barrage. The lasers fizzled and died in their energy shields. The fireballs dropped to the ground, neutered. "Come!" Hrulora yelled. A laser tore the ceiling apart over their heads. Will stepped behind Kade and angled his shield to cover them. They backed up in tandem, Kade fending off the fire, Will, the falling rock. Hrulora had the rover rolling as they jumped inside.

The rock made thunder on the roof. The wheels slipped in the rubble, caught. They sped through a black tunnel. The far mouth was filled with stars. Will climbed the ladder, opened the hatch, gripped the cannon, felt for the trigger. He pointed it at the ceiling behind them, fired glowing red rocks the size of softballs—*thoomp, thoomp, thoomp*—and watched as the tunnel collapsed and swallowed the chasing headlights.

They burst into starry black night. Burning cold slapped him in the back. He turned up the heat in his suit, turned into the roaring wind. The fractured surface glowed in the light of two hanging potato moons, one smaller and pale green, one larger and yellow with red lines like veins. Between them was a big blue star. A heaven. A future. A solution. A destiny. Impossible and unattainable until one day it wasn't.

It was not hard for Will to imagine, as he flew through that killing cold and radiation in the hours or minutes before the killing scorch, how any individual or collective conscious could become obsessed with that spark. How after centuries and centuries, the last few a bloody quagmire of oppression and inequality and lost, angry youth, they would turn to someone with the potential to deliver it, someone who told them they didn't need the help or permission of the murderous incumbents, they just needed each other. No, it was not hard for Will to fathom loving such a leader and his fellows and pouring himself into such a cause.

The rover skirted the edge of a canyon and swung back. Will climbed down into the cabin, sat beside Hrulora, and put a hand on her shoulder. -- Easy. It's just us. --

"No time," she said, glancing at the western horizon. They caught a slope down, and the canyon walls rose up on either side of them. "Maps. Hurry." She pointed to a box at Will's feet. Inside were metal wafers etched with cracked topography. But Kade did them one better. He found a holo map and projected it.

"Find flight on the edge," he said in a woman's voice.

Hrulora scowled.

-- The edge of what? -- Will asked.

But the woman didn't answer.

-- Sit down. Send it to me. --

Kade did as he was told. Will raised the map over his wrist. The rover was a black dot sliding over a gray land bridge. Ahead, the bridge split into three. Will dipped a pointer into the map, dragged it forward, and traced each path. Two broke off into nothing. The third led into a knot.

-- Stay left. It will narrow then bend right. --

Hrulora looked west again. "Won't make it."

-- We have to. You're doing it. Left coming up. Easy. --

The map proved imperfect. Twice they had to stop at cliffs and retrace their steps. But Hrulora made up time. She proved herself an invaluable agent of the unfolding plan. The ravines became thinning tentacles snaking off into an endless plain. She tapped an anxious rhythm on the joy.

-- Left and straight and that's it. --

They watched, the three of them, through the windshield eyes, as the last black canyons to either side of them wiggled and closed. Then Hrulora opened it up, and the machine gun fire of the spiked wheels melded into a blur. But they weren't done. The horizon grew spikes. A bed of giant thorns. A forest of branchless trees, gorrdrr trees, if Will remembered correctly from his readings. Stone-like bark that cracked open for a few moments at dawn and another few at sunset to collect photons and cosmic radiation. The trees rose and multiplied, thickened and towered, pricked the moons. The roots were a field of anacondas. Will braced himself against the dash with his good arm. Kade held onto the ladder. Hrulora leaned forward, eyes locked. They bounced violently.

"Through, then east," she said in Korial.

Will pulled the map forward again to the edge of the forest. It was further away than he would have liked. He swiped right, searching the tree line for a hole for them to tuck into. He found nothing. The sky was no longer fully black.

"Hurry. Please," Hrulora said.

-- I don't—wait. This? --

He showed her on the map.

"Yes," she whispered.

The forest thickened, then ended. They tore east, Nurin sniffing them out from behind, close on their heels. Will turned off his suit heat.

"Too late," Hrulora said.

-- Faster. --

"We passed it."

-- No. There. --

The surface transposed from dark gray to shimmering light gray, and Will was transported to summer days so hot that nothing moved, not the insects, not the air. Days when no one but he and George left their homes. Days when they would sit in the useless shade of a river birch with their lines cast and pour sweat and not say a thing or catch a thing because the fish had the good sense to stay down where it was cool. Days when Will felt that he was the luckiest kid alive because he was wanted.

To melt, it was almost pleasant. But to sizzle and burn was not. Will held a shriveling finger to a black dot drifting toward the center of the map. The holo faded into the growing, blinding light. Little suns exploded: retinal burn against the dark of a tunnel.

24

Radin awoke to the piercing cries of the winged animals. He raised his lazy lids in time to see, through the vines hanging down over his open door, a trio cut across the paling sky in triangle formation. He breathed the salty air in rhythm with the tide. He put his hands behind his head, arched his back, stretched, and groaned with pleasure. He thought there could be none more content on four worlds than he inside his seaside shack.

It was a timeless place, as he was timeless. The calm breath of the sea was *his*. The worlds were tuned to *him*. He rolled onto his side and traced the grain in the thin, wood wall with a finger. He opened his box, plucked a rubbery strip of the local algae, and laid it on his tongue. It took him back to his youth, as it had yet never failed to do. The particular blend of bitter, spicy, and sweet, by some poetic wrinkle of this system of solar systems, echoed the pulge he grew up on. He was sitting with his brothers and sisters at the feet of their father, watching him eat and drink, waiting for scraps. His oldest fear, rage, and helplessness were raw in his breast. But he felt them with a knowing, experienced heart. He felt *in* them the touch of the universe and its wisdom in shaping him how it did.

He took a fat pull of dust and walked out of through the vines onto the beach. Gorr cast a sparkling path of red light across the teeming, metallic blue ocean to *him*. The gentle tide reached for him with every flow, invited him in with every ebb. He was the subject of these forces.

The wave inside the eye inside the triangle inside the square. Four worlds, three systems, one eye. *His.* Every moment in his life had led to this. Every choice. Every piece of what once seemed like luck, good or bad, now understood to be intervention. No random, only purpose.

He heard a familiar sub-roar behind him, an eruption. He turned and watched a rocket rise from the bluffs. He smiled ear to ear and dove into the water, swam in Gorr's red glow as it dipped into the ocean.

Two shadows stood on the bluffs against the deep blue sky as Radin stepped out of the water. Two round mirror eyes flashed. How long had they been standing there? He waved them down.

Ravrada wore the brown robe, cropped brown hair, thick brown brows, and reflective lenses. Her disguises typically disgusted Radin, but this one he didn't mind so much. He liked to see himself in the lenses. He liked to imagine Ravrada's eyes scurrying around behind them in their little nests of artificial skin and trying to penetrate his thoughts. He hoped she'd try again.

"Dondante, how do you feel?" she asked in Vrrgrrul.

He waved away the question. "When?"

"Next cycle, Dondante. Early. We are all MaGog in awe. One thousand rings—"

"Who is he?"

Ravrada stood up taller on her good leg. "Dondante, he is *Dama.* Very eager to meet you. May he speak?"

"He's earned it."

"Dondante, thank you!" Ravrada placed a hand gently on Dama's back and urged him forward. He came in choppy steps. He was short even for a Qol male. His hair was dark and flat, his eyes tiny and penetratingly focused or completely absent. Ravrada beamed from behind him, and for good reason. She'd used her art of influence to great effect here. Dama she'd *raised.* Dama she'd taken as a youth and made a part of the long game. Dama she'd guided through life in developing the skills he needed to work his way into position inside the brain of the Qol defenses, all the while bending his will and spirit to the destiny.

"You've done well, Dama," Radin said.

Dama smacked his lips and spewed trill-less Vrrgrrul. He thanked Radin too many times. He told Radin things he already knew: that he'd waited for Radin; that he'd inserted a chemical or an invisible crawler (something here was lost in translation, but Radin understood well enough) into a nerve in the Qol system; that he'd been listening as Radin approached in the meteor; that he'd made the chemical burn or the crawler bite at the exact right time; that he'd waited so very long; that he wasn't done helping, was Dondante ready?

Ravrada patted Dama on the head. "See, Dondante, very excited."

"He'll take me?"

"No, Dondante," Ravrada said, and her mirror eyes flickered. "Dama, who will take Dondante?"

Dama's eyes locked onto Radin's forehead. "Dondante, I turned him."

A slow smile spread across Ravrada's lips, and Radin felt caught. He'd underestimated her, after all. If she could train Qols to turn more Qols, what kind of flock could she build? What could she do with it? How big was it now? How far and deep was her reach?

"Fascinating," Radin said, and he meant it.

Ravrada took a bow, but then, wisely, moved on. "Dondante, news."

"Tell."

"As Koren predicted. All ships gathered above Zone 3. She draws them into talks now."

"Love for Koren," Radin said, in awe of her too. She'd created all of this. He'd not be what he was—the *locus*—if not for her. His love for her was a festering wound. He loved her in the way that he'd always suspected his father of loving his mother, right up until to the point of bludgeoning her in front of Radin and his siblings.

"Yes, Dondante, yes. But more. Dawlis. Continues to be erratic. Split from his fellows. Creeps through the hive leaving a symbol and telling MaGog it is him and all of them and every Qol." She projected the symbol over her wrist device and described it as Dawlis had been.

Radin's initial thought was that he was the winged creature and that she, Ravrada, was the other, slipping her tentacles into cracks in Qol minds and wrapping them up. But it was far better than that.

"These creatures, Dondante. He tells MaGog that they are found where he is from. But they don't exist. Losing his mind and his way."

Radin laughed out loud.

Oh, but maybe they're real, Ravrada! Creatures from Earth, not Qol!

But could she know? Was she telling him these things to see how he would react, to see if *he* knew? Had Rasmussa, in the grip of her tentacles, told her the story of the bulb and the four worlds after all? No. It couldn't be. He said he hadn't, and Radin believed it. Not because he trusted Rasmussa but because he trusted in his own centrality.

He laughed at his fortune. He laughed at himself for feeling, moments ago, any shred of anxiety about Ravrada being a threat to his place in history and the universe. Indeed, there was such a gulf of knowledge between them as to render Ravrada's tinkering, however impressive and critical on the scale of this two-world conflict, insignificant in the grander celestial scheme that Radin was privy to.

She wasn't smiling anymore. She was struggling against the urge to reach into his mind and find out what was so funny. It told him everything he needed to know.

"I'll rest," he said.

"Dondante, yes, but please, one more thing. Brrumida and the female Ayn. Everything is set."

"Like the last two times? Why so much trouble for her?"

"Dondante, her connections. Even from her cage, she sniffs and could disrupt us."

"Who's protecting her?"

"I don't know yet. I'm close."

Radin turned and walked into his shack. He sat against the back wall and listened to the ocean whisper to him in its timeless rhythm. A flutter in his belly was the universe tickling him. A blinking dot on his wrist device was the universe reaching out to him right then, right on time, through Rasmussa. He'd done it, the message said. He'd found a passage between Qol and his world, Ashuwa. On Ashuwa there was a bulb, a nexus between worlds, waiting to be plucked. And Radin was the plucker. Radin was the nexus. But first, one more thing for his fellows.

25

Will and Kade stood in the entrance to the common, neon-purple to each other, invisible to the old, hunched, hairless fellow in drab-colored cloth scrubbing a stone slab—*scritch, scratch*—by the life-green light of trroorra flares. Will rolled camera. He liked to watch them first when he could, capture them in their day-to-day. He wanted the Qols back home (if by some miracle these videos got through to Nopa, and if, by just one more, she decided to risk her neck for him again and leak these clips out of a grounded battleship) to see what he saw: humble, hard-working human beings living their lives, doing their best, trying to make sense of an upside-down solar system as warships hovered over their home. This male and his fellows, they were the same, only different, as any human Will had yet to encounter on three worlds.

He approached the male from behind and clapped his black-gloved, gossamer-circuited hands. The male fell to his ass on the floor and whimpered. Will stood perfectly still, so the male saw nothing. Will circled him, so the male saw wavering air. He lasered his symbol into the floor, then projected his message in Vrrgrrul:

-- Your path to the blue world is through cooperation. She lied to you. Your Dondante has no hold on Qol. I wounded him, shattered his collar. I am here to end her and forge a bond with you. But you have to choose. Seek the oasis and the safehouses. The resistance will find you. --

Kade gassed him. Will caught him, laid him down, and took a close-up of his wrinkled, restful face, then a closeup of the symbol. They left him there for Hrulora and the others.

They ran through a black tunnel made pale blue by their night vision. A mile or so on, the blue turned trroorra-green, and they heard voices, grinding metal, and squeaking brakes. Will was pleased. Cart stations had proven good venues for creating buzz. He confirmed their location on the holo map in his googles as best he could (the guard had developed maps of the underworld over time with help from the resistance, but they were patchy in places), then stepped inside with Kade on his left flank.

There were half a dozen tracks and several dozen fellows in many colors of cloth, adults and young adults, hopping in and out of carts. Each fellow had a wafer punched with dots and dashes: assignments, directions, according to Hrulora. They'd follow them to a hollow, a mine, a farm, or the maze. They'd be handed heat weapons if they were lucky, pickaxes if they weren't, to wield against Qol lasers. They'd be given no training, there was no time. But perhaps Will could convince them they didn't need it.

He slipped through the crowd tapping shoulders. Fellows turned and looked at each other. He found an empty cart in a corner, pushed it a few feet down a track, then stopped it and pulled it back. A female in red cloth saw it move by itself. She stared, pointed, trilled. Others turned. He did the magic trick again, then turned off his camo. Fellows jumped. A male charged. Will gassed him, caught him, and lowered him to the ground. The others stayed put. Will lasered his symbol into the side of a cart, called up his message, cut an arc with his xim, then threw a gentle wave at the female in red. She toppled into the arms of her fellows. A male fainted. Will turned his suit back on and ran off with Kade.

They went deeper down and in. They were headed in the general direction of a census station, where they were to meet Hrulora and the
station lead. There was more than one winding path to get there, and
Will did not feel strongly about which one they took. He was content
for now to keep moving, keep disrupting, keep refusing to hurt anyone,
keep filming. They were somewhere in Zone 11.

Kade did not complain or opine. He'd been as mute as Will since
the start of their campaign two Gog cycles by (slightly more than three
days ago, slightly less than three spins past), but he'd executed flawlessly.
He was holding it together. He was keeping the voices at bay. Will was
proud of him. Will loved him very, very much.

They came to a farm, their first. Fellows in crimson cloth stood up
to their waists in circular pools, tending to gardens of a purple-green,
kelp-like plant. Pulge, Will recalled. They trimmed, raked, harvested.
Other fellows hung the pulge to dry on metal wires strung along the
walls. A female walked in Will and Kade's direction and took a seat
against the wall by the mouth of the tunnel, took a load off. Will bent
down, blew in her ear, captured her dumbstruck face, then hit her with
a mouth full of sleeping gas.

-- Here we go. -- he typed to Kade.

They walked to the nearest pool. Two males were underwater,
buried in the strands of pulge. They surfaced with handfuls of dark
green seeds the size of walnuts. Will slapped the water. Their mouths
dropped open. He slapped it again, and they screamed. He gassed them,
and he and Kade pulled them out.

Two females rushed to the aid of their fellows. Kade stepped in front
of them and put them to sleep. They went down like shot buffalo. Everyone else froze. Will paced, a wavering specter, a colorless jellyfish in the
diffuse, trroorra-green sea. He made a full circle arc to burn into their
retinas and their memories, then lasered his symbol and called up his
message.

They pounded the pavement. They ate what they could steal (not bad, the pulge and the crawler legs, kind of like crab, but the dried worms were tough to put down) and traded catnaps. They stayed ahead of the rumors, which meant that every fellow they introduced themselves to was completely and mercilessly unprepared for the two-headed Qol ghost. They left a growing spiderweb of confusion and speculation. Hrulora and her crew followed at a safe distance and engaged in conversation, under the auspices of being just as puzzled as any other fellow, with those witnesses most afflicted by uncertainty and curiosity. Will filmed every meet and greet and the increasingly unsettled day-to-day. He sent his clips to Nopa with his fingers crossed.

The web finally spread out around them. They were known at a mine. Destiny-anxious glome clogged the entrance, and so they took to the ceiling in their sticky blenders and crawled upside-down through the stalactites.

"Females. Young. They don't care," one glome said in Vrrgrrul.

"Mad," confirmed a second. "Just killing. Rogue. They have a symbol."

"Not rogue," said a third through his teeth. "They want us to think that."

Will was hurt but not surprised. It was a very human reaction to his and Kade's zero-hour knuckle ball (floating like a butterfly) to invent such things. MaGog were clinging to what they'd always known, to what Koren had drilled into their heads. The Qols were killers and oppressors, with no intention of sharing and every intention of keeping MaGog in their place. And perhaps she'd thrown some fresh propaganda into the pot. Perhaps she'd caught wind of the friendly ghosts and was playing defense.

It was effective. Will and Kade, as they worked their way further down and into the hive, heard more and more about the Qol wraiths running amok. But what mattered to Will, what exposed the MaGog

Self-doubt, was that *his message remained intact.* It went through the game of telephone and came out itself. MaGog would spit it out word-for-word, then punch a wall or stomp a foot or take a thick, chalky whiff of dust and yell things like, Wounded Dondante, ha! Here to cooperate with four warships, ha! Here to forge a bond, sure! Koren ever lied, die! Seek the oasis and safehouses, yes, we will! And those who were loudest and shrillest were often the same ones whispering later, asking another brow-wrinkled fellow if they thought the ghosts' blue arc energy could possibly have cut through Radin's stone-metal collar; if perhaps they'd underestimated the Qols and the resistance; if they'd ever felt, since Koren had unveiled the secret of their progress, the slightest bit untrusted or even betrayed?

A more insidious rumor grew. A mental and emotional cancer. A taboo that when brought up by the occasional particularly befuddled and distracted fellow was immediately shut down by any within earshot. Something to do with someone named Oorroom. But where in his readings had Will heard that name?

They made it to the rendezvous, a crack in the bend of a black tunnel not far from the census station. They waited inside for Hrulora.

--You first.-- Will said.

Kade was instantly asleep.

She came an hour or two later. It was the first time they'd seen each other since their ride across the surface.

--Is it working?-- he asked her.

She looked unsure how to answer that question. She looked at him like she had when they'd first met, after he'd burned his symbol into the stone floor between them, like she was trying to remember something or to place him. "You're shocking them," she said in trilled, broken Korial, smoothed out by Will's translator. "Half wake up fearful and vulnerable—we're getting some of those. Half wake up fearful and hungrier to fight."

--A start. What about the negotiations?--

"They've met twice. Koren demands safe passage for MaGog on Qol ships in exchange for minerals."

-- How many MaGog? --

"All. Qol says they'll give nothing until an apology and reparations."

-- Which Koren will not give. --

"She says things are even."

-- Because of the history. --

"Yes."

The grudge. The wedge. The ill-fated first mission thirty-three rings by and all the failed attempts at diplomacy since. Koren, of course, expounded the version of history in which the Qols fired first. Monte lo ara Bige expounded the same, while virtually every other Qol academic and journalist knew for a fact that the Marradar drew first blood. Regardless, what did she want? Was she really playing for a safe migration? Was it her plan all along to punch Qol in the mouth, show them what MaGog was capable of, and then use that as leverage to create a new life for her people? Or was this blind revenge for a sin Qol may or may not have committed? Did they have her in a corner, or did she have them exactly where she wanted them?

Hrulora was looking at Will in that way.

-- What is it? -- he asked.

She shook her head. "A story."

-- What story? --

"About Oorroom."

Oorroom.

The rumor. The taboo.

"Koren's brother. Her *illurrur*," Hrulora said and shuddered.

Will's glasses took an extra second to translate that last word to English. They came up with *magus.*

"Sees your heat," Hrulora said. "Your feelings. Moves things with his thoughts."

Will recalled passing reference to a sibling. But Koren, if she was the daughter of a fat cat, would have had many siblings, perhaps dozens. This one was special? Telekinesis?

-- What about him? --

"Tongueless."

Yes, Will remembered this character now. Sadly, he had taken the mutilation for granted, given the Marradars' history.

Hrulora's colorless skin, bathed in light blue by Will's goggles, dried. "Many versions of how he lost his tongue. You hear them all as Youth. Barra worms ate it. He was gone on dust and liquids and licked lava on a dare. Owed a debt to a Marradar and paid. But recently, before you came, another surfaced: Koren cut it out."

-- Why? --

"He saw something in the fabric. He is an illurrur. Someone would come for her."

Will was flooded with energy: the connective tissue, the implicate order, the fabric.

-- A prophecy? --

"Just a recent story. No one believes. No one speaks it. They love her too much."

But *Will* believed. For the energy was everywhere. It connected three worlds, and he was caught in it. He was a carrier of it. So were Kade and Ayn and Peis. Piper too. Hrulora. Radin. Koren. Oorroom. The Fenti. The wolves. The Nimar and Tiralee. It didn't stop there. It was two billion souls on Qol, seven and a half on Earth, and tens of millions on Gog. They were *all* carriers. They were all *It.* They were moving together through the perennial present toward some future-present that certain people—*human transistors*—could sense or see.

Yet, nothing was inevitable. Will had dreamt his death out on the Shole. Eamon, the Kyut chief, had drawn it on the wall of his cave three hundred turns earlier. But here he was, because of the choice he'd made between the butterfly and the squid. Somewhere Radin was making choices too. And Koren. The guards. The resistance. The Council. Countless others that had in the past or were now or would someday dip their fingers into the pool in some random or fated moment in some random or fated place and push their own ripples out into the interference pattern. It was out of control and oppressively empowering.

-- You sleep. -- he wrote.

Hrulora did not argue.

Will straightened his back, turned off his goggles, closed his eyes, and stared into the black that was not at all black. It was a swirling storm of pixels and shadow. He'd been seeing it—he was never not seeing it—but he hadn't *watched* it, communed with it, since their forced landing. He'd been consumed by the plan unfolding in real time. Now, in this crack in a tunnel wall, his mind churned like the infinitesimal bits of light in his head. It churned over Koren.

He'd come to the conclusion, based on his research and what he'd seen so far of these humans and their society, that she'd done more good than harm for them. He believed that the lives they'd been living since her bloody revolt were likely safer and more rewarding than the ones suffered for hundreds of rings under the Marradar. So, the question was why? Why had she dug this particular channel for MaGog's pent-up energy? Why had she so diligently and passionately stoked their fear and hatred for Qol? Why send warriors in meteors instead of diplomats in ships?

A hint came to him related to Bige's claim, floating irresponsibly without a single fact-stone of foundation, that Koren was the child of the Marradar who'd confronted the first Qols and taken their ship, and that she was the one who slit his throat. What if it was true? What could drive her to patricide? Neglect and abuse, yes, and Will had a place in his heart for any human being driven to such self-destruction. But there had to be more to it. She hadn't labored all these long rings just for herself and for control of the rockets. She'd built a better life for her people, centered around the protection of women and children.

That.

Perhaps *that* was it. Perhaps killing her father was a protest, a gospel, an expression of a philosophy that there was no true living, no freedom or happiness, and no fulfilling of any destiny without the nurturing of the young and the feminine principle.

Will felt the truth in this but not the whole truth. It struck a tuning fork in his mind, but the chord was missing a note. He knew the note. He shared the pain. It was Koren's mother, absent from her history as Will's was absent from his.

The fork rang brighter, but it quavered. The last note was there but not there, like a phantom limb. The feminine principle was a pulsing ember in the pit of Will's mind. He pondered its role in this collision of worlds, this awakening to the connections between them. He saw, in the center of the fizzing pixel sea, the spiral and the object at the bottom, the monolith. He rubbed his fingers over the necklace bumps beneath his suit: the snake tooth, the buma tooth, and the karma stone. He decided he would simply ask her. He would give her the opportunity to exorcise. He didn't expect to get the chance so soon.

He dozed.

He awoke, all three of them did, to a resistance fellow panting, shaking, telling them that Koren was near.

26

Droodroovid plodded through the stacks hiding the wafers of fellows far too old and far too young to fight (and all too young to die for Koren's agenda). It was more of the same, this latest wave of reassignments, more scantily armed, untrained fellows sent into the already stuffed tunnels of the maze to protect the rockets with their presence alone. Koren knew they didn't stand a chance against the guards and their weaponry. It was obvious to anyone not blinded by fervor and loyalty that her strategy for neutralizing the lasers of the three Qol battleships hanging over Zone 3, irate over the grounding of their fourth, drops of drool dripping from their triangle mouths and splatting onto the silo caps, was to surround the rockets with humanity. She was betting on Qol not having the stomach to commit genocide. And Qol had held its fire thus far, but what would happen once those rockets started launching? It was easy to predict.

He scratched an itch above his right eye, reopening a scabbed arrada worm track. It pussed and bled down the side of his mangled face. He slipped another fellow in the form of a wafer back into a random den in the form of a slot on a shelf. He hid this fellow from the impending massacre. But he was only delaying the inevitable. The destiny would ensnare them all sooner or later.

A runner came with fresh reassignments and fresh rumors. Negotiations had stalled. The oppressor Qols would not yield to Koren's reasonable, humane requests. Brave glome fought isolated skirmishes with the guard and the resistance. The two ghosts continued their campaign of propaganda and indiscriminate murder.

The ghosts, Droodroovid thought.

He'd been wondering about them. It seemed odd that they would preach cooperation and choice and then choose to kill women and Young. Indeed, there were other versions of the stories whispered by the occasional reckless fellow. "I heard they don't kill," Droodroovid said recklessly. "Knock fellows out and leave a message."

The runner spit on the ground at Droodroovid's feet. "You believe it? You believe they wounded Dondante?"

Droodroovid backed away. The analysts glared. Heavy, stone-metal footsteps stopped time. Dondarra entered the station in two lines. Rising from their ranks were her sharp shoulder peaks, her ridged, wrinkled skull, her giant eyes that sucked all light and hope, and her scythe that cut it to shreds. Droodroovid regretted being born. He shook. He dried with fear. Caught after all.

A Dondarra called for the station lead. Droodroovid couldn't speak, but he needn't have. Oorroom—*Oorroom!*—stepped out of one line with a sphere floating above an open palm. He read the guilt in Droodroovid's energy, pointed at him and smiled, open-mouthed and tongueless!

Two Dondarra took Droodroovid by either arm and led him into the stacks. Koren followed, filling the aisle, blotting out the wafers as she passed them, the lives. She towered over him and swallowed him whole with her eyes. "Here, fellow," she said, slicing his mind with her stone-metal trill. She reached inside her robe and pulled out a roll of wood. "A particular assignment."

Hope was a blinding, burning flash. Could it be she didn't know? Could it be he'd have another chance to kill himself?!

"Use your breath," she said. "Look." She unrolled the wood and held it against the wall, jabbed at it with a bony finger the length of his hand. Thirty reassigned to glome, she ordered. Strongest he could find. She didn't care where he drew them from. She understood that MaGog was thick in Zone 3 and thin everywhere else, but she wasn't interested in that as an excuse. He was to take them himself, to 4, to an edge of the hive, and deliver them to the lead digger there. Did he have it?

He did, and he didn't. He'd filled many hundreds of reassignments, just never one delivered by the leader of the underworld during the beginning stages of an interplanetary war.

She rolled up the map and leaned into him, her breath a hot mix of liquids and rot, her touch a barely felt slicing as she craned a finger and traced a curved scab down his left cheek. "We've both been scarred, haven't we, fellow? Perhaps you will go. Trust me. We are there. Do this work for MaGog."

"Koren," he croaked.

Then they were gone. Koren, the Dondarra, Oorroom. Maybe it had been a nightmare. But the analysts were staring at him.

"Reassignments," he mumbled. "I'll handle."

The crowd broke up and went back to work with electric vigor, charged by the close encounter with their beloved.

Something shifted in Droodroovid's periphery, in a back corner of the stacks. The wall rippled. A short, broad human in a shimmering black suit and black goggles appeared out of nothing, motioned to him, then disappeared again.

27

Grugreera passes Koren samples of irrudrr, rruvik, and grorum, and she passes them back after cursory examinations. She asks him what he needs. He tells her five more dens in Zone 9, seven in 10. The number of fellows choosing to stay is increasing.

She is pensive. "You were right," she says.

"So were you. Thousands of fellows on the lush surface already. More all the time."

Her eyes soften, weaken. "You don't want to go?"

She knows him better than that. She is projecting. She regrets not being able to go herself. He doesn't blame her, not after all she's sacrificed. It's natural that she should dream of being younger and making the crossing. But she is a skeleton draped in translucent skin and dark robes.

"Your role," he says. "You made all of this." The underworld, the womb, where she will live out her time with him.

She thanks him and asks him to forgive her these doubts.

"Nothing to forgive."

Hrulora places a warm hand on his shoulder and smiles down at him, fingering the dark arra pendant hanging from her neck. Their Young coos in its cradle.

Cries.

A foul wind gushes through the tunnel. Grugreera rises, tells Hru-lora to take their Young and run. The winged creature appears, snaps *its razor-sharp beak and beats its wings. The other slides out from behind it and reaches for Grugreera with ten oozing tentacles, stares at him with one gaping-hole eye. He points his pickaxe. The creatures become the two Qol ghosts. They are holding explosives. Grugreera rushes them, but he's too late. The bombs go off without a sound but with a feeling that all is wrong and all is over.*

Grugreera walked the maze, trying to rid himself of the dream. Koren's uncertainty plagued him.

He came to a slope of rubble, a crumbled dead end.

Sloppy, he scolded himself.

He never allowed his crew to leave any tunnel or intersection they dug anything but spotless and perfectly safe. But here he'd misjudged. Here he'd underappreciated the amount of brittle urramir in this alloy. This was one of the first tunnels they'd dug. Or one of the last. Why could he not remember? And where was their next assignment anyway? They'd been dormant for more than a full cycle now. Where were the glome? Why were these tunnels, so critical to Koren that she'd felt the need to hand Grugreera his assignment personally, not filled with ready fighters? The Qols, if the third- and fourth-hand reports one heard in the maze were true, were trickling into the hive in ever greater numbers. The two rogue ghosts were running amok and could be anywhere.

A noise seeped from the rubble and dried his skin. Unnatural, but not a bore and not a drill. An engine? It cut out. There were voices.

He held his breath. He was *there.* He was a layer of collapsed stone from the rockets. He tossed chunks aside, ignoring his guilt. Koren had sent him there to help protect the hangar, not bore into it. But the engineers and glome would need to know that there was a breach. The sooner Grugreera owned up to his mistake, the sooner he could help fix it. That was what she would want. And she would not begrudge him— no, not him!—one look inside.

The quiet was unnerving. A massive industrial site in its final stages of preparation should be raucous, clangorous, booming. Perhaps the work was done. Perhaps the engineers and glome were resting now, waiting for the call. But something wasn't right. That rev again. So smooth.

Trroorra light spilled from cracks in the stone and cast shadows in Grugreera's mind. Something to do with his dream, with Koren's sheepish look as she asked him, 'You don't want to go?'

He broke through, and his heart broke. He stared at it for some time, the Qol ship, the first to land on Gog. All MaGog knew it to be rusting in pieces somewhere. But it looked quite sleek and quite ready. Another sleek lie. A very ready chariot.

Thirty glome were waiting for him in Verderr's intersection. Thirty glome and the census male who'd changed his life twice before. Grugreera recognized him despite the worm scars—arrada worms, clearly, the type that had eaten half of Grugreera's right arm. They both sensed the synchronicity. "Hello, fellow," Grugreera said, but the male only stared at his stump. Grugreera took the wafers from him, skimmed them, tossed them onto the floor—*clang, rattle!*—then took command with a bright smile, a clear voice, and a quick step. He directed glome to this tunnel and that, escorting the last few himself. When they were all where he wanted them, all a safe distance from the rubble, he returned to Verderr's intersection.

"I don't think we're in the maze," Verderr moaned.

The census male nodded.

"Come, fellows," Grugreera said. "I'll show you something."

28

Kade was the girl with the broken heart, and she was lying on her belly at the edge of the cliff and staring down into the mist. In the next moment, he was back in a cart station in the underworld of Gog standing beside neon-purple Dawlis and watching Hrulora, who was speaking to a young male, who was having trouble breathing. Yes, the male managed to say, Koren and her Dondarra had been through here. She thanked him and told him, serve well. She spoke to the driver of a half-full cart string, then got in. Kade and Will crawled into the tight gaps between her cart and the ones on either side of it, crouched on the bars connecting them, stuck their hands to the walls, and they were off again.

They'd ridden several carts in this way since the census station. They'd sprinted through many tunnels. They'd nearly run into the stone-metal tail of Koren's Dondarra entourage more than once. It had not been very difficult to follow her. She'd taken a more or less straight line toward Zone 3 and left a wake of starstruck fellows. But they'd yet to see her again, yet to find an opening, and Kade was starting to fear that they wouldn't. He wished they'd jumped her at the station. He wished Dawlis hadn't held him back. They more than likely would have died, but they would have taken her with them. Dying, anyway, seemed only a matter of time.

It was not sane what they were doing, but they had their directives. His was to follow Dawlis. Dawlis's was to follow whatever forces had been driving him since coming alive in the boat in Nima, forces that spoke in prophecy and left very little to choice, despite the boy's symbol and message. Any choices they made were under coercion of these forces. They were flotsam on a slow-moving tidal wave bound to do what all waves do.

But maybe Kade, lying on her belly, listening to the rhythmic crash and roar, was thinking of the wrong kind of energy. Maybe it was more like an exploding star whose light rippled out through space in all directions forever until it touched things, mixed with them, continued to exist as part of them. This explosion, it happened some impossibly long time ago and started every chain of events and every life that ever was. Everything was made of this light and the shadows it cast, morphing incessantly, spreading out in fractal patterns and dark blooms.

Both seemed true, the cycles and the infinite. The girl was trying to make a point. She was stating a paradox. Or she was spewing depressed philosophy. Kade let it play in the background. He focused on the grinding, sparking wheels, the speed, the ache in his knees and back. The movement and the pain, they were his checks against the *others*.

They rolled into a small, quiet station with three tunnels along the back wall, three tracks leading into the tunnels, and three empty cart strings waiting on the tracks. A glome standing guard told them to stay in their carts. Two others walked the line checking wafers. Hrulora asked the one who checked hers (forged by Droodroovid) if Koren had been through here. He didn't answer. He didn't say no. He directed her and the others to one of the other strings. He chose who went where seemingly at random. Hrulora sat heavily in her assigned cart. Kade and Dawlis wedged themselves in and stuck on for the ride. They were reduced now to chance. No resistance or guard maps of *this* region of the hive.

The next station was identical to the last, except that there were only two cart strings sitting idle and a few fellows in one of them. All passengers swapped strings again at the whims of the glome. There was a third station like this, a fourth, a fifth. They were in the maze, Kade knew. Lost, quite possibly forever.

The next station was larger, louder, and more heavily guarded. The tracks all turned in a semi-circle and ran back out. There were six narrow walking tunnels. Glome shoved fellows into one or another without bothering to check wafers. Hrulora headed for the far right one. Kade and Dawlis rode the wall and followed her in. She stopped beneath a trroorra flare. A fellow passed. Dawlis, wise not to project anything, sent a message to Kade's glasses.

--Ask her if this is it.--

Kade knew the answer, but he whispered the question anyway.

"Yes," she said. "There are gates now."

One creaked and slammed shut somewhere around a bend. Nervous trills from that direction.

--Let's go.-- Dawlis typed, and Kade relayed.

"I can't," Hrulora said. "I'll never get out. You could."

--Zone 4 then. Where Koren sent Droodroovid.--

She nodded. "I'll see what's there."

--Thank you.--

Dawlis squeezed her hand and kissed her on the cheek. Her skin softened. They went their separate ways.

The tunnel opened into a high chamber dripping with stalactites. Water poured from a metal spout in the near wall and flowed down a metal trough toward a stone-metal gate fit to a wide fissure at the far end. Fellows stood in crooked lines looking at each other as though they couldn't quite believe that this was happening and weren't quite sure how they felt about it. A glome opened the gate and let a few fellows in from each line. Shut the gate. Dawlis pointed up at the ceiling. He and Kade scaled the wall and maneuvered through the stalactites. Dawlis climbed down the gate until he was just above the door, which was a few feet taller than the glome guarding it. The door opened, the crowd surged, and Kade would never forget it: neon-purple Dawlis letting go, hanging in a crouch, hands clawed, toes pointing into the rectangle of space between the glome heads and the top of the door, fellows frozen with shouts in their mouths and wafers held high, existence holding its breath—and Dawlis catching the bar that topped the door, going horizontal and nearly scraping his legs and chest on it as he swung inside. He landed softly and stood perfectly still. Two females looked right through him, looked at each other. The door shut.

Kade climbed down and got into position. When the door opened again, Dawlis reached through the bars and shoved someone, who shoved someone else. Kade flew through in the scuffle. They climbed a wall.

Fellows formed lines again. Glome handed out heat weapons, swords, and pickaxes and sent the newly minted protectors of the maze into a black tunnel. Kade and Dawlis crawled along the ceiling into a round, trroorra-lit intersection. Two bent-back old males dispersed fellows one and two at a time, distributing them evenly into the tunnels with slaps on the back and croaky trills of encouragement (streaming down Kade's right lens): "You can do it," "One MaGog," "MaGog is grateful," "Koren is grateful." Dawlis jumped off the wall and chose a tunnel. Kade jumped down and followed him into another hub and spoke where he picked a tunnel without thinking and without breaking stride. They came into a small, crowded den with a stream running through it. Fellows sparred with their new weapons, paced, argued over the latest hearsay. Dawlis panned the room with his goggles, captured the scene. He left his symbol in a dark corner behind a boulder for MaGog to find later.

Into another intersection, another den. On and on, and Kade's body finally started to revolt. It was not just the feverish pace and lack of sleep. It was the acid of uselessness and guilt burning in his gut. Before the maze, he might have admitted to having sensed at times the life in Dawlis's "plan," the mind of its own, the blow-less wind nudging them in some direction. Running into Koren in the census station might have been something other than coincidence. But this movement through the maze was willful abandonment to chance, and Kade was a mindless follower.

Keep him safe!

The butterfly and the squid? No. Kade had no choice. He hadn't made a choice in his adult life. He'd spent it waiting for the boy, then followed him to the island, into space, and down into this nadir.

They crept through intersections, tunnels, and dens choked with MaGog. They ran through others mostly empty. Wherever there were fellows, there were fellows speculating on when the guards would arrive, bragging about how many they would kill, and dreaming of being called to the rockets and the destiny, the new life. Dawlis left his symbol where fellows were thin and looking the other way. He raised his message only to stray individuals before knocking them out with his sleeper gun. The horror myths spread out around them, but the tales of the ghosts' indiscriminate murder were countered more and more, with less and less fear and trepidation, by the rebuttal of What if? What if there was something to the stories of non-lethal gas? What if Dondante roamed the surface of Qol wounded and collarless? What if the ghosts ever found their way to Koren? And nothing confounded and emboldened the rebutters more than the story of Dawlis and the dead female.

A Prime-aged male sitting at the edge of a pool of pulge in a small farm said to a captive audience, "Two creatures combined. One flies and is all the colors. One swims in the deep and never sees the light."

Dawlis stepped closer, recording.

"A choice," contributed an older female.

"Yes," said the male.

"Traitors. Resistance," said another male, standing up, shoulders hunched. His left eye twitched. He twirled his stone-metal pickaxe.

The female stood. "It's only what we've heard. We don't know. *You* don't know."

A swish, a crack, and a thud. Dawlis gasped. He turned off his suit. His chest heaved. The murderer, terrified, dropped the pickaxe and crumbled beneath Dawlis's black-goggled stare. Two fellows rushed, and Kade, still invisible, dropped them with his sleeper gun. Dawlis cut the pickaxe in half with his xim, gassed the killer, and kneeled by the body of the dead female. No one called for help. No one knew what to do. He caressed her right hand, closed her lids, and folded her arms over her chest. Then he untied her necklace, closed his fist around the purple-blue stone, stood, and projected over his wrist:

-- Your path to the blue world is through cooperation. She lied to you. Your Dondante has no hold on Qol. I wounded him, shattered his collar. --

Big MaGog eyes glanced down at the severed pickaxe.

-- I am here to end her and forge a bond with you. But you have to choose. So do the Qols. --

He lasered his symbol into the floor, then walked out. Silent fellows parted for him. Kade followed.

They were ships on the crest of a wave. They were riding starlight through space forever and ever. Kade's body was shutting down. Dizzy spells. Shards of pain through joint and bone. Dawlis too had slowed. They shuffled into a long, rectangular room. Open shafts lined the longer walls, each shaft housing a vertical stone-metal pole and chains hanging down. Two glome sat against the far wall beside a tunnel mouth. One was sleeping. Chains rattled in a center-right shaft. A stone-metal lift rose up out of the floor and kept going. A female in blue cloth trilled to herself, just passing through.

Dawlis walked the room. He reached a hand into the shafts, palm up, then palm down. He dipped his nose in and sniffed. He stood in the center of the room and turned in a circle, trying to decide. But he had no choice. A neon-purple guard came down in a lift and lasered the two glome through their heads. Dawlis stiffened, huffed, made hammers of his fists. Kade, blood pumping, took his xim, took his place on Dawlis's flank, and waited for the scout to notice the two other invisibles.

Cut chains and then lifts dropped out of the ceiling in free fall. One held three fellows in dark purple cloth, screaming. The lifts crashed like symbols far below, announcing the attack. Two came down slowly, each crammed with seven guards, heavily armed and quickly aware of Kade and Dawlis.

Dawlis turned off his suit and raised his arms. A guard aimed a laser barrel at the xim on his waist. "Take that off and drop it," the guard said. "Do it."

The others circled. Kade pivoted and went back-to-back with Dawlis, stroked his xim. He hoped it would happen. He would like to see them try. A glow in his periphery was a message raised over Dawlis's wrist. It appeared in Kade's right lens, in Korial:

-- You know who we are. --

"We know," said the guard. "Drop it."

-- We're reaching MaGog. Getting through. --

"That's what you call it?"

-- You believe the stories? You believe everything you hear? One dead in our path, and we didn't kill her. --

"Then you're just in the way."

Dawlis stepped forward. Kade stepped back. The guards set their feet.

-- At least one of you has a sleeper gun. You didn't need to kill those two. That was a choice. Those three screaming to their deaths? We'll never stop hearing them. Watch me. This is not a weapon. I'll go slow. --

Dawlis took the laser off his belt and burned the symbol into the floor. The guards grumbled and spit.

-- Where are the negotiations? --

The lead shrugged. "The emissaries went in and haven't come out. You still like your approach?"

-- Every choice counts more now. You must have a map. Send it to me. We're moving on. --

"You're not."

Dawlis turned in a slow circle. Kade matched his rotation.

-- Think of living under here for a thousand turns. You may not know the history. You should. They've suffered. They were pent up, and Koren gave them hope, but she manipulated it. I don't know why she did it. I'm going to ask her. --

One of the guards coughed.

-- They're afraid of death like all of you. Every choice we make will ripple out in front of us. Every kill will live with us forever. We'll look back and say we got caught up in it. Or we'll look back and say we tried to do it differently. --

He slapped the laser back onto his belt and walked, hands up, out of the circle. Kade followed with his hand on his xim, ready and willing.

-- Send me your map. --

A guard tapped a holoball down by her side, and a file landed in their goggles. They left through the far tunnel, past the two glome, who sat slumped against each other, heads hanging, free from all of this now, maybe living in a blue world heaven.

The map was a black blob with a handful of kinked, curved, and jagged lines leading from random points along the edges to random points inside. The lines were the paths that various guard units had taken into the maze. They were paths out for Kade and Dawlis, if Dawlis chose one. But he didn't. He chose instead to go deeper into the black, and it cost them everything. All in vain. Lorel screaming over the other voices in Kade's head: *Keep him safe! My only son!*

MaGog finally figured out a solution to their ghost problem. They rigged nets above the gates. Dawlis got caught in one and dropped like a sack. Kade fell on top of him and clung to him as a small army of glome dragged them away.

Kade spent the next two cycles sleeping, fighting off the *others*, and steeling himself against a slow, regret-filled death. Dawlis spent them sleeping and meditating by the door of their cell. They were naked. They had no light. They saw no one. They were given nothing to eat or drink. They were on the doorstep when she came, Koren. She told them about Ayn and Radin and left them to choke on that.

29

Ayn is back at that concert. The first neon marble rolls to her feet, and she picks it up and throws it out over the crowd. It flies in slow motion and leaves an arced tail of light. She smiles and waits for the others to start throwing their marbles, for the big light show. But there's no show this time.

Tontine comes back with the drinks. They each take a slug and smirk at each other. They say it without saying it: Yeah, yeah, I'm sorry, and you're sorry, and let's just move on. But they know there's really no doing that. The wounds are too deep. They take another slug.

She steps onto the deck in Rivel and follows the girls down the walk-way toward the ocean. The girls disappear behind tall, browned grass waving in the icy winter wind. The wind is exhilarating. Ayn feels alive. She forgets everything. She's caught up in the scene. Entranced. Trapped. There is no winter in Rivel.

Zee turns the corner on her board, screaming. Maya and Mycah come running for their lives. The wind whips and crackles with electric-ity. The girls reach Ayn and huddle behind her. A shapeless being glides toward them, a tall black nothing with glowing eyes. Ayn charges and dives into it. They merge, swirl, wrestle with their souls. She subsumes it. She wins. She breathes.

She looks down into a pond so clear and still, so lucid, the water is sensed but not seen. The bottom is a carpet of red, brown, and tan pebbles. The girls are down there hiding behind a boulder. Ayn signals *to them that it's safe. They come out and start up the slope, but it's steep, and the pebbles slide under their feet.*

Ayn jumps in. They climb on her back and weigh her down. Her feet slip, and she's running out of air, but she finds her footing and trudges up the slope. The girls reach the surface first and pull her up. She kisses them goodbye, and none of them asks when she's coming back. They spare her the heartbreak.

She's in Stilter standing before the first glass mosaic wall, the eye, the symbol of the Mind, floating in deep blue space. Above the eye is something she is sure was not there before: two crossing lines, a longer vertical one and a shorter horizontal one. She remembers standing here with Dawlis. She remembers walking him along the walls and explaining the images of Qol's evolution and history. But all of that is gone now. There's just the eye and this cross, which now holds an animal in each quadrant, a fish, a cat, a serpent, and an insect with a stinger. It's two ways of saying the same thing, the eye and the cross. Ayn understands, and she doesn't. Love mangles her insides.

She opened her eyes, touched her face, her chest, a wall. She was solid. The wall was solid. She was in a cell in a glass tower in the Wolla swampland. Her daughters were very far away.

How did she end up here? Why didn't she spend more time with them? Why did she prioritize her career and a missing boy? What did it amount to? Look at her now. Look at him. Think of Lorel and Shaw.

The halls were empty. Every cell door was open. *The game,* she remembered. Some important spiral game. Not spiral as the Tiralee played it, as Ayn had seen it played from a satellite just before everything unraveled—*an eye,* Ayn thought, *someone lost an eye during that game*—but spiral played inside giant oval tanks inside stadiums. The inmates had been given a break in the morning routine to watch, which worked out for Ayn. She could call the girls and then have her tea in peace.

Zee answered. She looked older, as though a whole turn had passed since Ayn last saw her instead of a single spin. "Fia!" she squeaked in Korial. "Early call! Are you coming home?"

Any little thing different in the universe might mean that her fia was coming home. "Not yet, little girl. How's it there?"

Zee's face collapsed. "Fine."

That was it. She looked older because she was losing hope. Ayn wanted to crawl into a hole. She didn't know what to do or say anymore. "Your sisters please?"

Jackson stepped into the picture and looked at Ayn as he always did on the holo, his head tilted like he was trying to figure out whether she was there in the room or not. He barked, and she jumped. "Damn it, be quiet."

Maya appeared. Her flat black hair was less flat. It was unclean, frayed. Her voice was deadpan. "Hi."

"How are you?" Ayn asked, hot tears in her eyes.

"I don't know," Maya said.

"Me neither. Except I love you. Mycah?"

"Cooking!" Mycah yelled from the kitchen.

"Come here, please," Ayn pleaded.

Orly stuck his snout in, turned and whipped Zee in the face with his tail. She giggled. Still just a kid. There was still hope.

"What?" Mycah said, leaning in, bowl in hand, flour on her face. The cramp in her brow was a dead giveaway that she was dealing with them elsewhere. Ayn remembered it well, that new level of pissed off, that disgust at nature for making this a requirement.

"Just wanted to see you."

"What's going to happen out there?" Maya asked, shoulders slumped, left eye hiding behind her hair.

"Who knows," Ayn replied. "Let's talk about something else."

Zee lit up. "Fia, I fell off my board and scraped my knee real good. Want to see it?"

"No way. Can you be more careful please?"

Maya smirked. "Some boy came asking for Mycah."

Mycah dropped the bowl. "Maya!"

"Fred growled at him, and he ran so fast. It was hilarious."

"I didn't invite him!" Mycah exclaimed, then burst into tears and grabbed onto her little sisters for purchase in this crazy universe. After half a ru of release, she poured out sniffling apologies for losing her cool and for all sorts of other things. They comforted her and shared a laugh at her expense. It was beautiful. It was a milestone moment. Everyone changing. Everyone a little older. Maybe everything was going to be all right.

Gode rolled by behind them, out on the deck. Grinning? Ayn wasn't sure she'd ever seen the man smile. She waved, but he'd turned his head. "When did Gode get back?"

"He isn't," Zee and Maya said in unison.

"Think again. Maybe he'd like some tea."

"I got it," Mycah said, wiping her nose. "Bye."

Ayn was suddenly restless. She needed to get back to work, back to the information game. She'd been sitting around feeling sorry for herself these last few spins. What searches did she have outstanding? What new guards and inmates should she be courting? Where was Daga with more information on the person with the white mask and green eyes? Where was Brava? Maybe she should dangle green eyes in front of him, see how he reacted, trade that for a private in-person meeting with Shaw.

"What are you thinking, Fia?" Zee asked, a woman's intuition in her violet, child's eyes.

Ayn blinked. "Just about you girls. Always. See you next spin." But she wouldn't.

––––––––––

All forty-something of the nineteenth-floor inmates stood packed in front of the wall screen, cursing and cheering. A digital hourglass in the top right corner told Ayn she had about five rus left in her little time oasis. She picked up her pace to the cafeteria.

Iora wasn't there. Must have had the day off. Some skinny guy Ayn didn't recognize was behind the counter chopping vegetables, back to her. He asked her in a gravelly voice and without turning what he could do for her. She placed her order. He made the tea, reached behind him, and put it on the counter. She never saw his face.

She sat in a glass chair out on the glass box balcony and sipped the tea. It tasted off. She'd forgotten to ask for citrus—Iora would have known to put it in—but she wasn't going to waste her last rus of quiet by going back to get a new cup.

The sky was as clear as the water from her dream. The earth was space black, the tree trunks snow white, the leaves blood red, the mud pools emerald green. Ayn swooned. She looked down at her tea, looked past it and through the glass floor to two pools at the base of the tower, darker than the rest, more viscous, the eyes of some underground creature watching her. They called to mind the glowing ones and the white mask.

She took another sip of tea and spit it out. But she'd had enough. The symbol on the cup, the jointed pipe, the logo for the company that serviced the tower, irked her for some reason.

The metal leg, she thought.

Of the half a dozen or so people known to have come in contact with the person, living in a rough semi-circle around Mon Teles, only one recalled seeing anything but that aberrant face, and that one recalled a metal leg. Which troubled Ayn on a very deep level, the more so because she had no idea why.

The tea was working on her stomach now, as the skinny guy from the cafeteria who'd botched it came and sat down next to her. He crossed his legs and looked out the glass wall. His wig was askew. He brushed the hair away from his oversized eyes.

Ayn shook. She was more angry than afraid, but she was plenty of both. Her head split. A blurry streak slashed her peripheral, and a grass fire flared in her gut. "Was it Brava?" she managed, as she keeled over out of the chair and hit the floor.

"Who?" the assassin asked in trilled Korial. "Oh, not sure about him."

"The metal leg," she groaned, pressing palms into the floor and pushing herself up onto hands and knees. Warm blood dripped off the tip of her nose and splatted onto the glass floor, right in the center of one of those green, mud eyes.

"Metal leg?" he asked.

She put a hand on the wall, lifted a knee, and planted a foot. "The mask . . . the green eyes." She just wanted to know.

"Oh! Disguises. She was first, Ravrada. I was second. I saw you at my landing site the very next cycle, by the way. You brought food for the guards. I took some, thank you. You talked to that one Brava. Ravrada was watching you long before that."

Ayn stood and almost fell again. Her stomach was ripping itself apart. "Should have . . . killed me sooner."

"No, it was fun!"

"You're responsible." Blood spilled from her nose and into her mouth. She smiled and bore her bloodied teeth. "You didn't kill me and I . . . got Dawlis on the ship."

He shrugged, but he seemed offended, petulant. "Ravrada didn't tell me he'd arrived. I could have taken him easily. But she'll answer, the lunatic gimp."

Gimp. Disguises.

Ayn stumbled away.

"Wait, describe the feeling!" the assassin requested. "It's a new mix."

Metal leg.

"Is it felt in the veins?"

Ravrada was watching you long before that.

Legless Gode. There in Rivel one spin, rolling by to check in and see what needed fixing, gone the next. There now. With her daughters. That grin from behind the glass door.

One of her legs was dead weight. She dragged it along behind her, past the empty cafeteria toward the pitched voices of her fellow prisoners. A horn sounded the end of the game. The last thing she saw was the girls at the bottom of that pond looking up at her.

30

Radin found sensory deprivation compelling. It made his memories very colorful and very loud. It made fertile space for the visualization of phase three. It challenged him with claustrophobia and itches of madness. He made good use of his time. He almost wished he had more.

It was nothing really, four Qol cycles inside the box, delivered to the launch site by the Qol who'd been turned by Dama, who'd been turned by Ravrada. He'd spent longer periods back home breathing through tubes inside boxes filled with the gooey virra, the eventual shock absorber for his crash landing and also a proxy for the fluid-like cushioning inside this box. He'd also spent fifty-seven cycles, more than half of his trip across the void, inside a cage inside a stone-metal meteor. But that was all before he'd lived on the surface under the infinite sky. Before he'd learned of other worlds. His mind had been greatly expanded and then bottled up. Inside the bottle, it poured out all around him: the dusty tunnels of his Youth and the always hunger; opening his father's neck; his father glowing red with mavzarra radiation even in death; the ecstasy of freedom and of knowing that he would never be hungry again; Koren reaching a hand down to him and telling him she knew his *exact pain*; slashing his fellows to pieces inside the pit and with each life *becoming*; his mother crumpled on the floor; standing at the edge of the crater, glowing red like his father; the rips; the best dust and liquids; any female or male he wanted, oh!; the power; his mother crumpled; the blue spark; the Qol artifact; racing down the winding rivers with the male Kade; his father's fist smashing into his temple; Koren reaching down; the always hunger; his seaside shack; fighting Dawlis on the island. A swirling, shadowed internal world that took no small amount of mental and emotional energy to navigate. But navigate it he did between naps long and short.

The box shook, the inside world collapsed, and Radin's heart thumped. The box lifted. He was being pulled off a shelf by a metal claw and placed on a vehicle, if Ravrada's intelligence proved correct once again. So far, all the feelings fit. The vehicle rolled toward the silo. Qol machines beeped and chirped. They sounded nervous, tentative, as though they sensed something in their midst but were too unsure and too scared to sound their alarms. It was music to Radin. It made him want to destroy them.

The box lifted again, then settled. He was inside the shining, blue-metal, cone-nosed, clipped-winged ship, one of the ones he'd seen rise and fall several times over the bluffs. The hull door hummed closed. A Qol inside said something in a muffled voice, and another laughed. But they had no idea what was so funny.

The launch was nothing compared to the bone-crushing thrust out of Gog's gravity. The cushioning in the box hugged Radin tight, reminding him again of the virra, of injecting it into the cage moments before slamming into Qol, of waking up choking on it, of clawing blindly for the lever, pulling it, and spilling out into the crater.

The cushion released him. He was deaf—no air to carry sound. He fingered his weapon. He knew he was prepared and knew that no amount of visualization could prepare him. But that was good. He would never get to do this again. He wanted to experience it in all its novelty. He hoped for a surprise or two.

Gentle pressure on the soles of his feet meant that the ship was decelerating. Dama would turn on his suit now.

Now.

Any moment.

Dama?

Dama would inject a chemical or crawler into the brain of the ship and blind the cameras inside the hull just long enough for Radin to open the box and slip out.

Dama?

Neon-red characters scrolled down his right lens. Four small green squares appeared in the left.

Good Dama.

He focused on each square and blinked. His suit warmed. His vision blued. The cameras presumably shut their eyes. The box opened. He swam out, a blur of air if anyone had been watching. He closed the box and ducked under the claw as it reached silently into the stacks and plucked another box full of food, parts, whatever. He kicked off the wall toward the open hull door at the rear of the ship. Starry space bloomed around the edges of the satellite outside. A vertical, box-sized slot opened in its near wall, and two jointed arms unfolded and reached for the ship. A guard watched a holo from behind the slanted wind-shield. The other got up from her chair to oversee the delivery. Radin reached the door, grabbed the frame, swung around, and stuck to the outside of the ship. He climbed to the roof, *saw*, let go, and drifted away, paralyzed.

He floated up and across the blue face of heaven. He heard it with-out hearing it, a silent breathing. He dipped his fingers into the ocean, traced the clouds, felt the cold and wet in his soul.

He could only bear it so long. He opened his palms and fired the jets. They made no sound. He clung to the roof and willed his heart to slow.

The satellite arms retracted silently. The guards in the windshield stared in the direction of Gog, and Radin saw it too, big, dull, and lonely. He'd never felt so close to it, so MaGog, so connected: a connector of worlds, a nexus.

He leveled his weapon and fired a charge at the satellite. It stuck. The ship rose, and the satellite slid underneath it and continued on in its orbit. Radin hesitated, fearful of the bliss, then turned his head to Qol and hummed with it again, sipped the salty ocean, breathed the swirling clouds, ran his fingers through the lush green forests of Qona, their future home. He cried for the first time since seeing his mother crumpled. They were tears of gratitude. He was here, alone on the edge of reality, breaking all the rules, making new ones, because of seeing her there. She was the sacrifice that demanded that Radin make one of his father. And *that* moment, more than any other, made him who he was, made all of this possible. That taste of familial blood and freedom.

Dawlis too deserved his gratitude. Dawlis, who'd shattered his collar and then flown off to fulfill Oorroom's vision. Oh, the universe and its clever irony! But Dawlis's romantic message was only partly true. They all made choices, but so did the universe, and there was only one at the center of its thoughts.

The next satellite rolled toward them in its orbit. The ship waited, reversed, and matched the satellite's speed. This one had a laser cannon on either side of its windshield, pointing at Gog. It reached out and collected its box. Radin breathed into the shot and the moment.

He stayed in the moment. He made it timeless, his celestial coronation. He bathed in Qol's energies, soaked them up insatiably. He fired a third charge. The ship accelerated up and away along an arced hypotenuse toward the meridian Ring. They delivered to three more satellites on their way back down to where they started.

Radin took his last look at heaven, then blinked at a square in his lens, zapping the camera inside the hull again. He swam inside and climbed back into the box with a full heart.

———————

He'd told Ravrada to tell Dama to wait until he was back on the surface and settled. He watched from outside his shack. The first satellite popped just above the black, glassy, watery horizon, a tiny spark amongst the stars. A spark in Radin's soul, the soul of four worlds. The second popped to the right, then the third further on, then one above the first and two more above that. It was the greatest thing he'd ever seen.

"Dondante?" Ravrada called.

"Ready," he answered.

They traveled in a wheeled Qol vessel for the remainder of the dark half. They penetrated deep into a forest where the trees swayed and bent in a screaming wind, panicked, crying: *Radin is here! See! Help!* But no one heard and no one saw.

Everything was right; everything was thrumming. And then everything changed.

Dama brushed the blanket of leaves and twigs off the other vessel. Radin and Ravrada were to take it to Qona and wait. But Radin had other plans. "I go alone," he told Ravrada. "The port city on Gala. Have Dama program it."

Ravrada tilted her head. She looked alarmingly unsurprised. "Dondante, yes. There is still some time."

No questions asked, and a smile in her eyes, buried in the false skin.

She knows, Radin thought. About the door. About Ashuwa. Rasmussa told her.

But no, that wasn't it at all.

"Dondante, one development," she said and showed him an image of a woman so intriguing in her expression of the orientation and choices of the universe that later, standing on the edge of the crack inside the cave and looking down into the orange glow, feeling its pull, listening to its call, Radin would tear himself away and put off his travel between worlds.

31

Will sat cross-legged and naked in the pitch-black of their cell facing the stone-metal door and meditating on water, trying to manifest it inside his body. It had been two cycles or so since they were caught. They had yet to hear about phase three or their friend.

He sat in a camping chair on Stinson Beach in Marin County, north of San Franciso. Raider was there, Raider the dog, his great friend. He wrote something down in his little blue book, something about life being like a dream, then cracked the binding of a book about a holographic theory of reality. But he didn't get past the epigraph, which promised an explanation for paranormal phenomena and synchronicity. See, because he'd become very sensitive to synchronicity of late, and he experienced the worst of them right then and there. A bee landed on the book, walked across those fateful lines, then flew off. It was the third bee to show up recently in his increasingly batshit crazy life. Three too many. He slammed the book shut, stuffed it into his backpack, and never looked at it again. But he knew a thing or two about it, because a professor from that school—*that school, that school, oh yeah, the Center for Holistic Studies*—had read a few excerpts from it in order to whet her students' appetites for alternate realities. One was about a woman who didn't eat for twenty-five years. She manifested nutrients with her mind.

Will was attempting the same, but his stomach was a desert-dry, shriveled sack eating itself. His shoulders and spine were curling over one micro-fiber at a time. But he didn't stop. He kept trying to make water and food molecules. He kept sending his intention out on the holographic airwaves, two Vrrgrrul words and two English ones: *Garra butterfly, garra squid.* We are the butterfly. We are the squid. He broadcasted through the rock, which was mostly empty space just like everything else.

Kade was passed out. He'd exhausted himself again arguing with his selves. It was a difficult thing to listen to, and all of Will's attempts to communicate with these *others* had fallen on the deaf ears they shared. But he'd come to accept it, because he'd come to know the *others'* purpose, one of them anyway. It was how he knew they would get out of there. The giant woman on the beach and her stick structure. She, Kade, had described it to herself on more than one occasion as a web. But it wasn't a web. It was a map of this maze. The part they were in now. Without suits or goggles, they were going to need it.

So, the question wasn't when the door would open; it would have to be before either of them died of thirst. The question was who would open it.

But Koren? She cast doubt on everything. She cast certainty of death. She stepped in, shoulders to the ceiling, arms akimbo, elbows sharp beneath her robes, trroorra torch in one skeletal hand, black-bladed scythe in the other. She sat on the square block in the corner, the cell's only furnishing. Her knees came up to her chest. Will stood up, bared himself, far more afraid than he expected to be. Her head was intensely long from this distance. Her eyes were eight balls without the white pupils. She reached into her robe. Kade struggled up onto his haunches, ten fingers splayed on the ground, eyes down. She put a vile to her thin nose and sucked on yellow dust. She tucked the vile back in, took out Will's wrist device, and back-handed it to him. He put it on, otherwise dressed as he was born. "I agree," she said in metallic, whirring Vrrgrrul. Will read the translation floating above his wrist. "Our lives are made up of our choices." She spun her scythe. It scraped the ceiling. "Tell me about you. Something relevant."

Will sensed the gravity of the event horizons of her eyes, and so it was too late.

Only human, he thought. *Hurt. Desperate for love. Just doing what she thinks she has to for her people. Just trying to make sense of this life like everyone else.*

That was all, and that was everything. He didn't know what to say.

-- I came to see you. --

And here he was. He hated her, and he loved her. He felt what they felt. He felt MaGog.

Kade spun him around. He wavered, stumbled, steadied. He looked at his friend, who was looking past him, toward Koren but down. Will loved him. Will would have died more than just the once without him. Will turned back to Koren and fixed his gaze on the scars crossing her protruding throat.

-- I think it's all a blend. -- he wrote, regaining his mind, his handle, his intuition.

-- Life. Of random and purpose. --

She read his floating words, shrugged her mountain-peak shoulders. "I don't believe in luck. You've been saying it yourself. Your side made choices. I made them too. It's your purpose against mine."

-- What about MaGog? --

"My purpose is theirs. They choose me."

Will chose sympathy and flattery. He reminded himself that he was dealing with megalomania and other psychoses.

-- You have some good ideas. You've done a lot for them. --

Her throat fans made a curious *hmmm.*

-- Your conviction and execution have been incredibly strong. I just wonder at stealing and killing instead of negotiating. --

"You'd have to know the history."

-- I learned as much as I could on the way here. --

"Then you know that they led with murder. That was their choice."

-- Qol scholars debate that. --

The tone of her fans tinted minor. "They weren't there."

-- I'll tell you something about myself. --

"Do."

-- I didn't choose to be lost for most of my life. --

He struck the chord, the infected nerve, that which drove her to launch a man in a meteor to kill him as a child, then again. The rumor. Oorroom's prophecy of a lost boy who would come for her. She smiled a mix of rotting teeth and sharpened stones. "He'll die slowly for spreading that lie, though I want him to see his error first. I was concerned about you, it's clear. But don't worry, I had a better reason for sending them. I'm surprised you made it here, but look at you."

-- I'm still alive. --

She scraped the ceiling with her blade again. Kade stood slowly. His bones creaked. He breathed on Will's left shoulder.

"You're in the dark," she said. "You have no bearing on anything in the end. That other reason: half of your Ring satellites are gone. It was Radin with help from the other two I sent. You couldn't kill him, too bad. The guard will panic and do exactly what I want them to. Just like the ships above us. They'll bring the remaining satellites together to stare and point their lasers in one direction. In case any ships in the fleet they expect to launch make it across."

Will swallowed.

Expect to launch.

"Another thing."

He braced himself.

"Ayn is dead. She also surprised me, I admit."

Kade stepped sideways and threw a wave. Koren ducked behind her forearms and fists, clenched her core, and just took it. A sharp black blur split the space between Will and Kade, cut sparks from the stone floor, and rang their ears. They hardly saw it. "No," she said. "I choose. Live a little longer. We're so close." She laughed as though at her own joke, a sound like a mad machine, stark raving.

Kade lay in a corner hugging his knees, eyes closed. He was preparing to die, settling down. He reminded Will of George's cat Boxer, killer of ten thousand chipmunks, dodger of owls and coyotes and coy wolves, revered by humans, cats, and dogs alike in the yards and woods of their Great Smokey Mountains foothill town. One day at dusk, in keeping with her circadian rhythm, Boxer sauntered into the kitchen, yawned and arched her back, sipped her water, ate some breakfast, meowed at the door, and then sauntered outside into her domain. She came home the next morning with a chunk missing from her side and a limp. George had always said that it would happen this way eventually. Will had always replied, well, they should keep her inside then, and George had always countered with, that would only piss her off and she'd shit on the rugs. She slept that day away and went out again at dusk and didn't look back.

Will sat down beside his friend, who was also a woman on a beach and several other people, and thought that maybe he was ready to settle down too. He found it amusing and merciless, the irony of his misinterpretation. The stick structure was not their salvation. It was not a map. The woman had been showing them their future, their death, a symbol of where it would happen.

Will remembered being dead. The two doors. Behind the first, the mountains, canyon, river, and butterfly that he'd made with his thoughts, which were made of sparkling light. Behind the second, the squid squeezing a bloated human carcass and reaching for him with one oozing tentacle. Heaven or the hard, soiled real worlds.

Choose.

He regretted nothing. He just hoped they'd made a difference.

He'd come this close to dying of thirst once before, in Needle Valley. The rain saved him then. This time it was Oorroom.

He was as much a living fossil as his sister but was childlike in his movements, fidgety, excitable. He wore a gaping, tongueless smile. He had eyes somewhere in size between Koren's and your everyday MaGog fellow's. He held their suits, wrist devices, and xims to his chest. Will thought of Peis for the first time in what seemed like a great long time. He pictured the two seers as poles on a tuning fork.

Oorroom dropped the bundle, scurried back out into the hall, and returned with a stone jug of water and a sack of dried pulge. Will and Kade shoved the salty leaf into their mouths and took turns chugging as they dressed.

Oorroom closed the door and rocked heal-to-toe. He took a wafer out of his robe and moaned with anticipation. Will zipped up his hood, blinked on his goggles, and took the wafer from the illurrur's out-stretched, cadaverous hand. Kade looked over his left shoulder. Their goggles translated the dots and dashes into English, running down their right lenses:

"She's my sister. I see her energy clearest of anyone's. I saw her death."

The tuning fork rang a two-note chord in Will's head.

"I saw you being born. I stood in the window. I felt a breeze and heard a squeak. A metal bird on the roof. Spiked blue fruit in the trees."

Will turned an ear to Kade.

"Shaw made it," he said. "The weathervane, Mind."

"Cracked mirror, mate!" the British prisoner bleated.

Kade, himself again, said, "The fruit grows in the forest surrounding Trill, nowhere else on Qol."

They leaned against each other, held each other up, read:

"I saw the blue world make a ring around Gorr then the number eighteen. Then the snowy crown of Damarra and you coming out of the white with three beasts of white. You sitting on an island looking at a lone mountain. You staring out the window of a ship coming here. You standing over her as she dies."

Must I? Will thought.

"I loved her. I told her because I hoped something could be done to stop it. She offered me my life for my tongue. A warning not to tell. I stayed by her side to watch it all unfold. I laughed when Ravrada failed and you disappeared as a child. I laughed when you came back and Radin failed."

-- Ravrada? -- Will type to Kade.

"The first MaGog to land," Kade said. "Must be."

Crashed into Fentum in a meteor. Arrived and befriended the Fenti and sent them after child Will.

"I laughed when Radin failed," said the dots and dashes. "But I set him free by telling him everything I saw, the only one besides her. Until recently." Until ratting her out to MaGog finally, spreading the rumor. To fluster her? Fluster them? To stir the destiny pot? "She sent him and the other two to end a threat to MaGog. She would never reveal that you were a threat to *her*. She will die not accepting that. It has driven her mad and made me laugh. All her life bent on something she's known deep inside she can never achieve."

Will handed the wafer back.

-- Where is she? --

Oorroom read the floating words as they morphed into Vrrgrrul above Will's wrist. He squealed with pleasure and opened the door.

The tunnels were empty. Maybe they were deep enough in the maze that Koren felt safe. Maybe she preferred to be alone in this space. They turned a corner. White light flickered from behind an open doorway at the end of a long hallway. Oorroom felt around like a blind man. Will held out his arm. The illurrur squeezed it and pointed to the door, tears of demented joy in his eyes. He was standing on his life's pinnacle. He was living his own prophecy, ferrying it along. Will patted him on his bony back and led Kade down the hall.

A compound eye grew in the door as they approached, bulging black and white lenses big and small, a dozen, then dozens. She paced into view, planting her scythe with each step as though planting a flag—*smash, smash*—stone-metal on stone. She spun and marched back across the corneas of the eye of the nervous system that she'd strung through the underworld. A pole connected to the seeing wall by a braid of wires had to be her microphone. Koren: skilled orator or ranting psychopath, depending on which Qol scholar told it. In either case, she'd made fair use of the technology stripped from that first Qol ship.

Will rolled camera and stepped inside. He scanned the eye, starting in the middle and then radiating out. He captured an empty mine, a bustling farm, a jam-packed common, an empty cart station, crowded tunnels that might have been right there in Zone 3, a big dead screen high and to the left. No, not dead. Little pricks of light in the black. Will turned off his camouflage.

-- I lost my mother too. --

She stopped short, turned her head slowly, read, then resumed her pacing. "You want to know why?" she crooned in Vrrgrrul. "You want to understand what you came up against? I find I want to tell you."

Confess, Will thought.

"The Qols killed her. The first to come. I saw it happen."

I'm so sorry.

For her. For all of them. For the mistakes and the chains of events.

"My father attacked them. The Qols were defending themselves."

So, Monte lo ara Bige, the estranged, contrarian Qol academic, had been wrong about that critical fork in the road. Gog had fired first. But he'd been right about Koren being the daughter of the Marradar who'd set the course. And Will didn't have to ask whether she'd killed her father for the actions that led to her mother's death. That debate was settled in his mind.

Neon-purple Kade took a few quiet steps to the left and closer to the eye. Koren paused beneath the black, star-speckled screen, as the silver nose of a Qol battleship pierced the right side of it and drifted toward the center. She took the vile from her robe and ripped dust up both nostrils. White lips spread over her cragged grill. "Come see. Closer."

Will followed her along the wall, mindful of the extensive range of those arms and that scythe. Screens flickered on the ends of frayed neurons. Others were murky with cataracts. A smallish one at the height of her shoulders was crystal clear. She stopped in front of it, blocking it, but not before Dawlis saw something missing. She spun her scythe. "You know the history? You know that the Marradar destroyed the rocket site to prevent me from taking it? They didn't. I staged it."

Will felt as he had at rare moments in his life when reading the ends of great novels or watching the ends of great films, when all the subtlety of plot development, character arc, and sensory experience fuse into a point of revelation, his emotions summed up in three words: *Of course*, and *Bravo*.

The destruction of the rocket site, the event that had set Gog so far back in the mind of the Qols and had allowed them to believe all this time that they were safe. Faked. Fictitious. The keystone lie Koren had built her society to protect. It was remarkable and remarkably sad. So much pain and effort. She was a hurt, scared, ambitious, psychotic girl.

-- You could have gone yourself if you did it differently. --

She hummed a smile.

Will pictured his mother, Lorel, standing beside Koren, just as he'd pictured Peis beside Oorroom. He saw himself next to Radin. Each a pair of opposite poles on a magnet.

He recalled a dream, from before the bee dream, of two screws, *his*, coming unscrewed. They were now spinning back into his skull.

He was down in a hole in Koren's eyes.

Kade yanked him out by the arm.

She smiled and stepped aside, revealing the screen where something was missing. A vast cavern. A forest of stone-metal beams. Trestles. Empty but for a lonely pod of cone-shaped rockets off in the distance.

Oh, no.

A blue-green light scorched Will's retinas. Kade's xim trembled beneath the black blade. They jumped back. Will threw a wave. Koren dropped her head behind her forearms and moaned like she liked it. "You know the history?" she screeched, standing tall again. "You know?" She laughed then and couldn't stop.

The fleet they expect to launch.

"Electricity!" her serrated cry. "The great gift of the first ship. They're still alive, you know, the two pilots. The Marradar tortured them for the ship's secrets. They were shattered when I rescued them. I gave them all the comforts. You know the history? The storms above our spiked mountain to the south?"

The praying hands.

The lightning flashes that took down a Qol satellite long enough for Koren to launch Radin and his party. Bige was right again. She didn't wait for those storms to wreak havoc. She wreaked it.

"Picture it," she whirred. "Great metal coils inside the peaks. Metal rings sliding down and around the coils, and the electricity rising and firing. So simple. Such pure, fundamental power. You see now, I can tell!"

Will did. Koren would not have shown her cards, would not have spent the brief period of that invaluable satellite shutdown to launch only a few dozen ships, even if one was pregnant with a meteor and her greatest fighter. The fleet was gone. It left when Radin did. It was some-where out there. Radin was fresh off decimating the Rings, and the Qol ships were here because Koren wanted them here. And what would they do when they found out about the Gog fleet? Carve up Zone 3 and risk slaughter just to take out a handful of ships? No, they'd turn around and play chase, behind by the length of the void.

"Truce. Just a little longer," she coaxed.

-- Alive. -- Will typed to Kade then turned on his camouflage and attacked with arc and wave. She backed up to the flickering, twitching eye and made a blurry black wall with her blade.

"Yes!" she mecha-brayed.

Lightning cracked the big black screen, three strikes fired from three fingertips of the praying hands. A Qol ship in the foreground dipped its nose and sank.

"Hold! Truce! Watch!"

Will breathed into his breaking heart. He'd failed: the death toll.

Another ship fired thick blue lasers at the mountain and sliced off two fingers. Koren cackled. Kade went low. She heard him or saw his warble in the strobe. Her speed was hard to perceive. Her strength was that of petrified bones and tree-flesh muscles. "Hold!" she pleaded, leaping aside like she was a quarter of her eighty Earth years. "Closer!"

She jumped and smacked another dark screen with her blade. Centered in it were three flat-tipped triangles of negative space surrounded by stars. Three volcanoes. The ones Gideon had seen in that eruption of awareness three hundred turns past, that instantaneous expansion of life and consciousness. If he could see them know.

"Wait!" she begged. "Wait. Wait. There!"

A string of purple sparks made a beaded necklace around the center volcano and lifted off its shoulders. A second necklace, lower down, rose. A third, lower still, rose. Black ships ascended on purple tails of fire and melded into a swarm of fireflies.

"Back here!" Koren cried, jabbing her weapon at the other night scene, as another Qol ship fell out of the sky and the last one fired at the swarm.

"There again!"

The Gog ships spit red sparks in a shotgun spray.

"Here!"

The Qol ships took shotgun fire.

"This one!"

The pod of rockets in the far corner of the mostly empty hangar lifted on purple flares, up through the trestles.

"Try and deny it!"

Will couldn't.

"Picture Qol. See it! The last satellites coming together in fear. Staring straight on. Always straight on! And the fleet coming up from the bottom."

Will no longer felt the awe. This was nothing but death. This was just one more mass tragedy born from one more leader's certifiable insecurity.

A screen above her ridged head showed a tunnel packed with clueless fellows, desperate decoys, pawns their entire lives, duped, decided for, manipulated. In the one above that was the final deception. Will turned off his camo and pointed to it, dialed up a precision rage. She followed his finger, grinned. "They needed to believe I wasn't going."

You're not, he thought.

It was the Qol ship, the first one. But it was not the cherry on top of her plan, executed to perfection over generations. It was the last piece of his, seeded on a muddy shore in Nima in the aftermath of his death and grown since then of its own fractal intelligence. He pointed to the ship once more, alive and well, warming up in its garage, then pointed to himself.

Maybe she saw it then, saw it all come crashing down, saw him standing over her like in her brother's vision. Maybe she didn't think it was so funny anymore that he and Kade had made it this far.

Will turned his camo back on. Koren backed up to the eye, bent her knees, wrung the well-worn shaft of her scythe, watched, listened.

--Alive. You go.--

Kade threw a wave at her legs and an arc at her head. One leg splayed, but she swatted the arc away and regained her footing. She made a wall with her blade, snorting like a bull.

--Again.--

She took his waves like a heavyweight, cut his arcs in half. A stone-metal chip shattered a screen.

--Again.--

Kade fired and threw. She was equal to all of it. She didn't wear down like Will hoped she would. But she got angry. Fed up. Late for her ride.

Will didn't move, didn't disturb the air but for typing with the holo-ball. He lulled her into the prospect of dealing with them one at a time. She went berserk on Kade. Will tip-toed up behind her and took off her left leg at the knee. It fell out of her slashed robe. She hopped back-ward and lacerated their eardrums with the angry, metallic screams of a tyrant losing control. Kade went for her neck, but Will blocked the arc with one of his own and pulled Kade out of the room. In the tunnel, Will gripped him by the back of the neck and stared into his neon-purple-rimmed black goggles.

--The sticks on the beach are a map. You have to follow it and get us out of here.--

But he didn't have to. Oorroom waved them on. Oorroom had been preparing for this eventuality for a long time.

Kade nodded to himself as though agreeing with a voice in his head. "This isn't it."

32

They sped along the greased tracks of Koren's express line, Oorroom driving, Dawlis in the cart behind the illurrur, and Kade behind Dawlis, hallucinating.

She was a hoverbird slaloming tree trunks. Her pebble heart fluttered as fast as her wings. Something was coming. It was time. For what she didn't know. She just knew with all her bird instincts that it was time.

He was a father weeping, heart and soul torn to shreds. He was kissing his dead girls all over their faces and saying all the things to his dead woman that he should have said.

He was covered in scales and walking alone on an ancient world beneath two blazing red suns.

She was lying at the edge of a cliff and dropping stones into the mist, calm in the knowledge that the cure for her broken heart was just a step away.

He was a prisoner trying to squeeze his head through the bars of his cell, bloody scrapes across his temples, screaming in English in a British accent, "Cracked mirror, mate, hahaha!"

He was in a cart on planet Gog, burning with revelation, the revelation of perspective, of *being* other people, of thinking their thoughts and feeling their pain. It was Dawlis's message all along: We're the same only different, and we can choose to remember that.

These encounters with the *others* needn't have been more than that, that penetrating, self-destroying, self-recreating lesson in empathy. But they *were* more.

The bird had been waiting, and the bird had a job to do, one that mattered, maybe a lot, maybe so much that none of this would ever happen if she didn't get it done. The one with the scales, he also knew something of the future. The prisoner knew something about the past. The father and the girl knew the greatest kinds of love and suffering.

But the woman giant on the beach. The sticks. If they weren't a map, then what?

Find flight on the edge.

She'd been right about that. Their way out of this nightmare was on the edge of the hive, somewhere in Zone 4 where Koren had sent Droodroovid and thirty glome. But if that was an impressive prediction it was also a useless one, for it was Dawlis who'd spotted the Qol ship on that screen, and it was Koren's tongueless prophet brother now escorting them to it.

But they weren't home yet, and the giant would soon assert herself. Oorroom knew where to go, but even he wasn't privy to the eleventh-hour expansion Koren had been running out there on the fringe.

They decelerated into a neatly bored, dead-end station with a single walking tunnel in the far wall and a glome on either side of the mouth. Another version of reality overlaid in sepia separated out. Neon-purple (brown) Dawlis gassed both (all four) of the glome, then grabbed Kade's hand and pulled him into the tunnel. The two realities collapsed back into one.

Oorroom led with confidence through the first intersection (unguarded), but he looked troubled at the second (Dawlis gassed the two glome), as though there were more tunnels to choose from than he remembered, and he looked utterly lost and betrayed at the third (unguarded). He turned in a circle. He panicked. A one-armed male stepped from a tunnel left of center. Dawlis turned off his suit, held up his hands, and raised a message. The words shifted in Kade's goggles, blurred, doubled: -- We know. Help us. We'll take you with us. --

The male looked from Oorroom to Dawlis, shook his head, and curled his fist into a ball down by his side. He had the bitter look of someone who could no longer be surprised. He spit at Oorroom, then bolted.

Dawlis grabbed Kade's hand, and they ran. Oorroom ambled after them, bleating miserably, begging them not to leave him behind. But he was not the physical anomaly his sister was, and his wails and shuffling footsteps soon faded.

Dawlis let go of Kade and grabbed the male's arm. The male swung him into a wall. He hit the ground. Kade kept going, kept his camo on. His vision and hearing tremored: the sepia reality, superimposed again. Which was real? Which held the real one-armed MaGog? He stopped at the next intersection, shoved his thumbs into his eyes, clenched his teeth, screamed back the other world, listened in this one, caught the male's footsteps, pointed left as Dawlis sprinted past him.

The ground was hard but not stone. It was hazy brown. Dawlis stepped in front of Kade and stopped short, raised his shield. It crackled under a barrage of red fireballs. Kade buried his head in between Dawlis's shoulder blades, and they drove forward. Dawlis handled the glome, but they'd lost time and lost the trail.

--Kade? --

He knew. The stick map, they needed it now. He closed his eyes and saw it, a crooked scaffold towering over him, wavy and incorporeal. Then he was inside a hollowed branch, standing on a swirling knot. Ahead was a gnarled joint.

"That way," he said, pointing, eyes shut but open to the other place. Dawlis took his hand and led.

Kade rose out of the stick, out of himself. The map branched off into mist, tending toward an unseen apex. It shuddered in the wind.

Kade chose, pointed, ran through the wood, pulled by Dawlis's disembodied hand, reaching him from the other side.

The wood and his head fractured.

He awoke to Dawlis slapping him in the face and a message in his glasses:

-- Get up. You can do it. You have to. --

Kade the woman giant drove her brick fists into the sand, pushed herself up, and looked down on her web and the two insect-sized men crawling inside it. "Second right!" she boomed.

They took the second tunnel on the right.

"First left!" she cried at the next intersection. "Third left!" at the next, her calls wild and joyful. They reached the apex, and she threw her head back and laughed. Kade's head cleared, and he was never her again.

They followed a trail of blood around a corner. Hrulora and Droodroovid were hiding behind a door at the end of a tunnel. They saw Dawlis, and their mouths dropped open. They pointed inside. Kade, invisible, took his place on Dawlis's left flank. They stepped in. The Qol ship, dull silver with rusty seams, sat humming with its ramp open and its nose pointed into the mouth of a wide tunnel on the far side of its garage. The one-armed male swung a pickaxe at a one-legged Koren, propped up on her scythe at the base of the ramp. She'd caught up during the time they'd lost in the maze. But Kade was pretty sure that it didn't matter at this point.

"Stay! Why?" the male cried. He gave Koren trouble. He was fast, strong, and desperate. But she was more of all those things, and she cut a line across his chest.

She spotted Dawlis and screamed to a dozen stunned glome to do something, as she hobbled up the ramp. But Dawlis went invisible again, and the glome seemed reluctant to try their luck against the Qol ghosts on behalf of the leader now abandoning them.

Dawlis hit her in the back with a wave and stepped to the side of the ramp. She fell forward into her planted scythe. Kade charged. She turned on her last leg, and Dawlis lopped it off. Her back cracked on the edge of the ramp. Her head hit the floor with a thud.

Dawlis turned off his camo and stood over her. She growled. She got up onto her forearms and started dragging her legless body away. No fellows moved or breathed. Dawlis stepped over her and up the ramp.

--Stay here.-- he typed to Kade, and passed into the ship.

Kade turned off his camo and raised his xim to the few glome edging forward. The rest were gathered around the one-armed male. Hrulora was down on her knees cradling his head and yelling for cloth and water. Droodroovid stood beside them staring at the ship with the great longing of his people.

Dawlis stepped out, pointed to Hrulora, Droodroovid, and the one-armed male. He projected: --Those three and two more.--

They were confused. They struggled to accept what was happening here, that the Qol ship was in one piece and might take them to the blue star, that Koren was dying in front of them. The one-arm male said something to Hrulora, who lifted him up by his half-arm. The curved slice on his chest seeped. A glome took his other arm. Two others came with cloth and water. He grimaced as Hrulora cleaned his wound. "Leave," he said to Dawlis in Vrrgrrul.

--None of you?--

A female stepped forward, head bowed as though ashamed to be one of the lucky ones, as though bracing for her fellows' protests. There were none.

--Lay it down.--

She laid down her heat weapon and climbed aboard.

Another stepped up. Droodroovid took Hrulora by the hand and tried to pull her toward the ship, but she pulled him back, kissed his scarred face, then gently pushed him away. She tightened her grip on the male's half-arm and fingered a dark pendant hanging from a string around her neck.

Dawlis nodded to her. She nodded back. Two more fellows came. No protests, only sighs.

Koren, a legless, twisted sack of bones, screamed metallic. True to her word in the end, she was staying.

33

Radin sat on the windowsill in Rasmussa's rented room in the port city watching on the holo projected from his wrist device and laughing from his belly. The harried, panicked, pieced-together footage. The shaking voices that kept asking themselves and each other how and why and who was to blame. Pure comedy. He leaned out of the window, took a big, long whiff of ocean air, then a fulsome rip of dust.

He was on Gala, farthest continent southwest, opposite Damarra, where Dawlis had apparently reentered this world. The footage was of Qona, which was northwest of Gala by the width of a narrow sea. Qona was smallish, mountainous, and tear shaped. It was covered in dark virgin forest and surrounded by sheer brown cliffs. It was cold and wet or stiflingly hot and humid, with little in between. It was outside of the Cooperative, and it now counted among its sparse, rugged population several thousand fellows.

Of the three hundred ships launched at the same time as Radin's force, thirty had flown straight at what was left of the Ring satellites, which had assembled to fend off what the guard would regret to learn was a sacrificial front. The rest, which had many cycles ago dipped down below the line of Qol's southern pole and slowed their pace, decay clocks synchronized, rose from underneath the blue world and made a constellation of craters in the dank Qona timberland. Radin watched it a few more times with a full heart. He then moved on to even bigger and better things.

Five cycles of perilous hiking later, by way of the jagged line on Rasmussa's map, he came to the mountain village in the Gontomon where Dawlis's father, Shaw, had spent half of his life waiting for his son to return. Three cycles after that, Rasmussa's tool, his gravity compass, began to point. Half a cycle more, and Radin was standing before the mouth of the cave. A beast lumbered out on four legs ('Each is guarded by people, secrets, culture, the land, an animal, a spirit,' Rasmussa had said of the passages. 'Agents of these energies, friend.'), covered in hair, shoulders nearly as tall as Radin. The Ursi, according to the local legends. Its head was colossal. Its eyes smoldered. Gaping, triangle ears twitched. Foaming at the mouth, it stood on its hind legs and roared and slashed at him with giant, bladed paws. Radin cut one off, then a tree-trunk leg, then the head. The latter took a few hard strokes, and the Ursi gargled in protest to the last. Radin smiled, wiped his blade on the Ursi's back, then stepped around it.

Deep inside the cave was the hole. Deep inside the hole was an orange glow like another world in space, Ashuwa. It welcomed him, pulled him. It told him in some language of light: *I've waited for you.*

He backed out of its gravity well. There was time. He knew where it was now, and Rasmussa posed no risk of revealing it to anyone else. Rasmussa was rotting in that room. Even if Ravrada knew something about it—*someone* had been to the port not long ago and tried for Shaw— she could never hobble through this range. Why not wait for Dawlis? It would be good to see him again. They could trade stories. Radin could complete phase one.

So, after crossing continents and mountains and finding the passage, Radin reversed course, having convinced himself it was for the chance of seeing his nemesis one more time.

———

He lived three cycles on the outskirts of Mon Teles. He slept during the light half and stalked the treehomes and glass towers by dark. He saw her once. That was all it took.

He was high in a tree watching the center, blue tower. A black vessel hovered into the thin, circular clearing surrounding it. He zoomed in through his goggles. Three guards stepped out of the vessel, then the one named Brava, then the other woman, the mother. Then her.

Alarm bells rang in Radin's head. A thrilling, foreign drum beat in his chest!

34

Kade the hoverbird darted through the trees. She paused, hovered, listened. She rose up over the forest, hovered, listened. Nothing yet. She felt compelled to bring the light another seed. She dipped her thin beak into a pod on a high branch, plucked a seed, dropped into the trees again, and raced for the cave. She left the seed in the growing pile at the edge of the crack and looked down into it, charging her spirit with the orange glow. It hummed, spoke to her. It was getting louder.

She roamed. She listened. She brought the light more seeds. Then she heard it. To Kade the bird it was the angry, tenor call in the distance of a rarely seen animal. Several of them. To Kade the human in another time and place it was a name being yelled: *Ingeo!* What other noises the animals/people made meant nothing to either version of Kade. Just those three syllables.

Kade the bird whizzed through the forest in the direction of the animals. She found one, and Kade the human helped her understand that this animal *was* the call. It was what the light had been telling her all along.

She led Ingeo to the light. The other animals came after him, and she dove at their eyes. She turned, and Ingeo was gone. The hill quaked and collapsed. Kade the human lost consciousness.

———

He awoke two Qol spin-equivalents later stuck to a wall, upright in a sleep sack (this old ship didn't have simulated gravity). He knew the name Ingeo. It confirmed what he'd come to suspect when the stick map turned out to be real. They were never personalities he'd invented to manage his trauma.

35

Will floated mindlessly. He was afraid of having a mind, of having thoughts. His head bumped up against the ceiling. He struggled to breathe. He was weightless, and yet he felt a crushing weight on his chest like the gravity of three worlds pressing down on him. He tortured himself by asking himself over and over, *What for?* and *What now?*

His goggles, floating in a high corner of the pilots' bunk room (which he had to himself; Kade no longer insisted on them sleeping in the same room, and the pilots never left their chairs) blinked. He had a signal. The first since before the underworld. So he thought.

It was a message from Nopa from a few Gog cycles ago. They would have been in the cell at the time.

Mute, I got your videos and leaked them. Don't know why I did it. Not sure what you expected to happen. I didn't message earlier because this amounts to a confession, but I don't care anymore. This all got out of hand very quickly.

You picked up a little following back home. I guess some people are into creepy videos of invisible men gassing MaGog, preaching to them, and then leaving a symbol of a made-up animal. Can't tell you I'm one.

Those calling for restraint have made use of you. Honestly, though, it's been hard for anyone on this ship to get on that side. Seventeen dead from when we went down. Over a hundred on the other ships and a ton of injuries. Try telling their families that MaGog deserves a choice. Try telling the families of the satellite operators that just got blown up.

Anyway, none of this is on you. You tried at least. Tried something different. I hope something comes of it. Who knows what they'll do to me for helping. Mixed emotions, you know? Maybe we can get that drink sometime.

Yeah, Will thought, *mixed emotions.*

He missed Kade very badly. Droodroovid floated into the room, scratched a worm scar beneath his left eye. "They're asking for you," he said in Vrrgrrul. Kade swam up behind him, clear-eyed, himself. They went together to the cockpit.

The two pilots, gaunt, wrinkled, colorless, toothless, random whisps of gray hair standing up in zero gravity, turned as they tended to—slow and at the same time—and looked at Will and Kade as they tended to—like they weren't real. One put a vile of dust to his meatless nose and pulled liberally. The other pointed to the blinking holo column in the center of the room and mumbled what they'd been waiting to hear: "The Council."

Eight of them sat in blue glass chairs around a blue glass table. The ninth chair was empty. Will and Kade would learn that it had once belonged to the representative from Findo, famous for his encyclopedic knowledge of Qol and Gog histories, his spotty attention span, and his erratic behavior. He'd made the seemingly innocuous decision to visit the artifact at the top of the tower on the night that Radin climbed in to take it. Or he'd helped Radin break in and had been helping Gog all along, expecting some reward and receiving the black blade instead. But that debate would rage long and ugly.

A severe-looking woman at the near head of the table introduced herself in Korial as Venn din sa Kinto, representative from Damarra.

She had flat, gleaming white hair down to her shoulders and sharp gray eyes. Flames circled the cuffs of her otherwise white suit.

Kade spoke for them: "Kade ru sy Bhomik. Dawlis lo sha."

Will wiped his tears and sweaty brow and read from his wrist device.

"Never chose your last name," Venn said to him. "We'll come to that."

Maybe we should, he thought.

Maybe he was ready to spill the beans about where he'd spent eighteen Qol turns.

Venn crossed her legs. "There is disagreement in this room as to whether you saved any MaGog lives," she said and let that sink in.

It did. It dug its nails into Will's heart.

"There is disagreement too as to whether you are responsible for dozens of guard lives."

A bald, flabby, black-eyebrowed, blue-suited man at the far end of the table drawled: "There is less disagreement about that."

Will felt the punishing weight. He stuttered and stammered before remembering he couldn't speak. He typed:

-- They're no different. No one wants to fight if they have a real chance at something better. Fighting was Koren's agenda, and you know it. You've known it for a long time. Now she's gone. --

Noses were scratched. Glasses of water were sipped. Surely they'd watched it all through his googles. Stood over her as he had. Venn clasped her hands in her lap. "You're questioning starts now, and it starts at the beginning. Where were you all that time that you didn't choose your last name?"

Will decided they weren't ready.

-- You won't hear about that part of my life unless I trust you. I'm open to it. It depends on what you do. Lead with empathy, despite everything. Remember that she was a tyrant. She was insane. You weren't there. I'll tell you everything starting with the Shole. --

Reliving it exhausted him. He was desperate for sleep, but Kade followed him back to the pilot's room. They floated before each other.

-- What is it? --

"They're past lives," Kade said in English.

Will heard it. Processing it was a different thing.

-- Past lives? --

"I was the bird again. I guided Ingeo to a passage."

-- How do I know that name? --

"Gideon's assistant."

-- A passage --

"Yes."

-- They're not personalities? Or dreams? --

"They're past lives."

Wait, Will thought.

-- Ingeo went through a passage? --

Time did a trick, and things came together:

In the clearing outside Peis's cave, at night, around a fire, the prophet told them what he'd found in a yellow-paged book concerning the symbol of orange gems. It was called Nuvium, which meant light path or light map. Eamon had seen it in a vision. Eamon was the Chief, the Kyut shaman who'd marched his people across the Shole in reverse of Will's eventual path, dug the cave in the rock wall at Needle Lake, then placed the symbol in a hole in the back. The traveler, the skeleton in the stone grave by the ridge on the Shole, had also been to the cave. He'd left his bird signature, left his rope, then risked the Shole and died holding his journal, which was written in Korial but was written, Will had believed all this time, for him.

On the left wall of the cave were black-tar frescoes depicting key moments in the Chief's journey. On the right were moments in Will's future, including his death. On the back was an image of Eamon sitting on the boulder in the middle of Needle Lake and looking up at a star, the Pymm, the Guide. On either side of him was a curved line, a bump, a hill. Inside each hill was a black dot, a cave, the one Will came out of and a third. Three caves in Needle Valley, which was not far from Teles, which was where Gideon saw what he saw and was burned for it. Where Ingeo saw too. Ingeo, who escaped with the knowledge and set it loose in Qol's collective consciousness. Kade, as a bird in a past life, had found Ingeo in Needle Valley and led him to the passage in the third cave.

-- Which leads to Earth? --

Kade picked up Will's train of thought without having to slow it down or back it up. It was clear he'd already run his mind around this same figure-eight track. He shrugged. "Perhaps."

Will didn't dare say it out loud: A *way back*.

Instead he typed: -- Ingeo was the traveler. --

Which meant that Ingeo had been *there*, in the hills of San Francisco, back when the redwoods were virgin and the Ohlone fished the bay from tule boats, foraged on Angel Island, and prayed to the Coyote, the Eagle, and the Hummingbird. But how did Will know all that? He remembered being dead and knowing everything.

"Who?" Kade asked.

Will told Kade about the traveler and the journal for the first time. He said they needed to go back to the island and get it. They didn't know that Piper already had.

Will grew sicker the closer they got to Qol. Run down. Headaches, body aches, nausea. No amount of rest or sustenance helped. He knew it was psychosomatic, but he didn't know the root cause and didn't want to. Yes, they were still waiting on the Council's verdict. Yes, he would look down at his hands sometimes and see blood. But there was something else. He felt no relief when word came of their tentative exoneration.

He tried exercise. He tried spending time with Droodroovid and the other fellows. He tried meditation. One time, eyes closed, trying to breathe away his perpetual heartburn, he saw the monument in the pixels. He likely figured out then what it was, but he didn't allow himself to believe it.

Kade avoided eye contact with him for days. He knew something. Will pried, but Kade played it off, sparing him the extra heap on his plate and setting him up to find out for himself. Will would come to be very grateful for that.

That he couldn't speak started bothering him for the first time. Then it started driving him crazy. He'd lose his breath, gasp like there was something stuck in his chest and trying to get out. Kade was always there in those moments with a glass of water.

Qol got bigger, and Will hid in his room. Kade pulled him out and led him by the hand to the cockpit, where they strapped in with Droodroovid and the others, their big eyes full of the dream.

They entered the clouds, jumped on the wind. They caught a tractor beam and landed at a base surrounded by high energy walls in an endless grassy plain. Brava was there with a dozen guards and two flyers. The fellows and pilots were led to one, Will and Kade to the other. Will looked back over his shoulder as Droodroovid did the same.

They took the flyer to a pill station and rode a pill underground through a silver trestle for a long time. They rose to the surface and snaked through a thawing, glistening everbluegreen forest. Will's heart swelled and pounded. He looked at Kade, who nodded.

--Is she alive?--

"Barely," Kade said.

--Let's go see her.--

"We're going."

Will's floodgates opened. It was being back there. It was picturing Ayn mostly dead with her daughters gathered around her. Kade squeezed his hand. The sinuous river glistened. Seven pastel glass towers rose from the trees, echoed inside of each other.

An echo barreled through Will's head, his own voice from the Shole during the whiteout: "I'm here! It's me! I'm alive!"

He remembered the true source of his pain. It was not the worlds that were heavy in his chest and snatching his breath. It was the monument, and he knew what it was all right, a monument to *her*. It was the karma stone hanging around his neck.

'Karma means things come around,' she'd said when she'd given it to him during set break at the Fillmore.

Kade led him into the Spire Stilter, into a lift, then down a curved hallway. The hall dead-ended in a cul de sac with two doors and two large glass windows. Ayn was behind the one on the right, chalk white and dead still in a glass box, connected by tubes and wires to blinking machines. Her girls were in a corner watching a holo.

Jackson howled from the room on the left. Orly and Fred scratched at the glass. Someone slipped out of view. Piper, his parents on either side of him, held the journal to his chest. A man who looked like Will rose from a seat and looked at him like he was a miracle. Lorel, his mother, stood against the back wall watching him take it in, healing patch wrapped around her left knee, arms crossed, tears in her eyes, a smile on her face like she couldn't wait for something. She motioned with her head toward the door as it opened.

Will found his breath and his voice. He said his first word since dying: "Elle."

And she said, "I heard you."

ACKNOWLEDGMENTS

Thank you to Laura Duffy for making another cover that I will love forever, to Karen Minster for making the inside beautiful, and to the editors of Yellowbird for their insights and sharp eyes.

And thank to my wife for her love and patience. As always, *It's all for you and the ones you grew.*

Please consider leaving a review of
The Butterfly and the Squid
on Amazon or Goodreads. It takes
a few clicks, and, if you want,
a few words.

Thank you.

– C.G.